DON'T TRUST ME

JESSICA LYNCH

Cover by MiblArt

For Suzanne.

You always said I could, so I did.

Miss you.

1

The cars ahead skated on a skim of water. The vivid red of countless taillights, brake lights bobbed in the pitch-black night that stretched endlessly in front of them, the only sign that they weren't alone in this storm. Sheets of rain fell sideways as it hammered down on the roof, a persistent drumbeat that even the radio couldn't quite drown out.

Despite the late hour, despite the treacherous conditions, going somewhere special made it worth the risk of travel. For Tessa Sullivan, it was an upscale spa and resort two states over from the simple suburban center she called home. She'd been looking forward to this trip for ages. The rain wouldn't stop her now.

It just made her a little worried.

Okay. Maybe more than a little.

As she prayed she would survive her husband's driving, she was reminded again that there was one thing she couldn't control: everybody else. It was a hard-earned lesson, going back fifteen years to when she was ten and her father was sideswiped in a storm just like this. Even if he'd been wearing a seatbelt, it wouldn't have saved him.

The SUV to their right suddenly cut over into their lane, spitting water up at the windshield, blinding her. Tess gulped, fervently wishing she hadn't let that last thought cross her mind.

She fidgeted restlessly in her seat, tugging on the strap by her neck as she checked its fit one more time. They had already been driving for close to seven hours with nothing more than an early supper and a bathroom break. Jack wasn't showing any signs of tiring, and his lead foot, heavy against the gas pedal, did nothing to help her nerves.

Not that he noticed. Or that she bothered to complain.

Except for the radio, he preferred silence when he drove if they were going somewhere new. She learned about that quirk on their honeymoon last year, where she struggled to keep quiet. It was a sad state of their marriage that she found it much easier this time around. There wasn't much she wanted to say to him.

Squeaky wipers slid across the windshield, but the

rain fell so hard and so fast, there was always a constant river streaking down the glass. She made a note to get them replaced after she returned home. The horrible scraping sound was grating on her already frayed nerves.

The music didn't help. Jack kept the dial tuned to whatever classic rock station he could find. If she heard one more power ballad with the crooner shrieking about lost love, she thought she might open the car door and pitch herself out into the storm.

She looked around, trying to find something else to occupy her.

There. On the opposite side of the highway, Tess could just make out a car sluicing its way through the rain. It had one wide white eye. The other headlight was blown.

Her response was automatic, ingrained in her from when she was a child and she played this game with her mother. Without even thinking, she leaned over and punched Jack in his upper arm.

"Padiddle!"

She knew right away that she made a mistake.

With all of his concentration on the road, he wasn't expecting the hit. His arm jolted which meant that his hand on the wheel yanked. He pulled suddenly to the left. The front wheels skid, hydroplaning on the slick road as the car slid to the other side. Jack struggled to right the vehicle, breathing heavily when he finally had it back under control.

"Jesus Christ, Tessie, I'm trying to drive here. What the—*whoa*."

A bump, then a squeal as they slid again, followed by a rhythmic *thump, thump, thump* as the entire car wobbled. He cut the speed drastically, the *whoosh* of the other drivers as they flew past causing their vehicle to rock.

Tess fell against her window. Her hand shot out, clinging to the grab bar over her head. She used it to pull her body up and climb back into her seat. Her heart thundered so fast, it was all she could hear over the drum of the pouring rain.

"What was that? What's wrong?" When Jack didn't answer, she let go of the handle and grabbed his arm instead. "Is something wrong with the car? Are we okay?"

He shook her off. "The tire," he grumbled, cursing under his breath. "Must've been when I jerked the wheel that first time. Damn it." With an aggravated sigh, he flicked on his hazard lights and coasted onto the shoulder.

Tess sank into her seat, crossing her hands in front of her like a child who'd gotten caught being naughty. Swallowing back the fear lodged in her throat, she murmured, "Sorry, honey."

As he maneuvered the car out of the flow of traffic,

Jack ignored her soft apology. Once upon a time he never would have. He would've assured her it wasn't her fault, maybe taken her hand instead of shaking it off, given her fingers a gentle squeeze. But those newlywed days were long gone. She felt the loss of them like an ache deep in her gut.

"Stay here," Jack ordered.

Bracing his big body against the door, he ducked his head and left her alone, disappearing into the night. Logically, she knew he crouched down to look at the tire. That was *logic*. Anxiety said only a few feet separated Jack from the cars whizzing by and she didn't have eyes on him.

Tess nibbled on her thumbnail, wondering if she should ignore his orders and go out to offer him some help. At the very least, she could provide some light for him. She wasn't *that* useless.

Grabbing her phone from her purse, she fiddled with it for a second before activating the flashlight app. That should make it easier for Jack to see through the nasty weather.

He was back before she'd reached to unclasp her seatbelt. The rain drenched him, leaving his t-shirt plastered to his skin. His sandy brown hair looked black as water dripped down his face. Shaking his head, he spattered her with chilly drops of rain.

Tess killed the flashlight as Jack slid back into his seat.

"No way I can do anything in this storm," he told her. "Tire's shot, though. Looks like we might have rolled over a nail or something earlier. How much longer did we have to go until we got to the resort?"

It was so disappointing to hear the weariness he didn't bother to hide. She'd been looking forward to this getaway for, well, *forever*. This second honeymoon was designed to help get them through this recent rocky patch in their relationship. Tess planned this trip down to its very last detail before they set off for the week away. At the time, the upcoming stormy forecast had been the least of her many concerns.

She was beginning to regret that oversight now.

"I'm so, so sorry. We've still got about two hours to go."

"What? Are you serious? It's after eight!"

"I know."

"Damn it, I thought we'd be there by now."

"We were supposed to be farther along—"

"You spent weeks getting me to agree to this, making arrangements." His voice was an accusation. Like she invited the rain herself, or caused the tire to go bad.

Tess sank in her seat. That part, at least, was true.

Jack glared at her, frustration coming off of him in waves. "Come on, Tessie. What now? This was your brilliant idea. Except now we're stuck in the middle of nowhere with a bum tire. Wonderful. And it's still another two hours? Really?"

"Dinner took longer than I expected, and the rain definitely didn't help." She bit her lip, then admitted, "We were already behind before the tire got all screwed up."

When he huffed and groaned, running his hands through his rain-dampened hair, she hurriedly added, "Don't worry, honey. Plans change, right? Plans change all the time. Our reservation will be waiting for us tomorrow. We just got to figure out something for now."

"Yeah?" he challenged. "Like what?"

Tess held up her phone. "It's okay. Really. I checked my maps app a second ago. There's an exit coming up in less than half a mile. I'm sure we can find something there. Someone to fix our tire, or maybe a motel for the night."

Another huff. "Well, it's not like we can sleep on the side of the highway. Okay. Fine. Let's go."

After turning his hazard lights off again, Jack waited until there was a gap in the traffic before he slipped back into the steady stream of cars coursing down the highway. He stayed in the right lane, hugging the outer line in case they had to pull over again ahead of reaching their exit.

If it wasn't for her phone insisting it was an actual road, she never would have insisted that they take it.

Nothing marked it as an exit. No sign, no arrows, not even a cone to guide motorists that way. Someone even honked as they turned off the highway.

Jack ignored them.

"I don't like this," he muttered. He pressed down on the brake, slowing his speed as he navigated the increasingly narrow strait.

She had to agree. The path was suddenly rocky, like they were driving on cobblestones. That couldn't be good for their bad tire. But, with the rain still coming down, there was no turning back now.

They couldn't even if they wanted to. The exit was obviously a one-way road.

A few minutes passed in silence as the exit turned into a street that seemed to lead to nowhere. Jack even clicked the radio off, lending all of his focus to his driving after the first time the car skidded and they almost ended in a ditch. Though the rain had let up on some of its relentless assault, the night had grown impossibly darker. Probably because there were far fewer streetlights than there had been on the highway.

It was so dark, Jack nearly missed it when the road split into two. Slamming on the brakes, they came to a squealing stop. Both of them flew forward before being yanked back in their seats. Tess shrieked and Jack cursed as their car came that close to diving nose first into a deep valley that bordered the necessary fork in the road.

There was no fence. No warning sign. Just a muddy path that disappeared into a gulley so deep, all he saw was the drizzle vanishing into a sea of black.

"What the hell?" He pounded the flats of his palms against the steering wheel. "Goddamn it!"

"Jack—"

"Don't *Jack* me. You see that? That hole? I almost just drove into—we almost *died*. No. That's it! I've had enough."

"But—"

"I said no and I mean it. I'm done. Okay? It's too dark to keep on driving, and it's definitely too late to look for a garage or someone to fix this damn flat. So do me a favor, pull up the closest hotel. I really don't want to sleep in this stupid car overnight and, right now, it's looking like our best shot."

She couldn't quite bite back her sigh. "Whatever you say, honey."

After giving her shoulder a quick rub, Tess leaned down and picked up her phone. It must have been flung there when Jack came to such a sudden stop. She paused to make sure the screen hadn't cracked before unlocking it.

Unlike her crumbling marriage, her phone was still in one piece.

Hiding her scowl from Jack, she went to pull up her maps app again when she noticed something strange: except for the battery indicator, her top bar was empty.

"That's weird. I… I lost my signal." She pressed the home button. No change. "I lost service. I can't do anything with my phone right now."

"Are you sure?"

She held it up so that he could see for himself. "Look."

"Check mine."

Jack always kept his phone stowed in one of the cup holders in the center console. She picked it up and shook her head. She didn't even need to put in his password to see that his phone wouldn't be any help either.

"The storm must have done something to the phones," Jack figured. "That's fine. Right now, I wouldn't put it past it. So no phones. Whatever. We'll just have to look for a sign or something."

"I can do that," Tess offered. "You keep your eyes on the road. I got this."

"Do you think we should go left or right?"

She blinked. It wasn't often Jack asked her her opinion about anything. She wasn't going to let this opportunity pass her by, no matter that it was for something so inconsequential. "Let's go right."

He took his time as he took the turn; with one bad tire, it was safer not to push it. So, as they coasted, Tess leaned as far as her seatbelt would allow, peering through the windshield. Between the rain, the clouds, and the lack of street lamps on this road, she couldn't see that far, but she was nothing if not determined.

"I think I see a sign ahead. It's coming up on my right. You see it?"

"Maybe. Let me get closer."

"It's there. You see it now? Look." She tapped her finger against the windshield. If he wanted to be pissy about the prints she left behind later, that was fine. "Jack. The lights. Over there. That sign... that looks different. Wait a second— is it handmade?"

He turned the wheel to the right, angling the headlights in the direction Tess was pointing. Through the curtain of steady rain, he could just about make out a wooden sign. Propped on a pole standing three feet high, the square sign was obviously hand-carved and painted. It read:

Welcome to Hamlet

est. 1941

Population: ~~193~~192

~ Hamlet Helps ~

Each letter was beautifully drawn in a script that was pure art. The sign was dark, the letters much lighter; the whole thing had an air to it that made it glow. Tess studied it closer. She had to really peer through the rain but she was almost sure that someone had used a different paint to change the population.

Jack noticed that detail at the same time. "Huh. Looks like someone left."

"Or else they died."

"Lovely, Tessie. How nice."

Didn't mean it wasn't true, she thought.

2

The road began to widen about ten minutes after they saw the sign. Lights were still sparse, the bumpy cobbles fading to a blacktop street flooded with rain. As she squinted, Tess couldn't find a sign that they weren't alone, which made her wonder if perhaps this Hamlet might have exaggerated its population.

When she pointed that out in an abashed murmur, Jack said, "Should I turn back around?"

Tess shook her head. He drove on.

A few houses eventually started to pop up on the outskirts. Taking heart in that, Jack continued to test the tire, pushing the car until he happened to see something that looked promising coming up on his side.

It was another hand-carved sign with that same

reflective paint. Hoping it wasn't announcing that they were *leaving* Hamlet now, he slowed down so that he could read it:

The Hamlet Inn
Hamlet's Finest Guest Establishment
A Luxurious Bed, Breakfast & More!

Inn. Inn meant boarding. Boarding meant a roof over their heads until the morning when he could find someone to provide him with a spare.

Thank God. He'd been beginning to think they'd be bunking in their old Honda after all.

The grand building beyond the sign didn't look like any of the hotels he'd ever seen before. It was more like a mansion, someone's home that was a few stories high, made up of countless rooms and had been converted into an inn. With a massive wraparound porch, a circular driveway that led to a set of double doors, and the single descriptor *luxurious*, Jack had the sinking suspicion that a night here was going to cost him a fortune.

His gaze slid to his wife. She was curled up into her seat, her slender legs tucked under her, one hand pillowed beneath her cheek as she rested her head against the window. Her soft, wavy dirty blonde hair covered her like a curtain. She stared straight ahead, silent as the night. He didn't think she even noticed he stopped the car.

Jack resisted the urge to run his hand down her thigh in a caress. It was a damn shame when a man couldn't be sure if his wife would welcome his touch. He could do one thing for Tessie, though. No matter what it did to his wallet, he was giving her a place to lay her head tonight that wasn't made of glass.

Flicking on the blinker, the static *click—click—click* drew her attention away from the rain. She turned toward him, her golden eyes vivid and bright. There was hope there.

Jack gripped the steering wheel so tight, his fingers went white. Was he so miserable to her that finding a hotel to stay the night in brought out a spark in her?

Stirring in her seat, she murmured, "You got something?"

He nodded. "The Hamlet Inn. I'm gonna go see if they have any rooms available."

Tess let out a soft sigh of relief. "Good."

Jack wanted to assure her that everything would be fine. He couldn't find the right words, though. Lately, no matter what he said, it always managed to be twisted into an argument.

He shook his head, then turned his attention back on the road. He followed the curve of the driveway, only coming to a complete stop when he pulled up in front of two massive french doors. After telling her to stay put, he slipped out into the rain and jogged up the front steps.

She watched him knock, wait a beat, then let himself inside.

Tess lingered a few minutes, her forehead pressed against the window pane in order to see if he would return right away. When it seemed as if he might be a while, she drew back, reached over, and turned off the car. Without the engine's hum, the pitter patter of steady rain was calming. Soothing.

Leaning forward, she grabbed her purse and pulled out her phone.

Still no signal.

No internet then, and no cell service.

Not that she needed to make any phone calls—or, really, had anyone left to call. Her family was all dead and gone and, since the wedding last year, she lost touch with any friends she once had. Even so, it made her uneasy to realize that she couldn't call out, even if she wanted to. The two of them were lost in some strange small town she had never heard of and there was no way anyone would know where they'd gone if something bad were to happen.

On the heels of that sobering thought, a sharp tap rapped against her window, breaking up her introspection. She screamed, a short, terrified shriek that burned her throat and caused her to fall back into her seat. Her purse spilled out on the floor of the car.

Out of the corner of her eye, she saw a dark shadow. Her imagination went into overdrive. She screamed again, her heart racing as frantic fingers fumbled with her seatbelt clasp.

Her only instinct was to get away.

The car door flew open. Jack's bulky body filled the doorway before one hand landed securely on her far shoulder. Caging her in, he dipped his head to meet her gaze as he tried to calm her down.

"Whoa, Tessie, baby, it's okay. It's me."

She ripped her seatbelt up over her free shoulder, clutching her chest with her other hand. Her heart felt like it was about to beat its way right through. Now that she was safe, anger rushed in. It didn't matter that her reaction was over the top. She hated being spooked and Jack *knew* that.

"What's wrong with you?" she snapped. "Don't do that!"

"Sorry." Since he tried to stifle his chuckle, she decided he might actually be. At least his mood had perked up some. "I thought you saw me running over. I swear, I didn't mean to scare you."

A deep breath to steady her nerves. When she muttered, "Whatever. It's fine," she almost believed that she meant it. She shook her head. "What did they say? Can we stay?"

After a quick once-over to make sure she was feeling better, Jack let go of her. He backed away, opening the car door wider. There was something tossed by his foot. Swooping down, he picked it up.

It was a folded umbrella. He must have thrown it when he heard her screaming.

"For you," he said, gesturing as he popped the umbrella up. With a quick shake, it opened wide. "I spoke to the clerk. There's plenty of vacancies. When I told her that I needed to head back out to the car, she offered me an umbrella. I brought it for you. The rain's starting to come down pretty hard again. I don't want you to get a chill."

It didn't matter that it was a short dash from the car to the front doors. Tess felt something inside of her tighten. "Oh, Jack. That's so... *thoughtful* of you."

"So, I'm forgiven?"

She let slip a tiny grin. "What kind of wife would I be if I held a grudge?"

Holding the umbrella down at his side, Jack leaned in and kissed the top of her head before giving her his hand to help her climb out of the Honda.

He insisted on walking her to the front of the inn. The umbrella wasn't very large. It covered Tess and might have shielded Jack from some of the downpour if he'd let her share it with him.

Which he point blank refused to.

By the time they reached the shield of the awning, he was soaked and her guilt had returned with a vengeance. Why was the pigheaded man so stubborn?

She tried to offer to go back and help him carry in the luggage, not at all surprised when he told her no. When Jack then tried to escort her inside? Tess let some of her own frustrations out as she denied him. If he wanted her out of the rain, she could damn well do it without a chaperone, especially one who thought she couldn't even manage to carry her own duffel bag.

She knew she was being tough on him. He thought he was acting the part of a gentleman, no matter that his overbearing personality stifled her. Tess might not be the type to hold a grudge, but all the little, niggling things that drove her crazy lately were quickly adding up.

Second honeymoon, she reminded herself. And she smiled.

"If I'm going in, here." She held the umbrella out to him. "Take this."

"I'm already wet. I don't need it."

He turned to hustle back down the steps, pausing when she latched onto his sleeve. She struggled to keep her smile in place.

"Please. Don't fight with me over something so stupid, Jack. Okay?"

A strange expression flashed across his handsome face, part leery and part confused. His sharp jaw tightened into a razor-fine edge. Tess was expecting *another* argument and then he surprised her.

"Yeah. Thanks, babe." His fingers folded around the handle. "I'll be back in a sec."

She made sure he lifted the umbrella over his head before she entered the inn.

As grand and intimidating as the estate was, the front room was exactly what she expected to find in the lobby of a hotel. The floor was covered in industrial carpet, patterned with cream-colored diamonds on a smokey grey spread; a matching set of overstuffed armchairs cornered the lobby. A potted plant stood on each of the opposing sides. To her right, a flat countertop ran the length of the room. There was a computer perched on the closer end.

It took her a second to notice that there was someone behind the counter. She was probably a good couple of years older than them, though Tess put her closer to thirty than forty. Her hair was pulled neatly back in a bun at the nape of her neck. While she had on a crisp white shirt, buttoned all the way up to her chin, she kept her plain face free of any make-up which only made her look younger to Tess.

The woman held a worn paperback with one hand. She had a small squint as she read, as if she normally wore glasses but forgot to put them on. From the bob of her head, Tess could tell when the woman got to the end of the page. She turned to the next one, then stuck her finger to keep her place.

That's when she finally acknowledged Tess.

"Evening, ma'am. Can I help you?"

Tess shook her head. Because her husband had left her in the car when he first approached the clerk, she had no clue what he told her. Admittedly bitter at the way he handled her outside, she decided to just let him finish registering when he was done with the car.

He wanted to handle everything? Fine. She didn't want to fight him anymore.

While Tess hovered near the threshold, the woman at the desk went back to reading her book. Every time she turned a page, she checked to see if Tess was still there, as if she expected her to vanish. Tess met her peeks with a small tight-lipped smile.

What was taking Jack so long?

Just when she couldn't take the awkwardness any longer, a tinkling bell rang and both women's heads turned to watch Jack hurry into the front room, a pair of stuffed duffel bags strapped across his body. In his right hand, he held her purse. He must have stopped to fold the umbrella on the porch because he had the handle tucked under his other arm.

Or, she decided with a small frown when she noticed the rain dripping from his sopping wet hair, he never bothered to use it all.

Eyeing him closely, she watched as Jack nodded his thanks at the clerk. He headed toward an intricate stand hidden behind one of the potted plants. After sticking the umbrella inside, he joined Tess and together they approached the counter.

"You're wet," she murmured under her breath.

He kept his voice just as low. "It's still pouring, Tessie."

"Mmm."

The clerk set her book aside as they approached. Her eyebrows rose when she recognized Jack, her initial curiosity shoved aside by years of working behind the front desk. Her surprise made Tess wonder if this was really an inn at all. The clerk hadn't seemed to think that Jack was coming back.

"Are you ready to register for the night now, sir?" she asked. "I can sign you in."

She changed from one second to the next, going from surprised to effusively helpful in a heartbeat. It was fascinating to watch the clerk slip right into her work personality, right down to the way her voice changed. A customer service voice, Tess thought. It sounded higher now.

She had one of those, too. The way she spoke, the smiles she offered, even the manner in which she held herself was different when she was standing in front of a class of her precious five-year-olds than when she had to deal with the parents and the administrative staff at her old school.

Of course, those days were gone. She gave up teaching when she married Jack. It didn't matter that she loved her work. He always dreamed of having a stay-at-home wife. It wasn't too long after the wedding when she realized that, in most things, what he wanted always came first.

Trying not to be *too* bitter, she clasped her hand in his, twining their fingers together as he walked with her to the counter. He glanced down in surprise at Tess, though he didn't say anything, then squeezed her fingers sweetly with his damp hand. And she wondered if maybe she wasn't the only one resenting the gap that existed between them.

Jack placed Tess's purse on the counter. Then, with his free hand, he reached into the back pocket of his jeans and pulled out his wallet. He flipped it open to show the woman his license in case that made registering any easier. "Yes, thank you. Hi. I'm ready now."

"What can I do for you, sir?"

"I'd like to get a room for the evening."

She turned toward her computer, fingers poised over the keys. "One room? For the both of you?"

"That's right. This is my wife. Tessa."

The clerk glanced at Tess, a quick flicker as she swept her from head to toe.

Tess was used to other women looking at her the same exact way: simultaneously dismissing her while wondering what it was that Tess had done to land such a strapping specimen as her husband. More than a head taller than her, broad in the shoulders and lean in the hips, Jack had a body most men would kill for. His shaggy, sandy hair was carelessly tousled just so when it wasn't rained on; even soaked, he exuded a safe masculinity that women always seemed drawn to.

She used to call him her teddy bear. But that was before. Lately, he was just Jack.

Tess couldn't mask her frown. The clerk cleared her throat, moved her glance to the computer in front of her, tapped a few keys before returning her adoring gaze back over to Jack. Honest to God, Tess swore she saw stars in the woman's eyes. And, after a second look, a big, honking ring on her finger.

"It looks like we have an empty house tonight so you have the pick of the rooms. Any requests, Mr. Sullivan?"

"Any requests, babe?"

"Something cozy," she murmured up at him. After all, this was supposed to be their second honeymoon. So they weren't staying at the resort for their first night. This place looked nice enough. "Something private."

Tugging on Tess's hand, he pulled her into the crook of his arm. His skin was slick from the rain and he carried a chill. She wrapped her arms around him, sharing her warmth.

He nodded at the receptionist. "You heard my wife. Cozy. Private." He still had his wallet open. Reaching around Tess, he rifled through it, yanked out a credit card. "I'll take the best one you've got."

3

Their unspoken truce lasted until Jack had let them into the room with one of the keys the clerk had given him. Tessa innocently asked to hold onto the other one. She didn't think it was an irrational request.

He flat out denied her.

"Why not?" she demanded.

She stopped right inside the doorway. With both of their duffels thrown over his shoulder, Jack maneuvered past her. He tossed the luggage on the empty seat of the nearest chair.

That done, he whirled on his wife. "Why do you need one?"

"There's two. Why do you need *both*?"

"If you think about it, we really don't need any now

that we're inside," Jack pointed out. "We're only staying the night. Once we leave in the morning, we're not coming back."

Tess wouldn't mind if they had to. As frustrated and annoyed as she was, she had to admit that the room was beautiful. Everything was done in soft, pastel colors: from the pale peach walls to the lemon-colored lampshades, and the pleasant floral quilted bedspread on the king-sized bed in the middle of the room. An oak nightstand stood off to one side of the bed. A matching set of dressers framed by a wide, gilded mirror sat along the far wall. Two overstuffed armchairs—similar to the ones in the front lobby—perched in separate corners. Jack had already claimed one with their luggage.

Across from the entryway, Tess saw a gorgeous bay window that stretched the length of the opposite wall. It was night, the curtains drawn and the blinds closed, but she thought the room would be even lovelier with sunshine streaming in through the window.

"Come *on*, Jack." Even Tess heard the whine in her voice. She couldn't help it. "I'm wide awake now. We've checked in two hours earlier than we thought by stopping over here. Why don't we go out, do some exploring?"

"Because the tire's shot. That's why we stopped. Remember?"

"We don't have to go far." She marched across the room to the window and pulled back the curtain with an impatient tug. "Look. The rain's slowed down some. If we baby the tire, we could probably find someplace local to eat. Let's *do* something."

"I'm not hungry."

"You can at least go and have a drink with me."

"Tess, I'd love to, but I'm tired." He kicked off his shoes, as if he thought he'd already won the argument. Sitting on the edge of the bed, he patted the spot next to him. "Let's just go to bed, get some rest. It's been a long day for both of us. You must be beat."

That wasn't exactly true. When she'd been trapped in the car, with the rain pounding the roof and Jack's imposed silence suffocating her, Tess had felt drained. Now, though, she was anxious. Jittery. She had no desire to climb into that bed and go to sleep.

Jack might be an early riser, always up before the sun while Tess slept in. She was his opposite; she'd always been more of a night owl. Sure, he'd made an attempt to be social while they were dating. Now that they were married, though, he gave up on trying to romance her with nights out on the town.

If he wanted to stay in the hotel and go to sleep at ten o'clock, that was fine. He could do what he wanted. Didn't mean that she wasn't still young enough to want to have some fun.

"If you won't come with me, I'll go myself."

JACK GLOWERED OVER AT HIS WIFE. SHE WAS DANCING ON her tiptoes, leaning forward, ready to take flight. Two minutes alone with him in the hotel room and she already wanted out.

Not him. He didn't want to leave the rented room. He sure as hell didn't want his Tessie going out without him either. At least it explained why she wanted to have her own key.

And only made him more determined not to give her one.

"No."

"No?" Tess echoed. She landed flat on her feet, stunned, but quickly shook it off. "Last time I checked, you were my husband, not my father."

It was a cheap shot. Her father died when she was a child. Jack never knew his. The whole topic made them both touchy.

He rubbed his mouth with the back of his hand. "I know I'm not—"

"We're supposed to be partners."

"We are."

"Ha! Partners are supposed to make decisions together. You always try to tell me what to do."

"No, I—"

With her hands on her hips, she snapped out, "I'm not a child!"

Jack opened his mouth to attempt to argue again when he realized something: Tessa was right. He hated to admit it, but his wife was absolutely right. If he treated her like a child—if she even *thought* he was—then she would only come to resent him even more.

And if he couldn't trust her to take care of herself, he would drive them both crazy with his stubborn refusal to let her be his equal. This trip was all about salvaging their marriage. He couldn't expect Tess to make all the sacrifices.

Maybe it was time he gave it a try.

"Okay. Fine. Point made."

"I— wait, what?" Tess obviously never expected he'd give in. How could he blame her? All they did was fight anymore. Knowing his wife, she was probably already plotting her next argument three steps ahead of where they were. Her brow furrowed, as if sensing a trap. "You saying I can go?"

When had she ever needed permission from him before?

"You're an adult. You were right. If you want to head out, I can't stop you."

"And you'll come with me?"

He wasn't willing to go that far. "Babe, I'm tired."

"It's not even nine yet."

"I know. I'm sorry, but I was driving all night. All I

want is to relax, maybe watch a movie. You want to explore, fine. I don't have to go."

Tess frowned, then shook her head, tugging the curtain shut as she did. "Forget it. I'll stay."

"No. No, Tessie, that's not what I want. I wasn't trying to manipulate you into staying." Jack could feel the beginning of another of his killer headaches forming behind his right eye. Rubbing his temple, he climbed into the bed, stretching his legs out in front of him. He exhaled roughly. "Look, I don't want to fight anymore."

"Me neither," she told him honestly. She edged closer to the bed. When he winced, she caught it. "What's the matter, Jack? Does your head hurt?"

Jesus, yes. The throb could be absolutely excruciating at times. It only got worse after one of their fights. He would never admit it, though. "Only a little. I'll be fine after I get some sleep."

"Hang on." Tess walked over to the dresser. "I've got a surprise for you. I was gonna wait 'til later but... well, you'll see."

Slipping her hand into the side pocket of her duffel bag, she pulled out the small bottle she purposely tucked there last night when she finished packing. It was made of plastic—due to their travels—but the familiar red cap and logo on the label made her think they were at home.

After a long day at work, Jack had a nightly habit of

having a single shot after dinner to help him to relax. She made a point of bringing a small bottle with her for their trip because she knew he would miss it.

But even with all her planning, she hadn't remembered to pack a cup. Heading for the bathroom, she settled on taking one of the plastic dixie cups that the hotel staff left on the side of the sink. It was wrapped in plastic, nestled between the flat bar of soap and a small bottle of rose-scented shampoo. Perfect.

She poured out a shot of Jack's favorite vodka before twisting the cap back on and tucking it in her pocket. Walking back into the cozy room, she handed him the cup.

"Ah, hell. If this is what I think it is, you're a lifesaver, Tessie."

With a mischievous grin, she held up the bottle and wagged it in his direction. "What do you think?"

Jack took a small sip. Savoring, he let out a short moan. And Tess knew she was forgiven for her part in their argument.

"Mm-hmm. Just what I needed to unwind from the drive. You know me so well."

She did. She absolutely did.

"Enjoy your drink, honey." Bending slightly, Tess ran her fingers down his leg. "Relax. You deserve it. Remember, you're on vacation."

"You, too, babe. And I meant what I said before. Go out, get a look at this Hamlet if you want," he told her.

"If you're really sure it's okay," she hedged.

"I am. It's fine. Here." Lifting up off the bed, Jack slipped his hand into his back pocket. When he pulled it out again, he was holding onto one of the keycards. "Take this. You can have it. I shouldn't have said no before."

She took the keycard from him, hugging it to her chest. "I really want to do just a little sightseeing. That's all. At the very least, maybe I can find someplace to buy you some headache medicine. I won't be gone long."

His eyes were starting to close. Jack yawned, resettled himself in the bed. Tilting his head back, he tipped the rest of his nightcap into his mouth and swallowed. "Oh, yeah. That hit the spot."

Watching him lay by himself in the bed, the guilt started to eat at her. They were supposed to be doing their best to make their relationship work. So what was she doing? Walking out on him the first chance she got, that's what. Just because she had the itch to explore and her plans got shot to hell the instant she yelled *padiddle*.

She couldn't do this.

She shouldn't—

Tess wanted to.

"Jack?"

"Mmm?"

"You... you *sure* you don't mind?"

Jack opened his eyes. They were already starting to glaze over. From the way he seemed to struggle to lift his eyelids, she figured he must've been more beat than he let on.

"I want you to be happy, Tessie. Just go easy on the tire, okay?" Reaching over, he placed his empty cup on the nightstand. It toppled over. He left it like that. "And don't stay out too late."

"I won't. Trust me. I'll probably just go out, get some fresh air, and come right back."

"Okay. And do me a favor—if I'm sleeping when you get back, wake me up. I haven't forgotten this is our second honeymoon. I'll make it up to you later."

Tess let out a sound that was half giggle, half snort. Just like that, Jack put her mind at ease. Her husband might be tired now, but he had a voracious appetite after he got a couple hours of sleep.

In the first couple of weeks after they got married, he was the one who did the random waking. Lately, though, she'd been sleeping through the night. It made her wonder if Jack didn't find her attractive anymore. It felt good to be wanted. That was the one thing—the *only* thing—she ever asked for. To be loved and desired.

Grabbing her purse, Tess made sure to turn all the lights off so that he wouldn't have to. Then, leaning down, she pressed her lips softly to his cheek. "Love you, Jack."

Her only answer was a snore. He was fast asleep.

SOME TIME, ESPECIALLY IN THE LAST YEAR, SITTING IN A dark bar seemed to lose some of its luster.

To be honest, Tessa hadn't had much hope when she took Jack's car and went looking for something to entertain her. There was only one inn in Hamlet, and the woman at the front desk was no concierge.

Like most small towns, she was used to her guests being locals and couldn't give a coherent direction to save her life. When Tess asked where the best place was to get a drink, the answer was full of "down the street", "at the light", "past the tree" and, her personal favorite, "don't fall into the gulch".

It was pure dumb luck that led her to stumble upon Thirsty's—mainly because it was the only building in town she passed that had more than two vehicles in the lot. While it was a sorry crowd by the standards she was used to, when she finally got up enough nerve to walk inside she was surprised to find that there were about twenty others filling the big room.

Though a couple of tables were occupied, the majority of the crowd was seated at a long countertop that ran the length of the place. The local watering hole, she figured. She made a point to take a table as hidden as possible. She wanted to be the one to observe for once.

It took a few minutes before a waitress noticed her. It was obvious that the woman was surprised to find an unknown face visiting the establishment but a table was a table and she got over her shock quick enough to bring Tess a menu and a glass of water.

After waving off food, Tess ordered a simple gin and tonic. If that drink passed her test, maybe she would indulge in something else. Until then she contented herself with watching the other patrons. She didn't think she could manage to completely banish her guilt. Since she had already abandoned Jack, she decided she owed it to him to give it a try.

It was a shame she hadn't been able to convince him to leave the hotel room. Her husband would have felt right at home at Thirsty's.

There was an honest to God jukebox in one corner of the bar and whoever stocked it had the same taste in music as Jack. The first time Cinderella's "Don't Know What You Got ('Til It's Gone)" played, she cringed. The second time, she flagged down her waitress again. When the opening chords to Whitesnake's "Is This Love" echoed through the room, she tilted her head back and swallowed the rest of her drink whole.

Her mood perked up a little when the music did. Still firmly lost in the eighties, someone put on Def Leppard. Just as the singer demanded someone pour some sugar on them, a movement by the bar caught her eye.

Tess watched as a woman stood up on her stool before pressing a booted heel onto the countertop. As she marched down the bar, all of the nearby patrons hooted and hollered, laughing as they moved their drinks in order to give her a clear path. Once she didn't have to worry about tripping over someone's beer, she started to dance.

Tess couldn't tell if the woman was pretty but she sure was wild. Dressed in jeans that seemed to be painted on and a button-down shirt that was buttoned up just enough not to be obscene, the dancer had long red hair that spilled down her back and rippled like a flame in the neon lights surrounding the bar. A cowboy hat was placed smartly on her head, an odd accessory considering they were on the East Coast. Amazingly, no matter how she threw her head or how she moved, the hat stayed in place.

As she swirled the straw in her latest drink, Tess was mesmerized.

So mesmerized, in fact, that she didn't notice it when a shadow fell on her table.

"Hello."

Tess jumped, her hand slipping off her straw and knocking into the rim of her glass. Amber-colored drink splashed her skin and the table in front of her.

With a shaky hand, she just managed to steady the glass before the whole thing toppled over.

As she reached for a cocktail napkin and started to sop up the spill, she glanced up to see who had startled her.

It was a man, about her age or maybe a year or two older than her twenty-five. There was something almost babyish remaining in his chiseled features, though, a softness that said while he'd seen a lot in this world, it still held some wonder for him.

It was his eyes, she decided. A warm sort of cocoa brown, they were big and wide and utterly adorable. Tiny lines framed them. Laugh lines.

He was smiling at her. She was used to bar crawlers smiling at her but there was something kind in his grin. It could've been pervy. It wasn't. And that made her a little bit wary.

"Sorry about that, miss. Didn't mean to scare you."

"You didn't." Her thundering heart called her a liar. "Something I can do for you?"

He must have just come in from the outside. For one, she was pretty sure she would have noticed him during her perusal of the other patrons. For another, his cropped hair glistened with the raindrops that clung to the short strands. His coat was buttoned up to his chin. She could see that his shoulders were dotted with big, wet splotches. Ran in from his car, she guessed.

"You can answer a question for me."

"Sure."

He nodded at the empty seat across from her. "You waiting on someone?" His offer was left unsaid. If she gave him the go sign, the seat wouldn't be empty for long.

Tess could tell that he was hitting on her, but he did it in such a transparent way, she wasn't offended. The curious stares and open leers from some of the other men in the bar had rubbed her the wrong way. This guy was cute. It was almost a shame that she had to turn him down.

Picking up her glass, she made sure to use her left hand. If he missed the wedding ring on her finger, then he was blind. "My husband wasn't feeling well. I left him to get some rest back at the inn. If anything, he's waiting on me."

The handsome stranger never lost his smile. He took the rejection incredibly well. "Have a nice evening, miss. Enjoy your time in Hamlet."

"Thank you. I am so far."

With a friendly wave, the man shook his head once before he backed away from her table and turned to search the rest of the bar. Because she was married but could still appreciate a good looking man, she sipped her drink and watched him go.

He greeted a few of the others, some at their tables, some while they moved on the dance floor. All the same, Tess had to admit she wasn't surprised when his path led him directly toward the redhead still gyrating outrageously on the far side of the counter.

Though maybe she did choke a little on her drink when the dancer removed the cowboy hat from her head, letting it fly across the dance floor before she launched herself right at the man.

4

Underneath the weight of his boss's slight frame, Mason locked his knees so that he didn't fall over when she jumped off of the bar and landed right in his arms. He was a strong fellow, and Caitlin De Angelis was by no means a big girl, but he hadn't expected her to jump when she saw him heading her way.

Then he saw the glassy look in her bright green eyes and he realized he should have.

"Hitting the bottle kind of hard there, huh, Sheriff?"

She leaned in, a strand of her ruby red hair clinging to her clammy cheek. Whispering loudly, Sheriff De Angelis told him, "I'm off duty," before reaching down to grab his ass with both hands.

"Yes," he agreed as he eased her gently down until

she was standing on her own. He was ready to ignore her wandering hands when she gave one ass cheek a squeeze. His smile became a little strained as he reached behind him and removed her hands. "But I'm still on duty so maybe you can keep these to yourself."

She took his gentle refusal with a sniff and a flounce. "I can have any man in Hamlet," she announced to the crowd before raising one of her hands royally. As if to prove her point, three bar hounds fought for the pleasure of helping Caitlin climb back onto the bar. She sat down on the bar top, crossing her legs and placing her pointed chin into her hand. "That's why I've got to celebrate, Mase! Almost got trapped once, didn't I? Now I know better. Why settle for one man when I can have anyone I want?"

Mason wasn't an idiot. Whether or not he was attracted to his boss—and, while she was a beautiful woman, he was most adamantly *not*—he knew better than to mix business with pleasure.

He also knew better than to rile her up when she was brooding over her divorce. Three years after her marriage fell apart, everyone in Hamlet knew that Caitlin De Angelis might be able to get anyone she wanted—but she hadn't been able to keep the only one who ever mattered to her.

That was why he put up with her drunken behavior and outright harassment. For three hundred and sixty-four days out of the year, Caitlin was an ideal sheriff. A tad paranoid and fanatically loyal to Hamlet, she was the law in their small village. She never abused her power. If she wanted to make an ass out of herself on the anniversary of her divorce, the townsfolk let her. And her deputies made sure no one held her accountable the morning after.

Which was also why Mason was checking in on her now. Willie dropped the sheriff off at Thirsty's when they both went off shift but she had three kids at home. She couldn't spare the time to babysit her thirty-year-old boss. So Mason promised to check in on Caitlin during the night, and Sly was on call to drive Caitlin home when she was finally done—if she didn't find her own ride home first.

From the way some of the fellas were eyeing her in her civilian clothes, Mason didn't think she'd have any trouble getting to her place.

His mind at ease, Mason took Caitlin by the elbow and gently helped her down from the bar top before guiding her to the closest stool. She was already wobbling in her thigh high boots. The last thing he needed was for the sheriff to take a tumble and break her neck. He'd almost had a heart attack when he saw her swaying on the top of the bar. And then, when she jumped at him... if she kept this up, he'd need a drink himself by the end of this shift.

He used the excuse of retrieving her hat to put some more space between them. Leaning in, he plopped her hat back in place before backing away from her again. "Okay, Sheriff. I'm doing the overnight. I've got to get back out there. If you need me, give me a buzz."

She was already accepting another drink from Georgie, the bartender at Thirsty's. Waving off Mason's concerns, she tossed the shot back before slamming the glass on the bar. "Another!"

The men surrounding her let out a cheer. Mason wasn't *too* worried. Apart from the outsider sitting alone at a table, everyone inside of Thirsty's was a local. They all knew Caitlin. One or two of them might take her up on her boast that she could have any man, but not one of them would hurt her. If anyone tried, there were at least five more who would nip that in the bud before it began. Mason was well aware that the only danger to the sheriff was Caitlin herself and the hell of a hangover she would certainly have tomorrow.

So, with a respectful nod to his boss, and a stern glare at her fan club, Mason backed away from the bar. Now that he'd done what he came down to Thirsty's to do, it was time to get back on patrol. With only four full-time members of the sheriff's department, they were running a little shorthanded lately. Willie was home with her family. Having come off a double that morning, Sly didn't start his next shift until five a.m. unless one of the others needed him earlier. Caitlin purposely took the night off. Mason was the only one on duty.

He wasn't worried, though. There was never any trouble in Hamlet—not unless it involved an outsider.

Without even meaning to, he searched out the lonely brunette with the golden eyes. She was still nursing the same drink she'd had when he first saw her. And, like before, she was sitting by herself, frowning into her glass. She looked so lost and alone, it made his heart ache.

Mason was born and raised in Hamlet, never left the small village he always called home. With such a tiny population, he knew each and every one of his neighbors. On the rare occasion that an outsider found their way into Hamlet, they usually stuck out like a sore thumb.

Not that one. Something about her called to him. In his eyes, she shone like a diamond. Her lonely presence lured him over to her the instant he entered the bar and, as he walked out, he had a strong desire to stay.

It appealed to him that she was a mystery. Unlike all the other girls in town, he hadn't known her all his life. He could discover everything about her in time, if she only let him.

It was a pity that she made it very clear that that wouldn't be happening. And, yet, he couldn't bring himself to go back out into the rain.

Standing in the doorway, hidden in the shadows, Mason continued to watch the pretty little outsider. He respected the ring she wore, and while her sad eyes and wistful smile were very tempting, he knew better than to poach when a lady said she was spoken for. Even if he couldn't understand what sort of man would leave his wife to drown her sorrows all alone.

If she belonged to him, he would never give another man the chance to observe her as closely as he was.

He glanced back at the sheriff. She was dancing with Rick, one of the fellas from the barber shop down on Main. Ex-military and a Hamlet local, he was a good man. He could keep an eye on Caitlin.

And maybe Mason should keep his eye on the outsider.

Someone had to.

When Tess realized that she had not only lost track of time but also of how many glasses the waitress had placed before her, she figured it was probably a good idea to make her way back to the hotel.

At least she didn't have to worry about her husband. When Jack knocked out, he was *out*. Especially after he had his nightly vodka shot. Since he'd been snoring when she left, there was a good chance he hadn't even noticed she was still gone.

Good. She wasn't in the mood for another fight tonight. And considering she stayed out way later than she intended, she had a feeling that another fight was exactly what she was going to get.

She bit back her pout. Some romantic getaway. She got tipsy all alone in some strange bar while her husband slept by himself a few miles down the road.

The waitress had dropped the bill off the last time she made her rounds so Tess didn't have to wait. Squinting at the total, she pulled a handful of bills from her purse and left them under the receipt. Feeling a little sorry for herself and her cracking marriage, she added a healthy tip before slipping out of the booth.

The wild redhead was still at the bar, surrounded by a small circle of men and women that she tried—and failed—not to notice didn't include the handsome blond man from earlier. The terrible music had only seemed to grow louder, or maybe that was just Tess's irrational sensitivity to it.

Laughter filtered from their group, too, even more shrill to her ears. She was tempted to join them—anything, to prove that she could still have a good time—but she knew better. The way the redhead's friend approached her like she was some unique specimen told Tess that this small town didn't get too many visitors. Besides, in the mood she was in, she doubted she'd make a good first impression on anyone.

Out of habit, she checked her cell. Still no service which meant there was no message from Jack. Tossing her useless phone back into her purse, she pulled out her car keys and made her way outside.

The rain had let up some, leaving a musty smell in the air and a chill that had Tess wishing she'd brought her coat. She'd been so anxious to get away from Jack that she hadn't stopped to grab anything except her purse.

The road behind the bar was all cobblestones. She'd forgotten that. After her ankle turned on her first wrong step, she carefully made her way to her car. It frustrated her to see that the flat had gotten even worse. One whole side of the car seemed to tilt down. She had half a mind to abandon it at the bar. Since that meant walking all the way back to the hotel, she said a quick prayer to the car gods and climbed in.

The car started on the first try. There was a small groan and a grinding screech as the poor flat tire feebly protested. Tess pushed past it. Maybe the vehicle took pity on her, or maybe she should've been sleeping long before she decided cars had thoughts and emotions, but though it didn't seem happy, the damn thing moved.

"Thank you, car gods," she muttered.

It didn't take too long before she realized that one of the car gods cursed her.

She'd made it maybe half a mile down the road when her rearview mirror became an angry flash of red and blue lights. The crazy impulse to take off lasted for a single heartbeat before sanity returned and she slowly coasted to the side.

Cursing under her breath, she slumped in her seat, her head thumping against the headrest. In a town that boasted a population of a couple of hundred and probably had two backwater cops, wasn't it just her luck that she would manage to get pulled over?

Or that the face looming right outside her driver side mirror would belong to a man she had already met?

A brisk knock against her window had her rolling it down. Without the rain-spattered glass separating them, Tess could see that she was right. Closely cropped blond hair, chocolate-colored eyes, and an inviting smile. The pretty boy charmer from the bar. Of course, it was.

And, of course, he was a damn cop.

"Well, hello again," he drawled. He shook his head, wiping the rain that trickled down his forehead. He never seemed to lose his grin.

She gulped. This was bad. Very, very bad. "Problem, officer?"

"Might be. Remember me? I believe I saw you over at Thirsty's earlier tonight."

Fighting the urge to hurl, she nodded. It probably wasn't a good idea to open her mouth.

"Okay. So, well, that makes it a bit easier then. I know you've been out drinking. And now I see you're behind the wheel. That's not good. It's not safe."

It took her a second to find her voice. "I'm... I'm okay. I'm just going back to the hotel."

"That's still a problem, miss. Quite a big one, actually. You see, the Hamlet Inn is a good five miles from here." She only had a split second to see the flashlight in his hand before he clicked it on and her retinas burned like they'd been seared. Black dots danced before her eyes as he said briskly, "License, please."

Her heart started to mambo in her chest. Trying desperately not to slur her words, she projected pure innocence as she yanked her driver's license out of her wallet and handed it over to the cop.

"Tessa Sullivan," he read. Handing it back, he opened the car door. His grin had slipped into a thin line of duty. "Step out of the vehicle please, miss."

She climbed out of the car, glad to see that the rain had finally died away. The chill was still in the air, though, and she shivered as she crossed her arms over her chest.

"Over here." The officer directed her to the painted

line that split the paved road. "I'm gonna have to ask you to walk that line for me."

Oh, lord. He was giving her some sort of sobriety test.

It was hard to think but she had to try. Rubbing her eyes, warding off some of the wooziness, she looked up at the officer through the fringe of her eyelashes. "Are you sure I should?"

"Traffic is slow this time of night," he assured her. "It'll only take a minute. Arms out, miss. Fifteen steps down the line, fifteen back."

Tess took in a deep breath. Thirty steps. Piece of cake. She could so do this.

Holding her arms out, wondering how the hell she got into this mess, Tess held her shaky head high and took the first step. One... Two... Three. She wobbled and just barely kept her balance. Four. Five— *Damn it!*

The officer rushed over to her side the instant she started to stumble. With a rock solid arm around her waist, he hefted Tess back onto her feet. Once she was steady, he didn't let go. Instead, he guided her toward his cruiser.

She didn't realize how much trouble she was actually in until he helped her into the backseat.

5

Nothing, Tess discovered, sobered her up faster than the harsh sound of cell bars clanking shut.

She jumped at the ringing noise, then stumbled forward. Her knees knocked into the edge of the bench seat that took up the length of the cell. The lingering fog in her head disappeared. Turning, she watched the broad back of the blond cop as he started to head away from her.

"Wai—" Her throat dry, the words seemed to catch. Swallowing roughly, she tried again. "Wait! You can't leave me here!"

When he turned around, the expression on his face was apologetic. "It's for your own safety, miss. Even if you were in any shape to drive, your car wouldn't make it far. I saw the flat myself, and the way the rim is starting to bend out of shape. No, it's better if you stay here, sleep it off."

Tess started to argue. He cut it off with a small shake of his head. "If you make it easy on both of us, all you'll get is a warning and a ride. In the morning, I'll take you down to the garage so you can get your car looked at. How's that sound?"

"No, no. I won't be any trouble, I promise. But, please—" She squinted at his nameplate. "—Mr. Walsh, I can't stay. I—"

"Deputy."

Tess blinked at his interruption and went right on without missing a single beat. "Right. Deputy. As I was saying—"

"You can call me Mason, miss. We're not so formal in Hamlet, and you saying Mr. Walsh makes me think my dad is here."

He *was* charming, she realized. And that could be dangerous. She shook her head, desperate to clear it. Much of the night was hazy, but she definitely remembered him stopping by her table at the bar.

Tess raised her hand, careful to show off her wedding band again.

"My husband," she blurted out. "He'll be angry if I don't come back to the hotel tonight. We're not from around here, and he'll worry something has happened to me."

The deputy—Mason—pursed his lips, a few lines

marring his brow. The keys to the cell were hanging loosely from his belt and while he fingered one absently, she could tell from the set of his jaw that she would be trying to make herself cozy on that bench shortly.

And then he said, "Well, I don't suppose it would do any harm to give him a shout," and Tess was so relieved that even the prospect of a sore back and a stiff neck didn't seem so bad.

Reaching behind him, Mason produced something that looked like a walkie talkie. It was bulky and thick, mostly black with a yellow case and a flashing red light next to an antenna that reminded Tess of her pinky finger. He fiddled with one of the three knobs on the side before pressing a button.

A shock of static cut through the air, followed by a soft voice. "Hamlet Inn. Who are you trying to reach?"

"Caroline? It's Mason, down at the sheriff's office. How's everything going?"

"Going fine, fine. Little late for a buzz, though, isn't it? I was just going to wake up Roy, have him take the desk for a couple hours so I can get some shut eye."

When the deputy glanced behind him to look at the clock, Tess followed his gaze. It was already half past one in the morning. Her shoulders tensed and her stomach dropped. How had it gotten so late?

"Sorry about the buzz. But, hey, you got some guests fresh in tonight. Yeah?"

"We did. Two outsiders. First ones we've had this fall so you know that storm was real wicked earlier. That's why I'm making my husband take over for me. I would've locked up otherwise. Hold on, I got their check-in right here."

The walkie died for a few seconds, then Caroline was back.

"Mr. and Mrs. Sullivan. Good looking man, and the wife seemed like a shy little thing. We have them up on the second floor. Something wrong?"

Mason chuckled. "Let's just say that the shy little wife is going to be my guest in the holding cells this evening. Nothing serious, but she'd feel better if someone let her husband know that she had a little too much to drink and is crashing somewhere safe. Do you think you can do that for me, Caro?"

If she wasn't so nervous, Tess might have been concerned with the way the loose-lipped deputy was spreading gossip about her when she was standing right there. At that second, it didn't matter. Not if he got the hotel clerk to talk to Jack.

"You're in luck. The wind didn't knock out the boards tonight. I'll connect to his room and see if I can get him on the line for you. Just give me a minute, Mase."

"Thanks." Clipping his communicator back onto his belt, the deputy offered Tess an explanation. "The phones don't always work here. You've never seen dead air until you try to make a village between a mountain and a valley," he added with a crooked grin. "Everyone in town who needs one has a channel, has a radio. No cell service in Hamlet. The switchboards are the best we have and who knows if they'll ever work. If she can't get through to him, I can always ask Caro to go up and knock. Or Roy could, I guess."

He was being too nice. Normally, she would be suspicious, but not when she was desperate enough to take his help without wondering why he was so eager to offer it. Shuffling as close to the cell door as she could get, Tess wrapped trembling fingers around the cold sting of the metal. Biting down on her bottom lip, she waited.

It seemed like an eternity before the static echoed through the wide room again.

"Hello? Can you hear me?"

At the sleep-roughened yet undeniably curious tone, Tess relaxed. She knew that voice. Everything was going to be okay.

"He must've figured out the radio," Mason murmured to Tess. He grabbed his own and pressed the button. "Yes, I can. Evening, sir. My name is Deputy Mason Walsh, with the Hamlet Sheriff Department."

"They told me this had something to do with my wife. Where's Tessa—where's my Tessie? Is she okay? Is she safe?"

"Mrs. Sullivan is fine, sir," Mason assured him.

"Little car trouble, though. Did you know your tire was flat?"

"What— oh, yes. The flat. That's why we've stopped over. I plan on having it looked at first thing in the morning. I'm sorry— what did you say your name was again?"

"Walsh, sir."

"Walsh. Yes. Sorry, I was sleeping. Can you please tell me what that has to do with my wife?"

Mason hesitated before answering. Tess could've sworn she forgot how to breathe.

"I was on patrol tonight when I encountered your wife a few miles from the hotel," he said. "Her car was swerving—probably because of the flat—and I brought her down to the station just in case. With the poor weather, the flat, not to mention the late hour, it seemed a smarter idea all around for her to pass the night here. She insisted on a courtesy call, though. Didn't mean to wake you, sir. My apologies."

The other end was quiet for a moment. Mason waited to see if her husband would believe him. Tess thought she might pass out from lack of oxygen.

Then, "Where is she? I'll come get her."

Tess discovered she had enough air in her lungs to let out a fretful shout.

"No!"

Mason turned to look at Tess. His eyebrows raised, he took his finger off of the radio's button. "Miss? Is something wrong?" While he kept his voice friendly and calm, there was steel there, too. Like he'd stand in front of her if she asked him to.

She shook her head quickly. "I don't want him to see me locked in here. He'll be so angry if he finds out I... I..." Gulping back her panic, she looked imploringly at the deputy. "I'll stay. I'll be quiet. Just don't let Jack come down here. Please."

For a moment, Tess was certain that Mason would refuse. But then he nodded. "Mr. Sullivan?"

"Yes?"

"There's no need for you to come to the station. Your wife will be nice and safe until morning. If it makes you feel better, I'll personally return her to you as soon as I'm off duty."

A pause. Tess clasped her hands together, covering her mouth with her fingers.

"Not that I don't believe you or nothing, Walsh, but my wife and I are strangers here. What would make me feel better was if I spoke to her myself, made sure she was okay. Is she available?"

Mason's dark eyes scanned her pale face. "Are you?"

"I'll talk to him." Slipping her hand between the bars, she took the radio Mason offered her. She pressed down on the button the same way she saw him do it. "Honey?"

Crackle. "Tessie?"

"Yeah. It's me. Hi. Sorry about all this... but, trust me, Jack, the deputy seems like a very nice man. We'll have to invite him to breakfast tomorrow."

Another pause. "If you say so, Tessie." His flat tone made it clear that he wasn't so sure. "But we'll talk about all this later. I'm not quite sure I get what's going on—" His words were slurred, the tail end of a yawn coming through the radio before he added, "—and I'm too tired to figure it out. It's too late to argue about it. Okay?"

She nodded her head, then seemed to realize that he couldn't hear her. She pressed the button again, the ridges biting into the soft flesh of her thumb. "Okay. Love you."

"Love you, too. Night."

Mason moved forward to take the radio back. A curious expression flashed across his face, there and gone again in the time it took her to blink and focus. His genial grin back in place, he twisted a few knobs on his radio and clipped it back on his belt.

"Feel better?"

"Yes."

"Good, 'cause your husband's right. It's late and I've got to get back on patrol. Sly will be in shortly to check on you. Sleep it off. I'll be back in the morning."

"Thank you." The words didn't seem adequate, and it was weird for her to be grateful when the man had kind of, sort of, maybe arrested her. Tess was tired, she'd been drinking, and she was so far out of her element, she felt like she was floating. But he had helped her when he didn't have to, and she was grateful. "I mean it."

"Rest. We'll talk tomorrow." He winked, a gesture so very at odds with what had happened that evening that Tess just stared at him. "I'm very much looking forward to breakfast."

MASON NEVER MADE IT BACK TO THE STATION HOUSE.

About ten minutes after he left, a tall black man wearing the same uniform came in to sit with her. He introduced himself as Sylvester Collins, and assured her that what Mason did was local procedure.

With as little crime as Hamlet saw, he told her, if it wasn't for the occasional drunk and disorderly, the jail cell would never have any occupants. Tess almost wanted to argue the disorderly part then decided that doing so would just prove the deputy's point so she kept her mouth shut.

After offering her a wool blanket and telling her the night would pass much faster if she got some sleep, Collins sat at one of the two desks in the wide room. Tess watched him pore over a pile of paperwork—no crime certainly didn't mean that their paperwork was any less—before taking his advice and finally catching a few hours.

Before she knew it, she heard the rustling of keys and the sliding of her cell door. Collins, looking as fresh as he did all those hours ago, stood in front of her with a muffin in his hand.

"Hungry?" he asked. He had a pleasant voice, deep and resonant. Too bad he looked like any sort of smile might cause a crack in his cheeks. As pleasant as he was, Tess thought of him as a glass empty sort in contrast to Mason Walsh's glass full demeanor.

Her stomach flip-flopped at the sight of the muffin. It smelled delicious but Tess felt like something had taken residence in her mouth the night before and quite possibly died in there. She swallowed. Her throat was so dry, she didn't see how she could get that muffin down even if her stomach wanted it.

"No, thank you," she croaked. Wincing, she rubbed her throat. "You wouldn't have any water, would you?"

"Sure thing." He left the room without another word.

Tess wasn't sure what to do. He'd unlocked the cell door for her. Did that mean she was free to go? Or was she supposed to wait for him? Come to think of it, she didn't even know if she'd actually been arrested or even detained last night. Mason had told her to sleep it off and she guessed she had.

It was time to get back to the hotel, get Jack, and get out.

Deciding the best spot to wait would be outside of the cell in case Deputy Collins got the idea to shut the gate again, Tess tried in vain to smooth some of the wrinkles out of her blouse before giving up. A finger through her wavy, tangled hair was the best she could hope for.

When he returned with a cup of ice water, she thanked him before gulping it down greedily.

He stared but, unsurprisingly, didn't say anything.

Tess felt her cheeks heat up, certain the deputy was judging her. "Am I allowed to go?"

Collins nodded. "Yes, ma'am. Mase buzzed earlier and said to let you out as soon as you were awake. He got held up, but mentioned you might need a ride."

That's right. It dawned on Tess that she hadn't driven to the station in her own car. Mason drove her over in his cruiser which left her car abandoned on the side of the road somewhere in Hamlet. She closed her eyes, exhaling softly. Great. How was she supposed to explain that?

First things first. Before she started to worry about how she was going to retrieve the car without Jack finding out, it might be a good idea to return to the hotel. After a shower and a fresh change of clothes, she'd certainly feel more human.

With that to look forward to, she shook her head.

"Thanks, but don't worry about me. I'll find my way back to the hotel myself."

Collins narrowed his eyes on her. They were a beautiful color, a striking copper shade that popped against his darker skin. "This your first stay in Hamlet?"

"Yes."

"Thought so. One thing I learned living here is that outsiders have a hard time accepting help," he said, unable to hide his derisive snort. "Always think that there's a price for everything."

Something in what Collins said triggered Tess's memory of a hand-painted sign and a slogan drawn prettily near the bottom. "'Hamlet helps'," she quoted.

"That's right. Hamlet's full of good folk. We look out for each other. Mase says you're a fine girl and you need a ride. I trust him so a ride to the inn is what you're gonna get. Now, you want to ride in the front of my car or the back?"

Part of Tess wondered if she should take his no-nonsense tone and harsh words as a threat. To her surprise, she found that she liked his blunt attitude. He wasn't being rude so much as he was definitely a direct kind of guy. If she wasn't so desperate to escape his company, she might have even liked him.

"Am I a prisoner?" she wondered.

Collins nearly glowered. "A guest."

"Then I guess I'll sit in the front."

"Good choice."

DEPUTY COLLINS DROVE HER RIGHT TO THE HAMLET INN. She didn't know how he knew where to go until she remembered that she was stuck in a town with less than two hundred people living there. It was *the* Hamlet Inn, after all. For an outsider staying at a hotel, it was a pretty safe bet that this was the place.

He pulled up to the front, dashing her hopes of sneaking around back and trying to find another way upstairs to her rented room.

"You want me to walk you inside?"

She knew she looked like something the cat dragged in. Her hair felt like a rat's nest attached to her head. Her back ached from sleeping on the hard bench in the cell. She was wearing the same clothes she put on yesterday morning. It was bad enough she had to do the walk of shame through the front lobby of the hotel. If she didn't have to have a police escort, she sure as hell didn't want one.

"Thank you, Deputy. I think I can manage on my own."

"Alright then. Try not to get into any more trouble." His grave voice washed over her like a warning of doom. She had to fight the urge to shiver. "And remember: if someone needs help, offer it. It's the right thing to do."

He wasn't wrong. It was something to think about. So, solemnly promising him that she would, Tess managed to escape from the cruiser.

She could feel his dark eyes on her back as she trudged up the steps and let herself into the inn. The front lobby looked exactly the same as it had before her major lapse in judgement, right down to the woman working the counter. Except, this time, she wasn't ogling Jack. She watched Tessa with open curiosity.

"Good morning, Mrs. Sullivan."

It was the exact same woman who checked them in last night. The one who warned her about the gulch. Too bad she didn't tell her that their precious town actually had a drunk tank.

Since it wasn't her fault that Tess was the idiot who decided to drink and drive last night, she kept herself from scowling at the woman's too chipper greeting. It was tough, though.

Especially since she looked well-rested and fresh, her hair slicked back, obviously wet. She must have already showered. Tess vaguely remembered the woman—this Caro—answering Mason's radio call at close to two in the morning. She probably hadn't gotten any more sleep than Tess had.

Tess decided to hate her on principle. Faking a

tight-lipped grin, she offered a quick wave, leaving the greeting at that as she purposely headed straight for the stairs.

The Hamlet Inn didn't have an elevator. As she dragged her weary body up the narrow flight of stairs, she searched her purse. She saw her wallet, noticed that the car keys were missing—*wonderful*—and continued digging until she found the room key she made Jack give her. At least that was one thing in her favor. Who knows what she would've done if that was gone, too?

Her eyes, like the rest of her, were tired and achy. Tess squinted, trying to make out the number scrawled across the top of the keycard. She remembered that their room was on this level and toward the back. 203 maybe? Or was that a 5?

It was a 3. A *Do Not Disturb* tag was on one door only, and that was to room 203. She'd hung that there herself before she left last night so that Jack could rest peacefully, then promptly forgot she had. It was a good thing the clerk woman ignored it last night or she'd be in even worse trouble for spending the entire night out without checking in.

That was if Jack had even realized just how late it was.

When she let herself in, she discovered that he was still sleeping. The room was dark, the curtains drawn, but she could make out that shape of him sprawled out beneath the floral-print quilted bedspread. His head was covered. He must have passed out hard after the late night wake-up call.

Unusual for Jack? Definitely.

Was Tess grateful for the fact that she could put off the inevitable for a few minutes more? Oh, yeah.

So desperate to feel clean again, she tiptoed carefully past the bed. Tess knew her husband. Once he was up, he'd start grilling her about what happened last night. She wasn't proud of her temper tantrum—looking back, her insistence to leave the inn had been childish—and it was humiliating that she not only spent the night drinking, but then she got caught driving afterward.

What was she thinking? She knew better than to do something so reckless. So *stupid.* The deputy had let her off way too easily. Tess was aware she deserved more than a chaperone and a night in the holding cells. The lecture she was sure to get was going to suck, no doubt. She couldn't deny that she'd earned it, though.

It took her a minute to find her luggage. Jack must have gotten up and moved their duffel bags sometime last night. She remembered tossing it back onto the armchair. After tiptoeing around the darkened room, searching, she finally found the two bags stacked one on top of the other underneath the window. Picking up her bag, she purposely left the curtain alone. No reason to face the light of day just yet.

Tess locked herself in the bathroom. Avoiding her reflection, she quickly stripped out of her rumpled clothes and jumped into the shower. The first spray of the hot water in her face made her groan. The knots in her back relaxed as she turned and let the water beat down on her. By the time the hot water had cooled down to lukewarm, she was starting to feel back to normal.

To her surprise, the towels hanging in the inn's bathroom were fluffy and luxuriant. She was used to staying at hotel chains where the guest towels were one step up from toilet paper. The oversized towel she wrapped herself in felt like she was being swaddled in a cloud, it was that soft.

If she thought she could get away with it, she'd hide one of them in her duffel bag before they checked out. Except, she admitted, that wouldn't be very helpful. So, with Deputy Collins' solemn voice still running through her head, she reluctantly hung the towel back up when she was dry.

She didn't know how long she hid in the bathroom. She did, however, admit that she was stalling. Since they would be heading back out on the road soon, she threw on a comfy pair of jeans, a tank top, and her favorite hoodie. It had the name of her alma mater on it and, though she graduated more than three years ago, she liked to wear it whenever she had the chance. Slipping on her sneakers, she mentally prepared herself to face her husband.

Tess opened the bathroom door. "Honey," she called out, "you awake?"

Nothing.

Okay. That was weird. She'd expected the sounds of her shower to rouse him. Now that he was still sleeping, she didn't know what to do. Glancing around the bathroom, her eyes fell on the hairdryer resting on the top shelf of the towel rack. She grabbed a chunk of her damp hair, letting the strands slide through her fingers.

Plugging the hairdryer into the outlet, Tess let her lips curve slightly for the first time since yesterday.

Back home, he always complained that it was impossible for him to sleep when she was drying her hair. The blow dryer the hotel provided was so loud, it sounded like there was a small airplane in the bathroom with her. There was no way he could sleep through that.

Except he had.

When she finished fluffing her hair, brushing the dirty blonde waves out, she placed the dryer on the side of the sink before gathering all of her belongings together. She stepped back into the room, expecting to find Jack waiting with his eyes open.

Nope. As if she hadn't made a peep, he was lying beneath the covers. Quiet. Unmoving.

Throwing her duffel bag on the floor, tossing her brush angrily on top of it, she scowled at the lump on the bed. "Come off it, Jack. Stop fooling. I know you've got to be pissed, but pretending to sleep isn't going to work."

His silence was the only answer she received.

That made her furious. He always did this. Either he shot down her arguments, or he acted like she didn't have any at all. And, yes, she knew that she was the only one to blame for what happened, but she'd spent the whole morning and most of her shower trying to figure out how she was going to explain her actions to her husband.

And now that she was ready? He didn't want to hear any of it.

Uh-uh. No way.

Tess stormed over to the bed, snatching the blanket off of him. He was lying on his stomach, his face turned away from her.

"Jack!" she snapped, slapping him on his back to get his attention. "Are you listening to me?"

The instant she touched him, she knew. His body was stiff. Cold. He wasn't moving. She knew. In the pit of her stomach, where panic sparked and bloomed before overwhelming any common sense she had left, Tessa fucking knew.

That didn't stop her from what she did next. Nothing could.

His name stuck in her throat. "Jack." It came out like a whisper, a soft rasp strangled by her frantic breath. Her hands started to shake. She didn't look. She couldn't look. Breathe in, breathe out. She was the only one making any noise. He was still. Too damn still.

She grabbed at her husband, yanking on his shirt, pushing him. He didn't move. Terror coursed through her veins, cold and terrible, and she heard someone chanting *no, no, no* before realizing the anguished squeal was coming from her.

She never knew where she got the strength from. Half his size and admittedly a weakling, Tess hefted Jack until his body flopped from his front to his back. His eyes—and his tongue—the blue lips. The waxy, white skin. Her hands flew up to cover her mouth, horror and shock and devastation crashing over her like a wave. It threatened to drag her under, drown her, leave her battered and broken against the shore. Without even giving her body the order to move, she took one step toward the bed again.

And that's when she saw the noose tied tightly around his neck. She blinked. Stared. Then, as loud as she possibly could, she started to scream.

6

Lucas De Angelis was dreading this call.

He knew it was coming. Every morning after for the last three years, the call came through first thing and Lucas knew better than to ignore it. It was like a band-aid. Grab it quick, give it a tug, and get it the hell over with. Yeah, it might hurt. It was still better than dragging it out.

If only she had the decency to wait until he was up and ready to deal with her. It was Sunday, the only day that he shut down his office and allowed himself any rest. He would always take in any emergency patients, of course, but at least the rest of the townsfolk were considerate enough not to bother him on Sunday if what ailed them could damn well wait until Monday.

Lucas didn't even open his eyes. When the first buzz came through on his Hamlet radio, he blindly groped outward until his fingers brushed one of the knobs on the side. He always slept with his communicator on his nightstand in case of some medical emergency. Stifling his groan, he mentally prepared himself for what was coming.

He already knew who was buzzing him today.

His fingers tweaked the nearest knob. Pressing the side button, he answered. "Hello?"

No response.

A second later, another buzz.

His eyes opened to slits. That wasn't Caity's call signal. It was the sheriff's—and it *was* set to emergency.

Sitting up, Lucas clicked his radio over to the right channel. "This is Dr. De Angelis. What's the emergency?"

"Luc. Hey. You up?"

He was now. "Yeah. What's going on?"

There was a pause. "We've got something over at Bonnie's inn. A real live DB. Do you think you can come over and check it out?"

DB. Dead body. As the only trained medical doctor in town, Lucas knew his way around a corpse, both in his practice and because of his adopted duty as the local medical examiner whenever necessary. Only a few months ago he'd had to wheel Mrs. Birmingham's withered old body out on a stretcher. It wasn't his favorite part of the job, but he could handle it. He had to. No one else in Hamlet would.

"Of course. I'll be right on my way." He was already out of bed, searching for something to wear. His gaze fell on the alarm clock resting on the edge of his nightstand. It was 11:33. Even for a Sunday, he'd slept in much later than he usually did—and Caitlin hadn't buzzed him before this. Yesterday was the anniversary of their divorce. She should've called him hours ago, drunk and babbling and begging him to give them one more shot.

Something wasn't right.

Grabbing a change of underwear from his dresser, he signaled back to Caity. "Is there anything else I have to know before I go?"

"Shit, Luc. I think we've got a homicide."

With one sock halfway on his foot, Lucas froze. He gripped his radio so tight, he nearly cracked the plastic side. "Anyone we know?"

Caitlin might be, in his very experienced opinion, a paranoid shrew who drove him absolutely batty with her insecurities, but she *was* loyal to a fault. As far as she was concerned, when the people of Hamlet voted her in as their sheriff, she became their protector. If one of them was hurt, Caity wouldn't stop until she found out who did the hurting *and* made them pay for it.

"Negative. It's a— he was an outsider."

Lucas let out a sigh of relief. He was a doctor. He hated the loss of any life but, well, he was loyal to their village, too. If someone had to die, at least it was just an outsider.

"Gimme ten, Cait. I'll be there as soon as I can."

"Don't worry about rushing." Her laugh was hollow. "Trust me, he's not going anywhere."

LUCAS USUALLY FOUND A HUNDRED DIFFERENT REASONS to avoid Caitlin, especially so close to the anniversary of their divorce. As bitter as it was when they first split, they both eventually agreed that they were much better friends and neighbors than they had ever been lovers or partners.

Most of the time Caitlin remembered that—until the reminder came that he was the one who instigated the divorce and she gave him hell for it.

It wasn't too difficult to avoid her. There was a handful of professionals who made their homes year round in Hamlet. As the only doctor and the town sheriff, they were often too busy for Caitlin's childish tantrums. He humored her on the anniversary of their divorce because he still cared for her, even if he wasn't in love with her anymore.

If he was honest, he didn't think he *ever* actually loved her. She'd just always been there, as constant as the sunrise.

That was why he answered her buzz that morning.

He expected the leftover ramblings of her annual drunken binge, the pleas that they could make it work again. Instead, he received a summons *to* work.

A summons to death.

Standing outside of the hotel room, Lucas watched the scene playing out in front of him before going in. He preferred to observe first, make his own assumptions. It was too easy to be swayed by someone else's preconceived notions.

The one time he stayed in Bonnie Mitchell's inn, he had a first floor room. Except for an entirely different color scheme—the room he rented when he first moved out of his and Caity's place was more wintry grey than springtime peach—this one was set up just the same. Two chairs, two dressers, a nightstand, and a very wide window. Then, of course, the large bed that took up much of the space.

Lucas's attention was drawn immediately to the still figure sprawled flat on his back. The tail end of the rope tied around the dead man's neck spooled on the thick, cream-colored carpet. Ligature strangulation, if he had to take a guess.

Caitlin was standing at the foot of the bed, a notepad in one hand and a pen in the other. Most unusually, her long red hair was hanging loosely down her back; it was her habit to wear her hair plaited away from her face when she was working. She was also wearing a tinted pair of shades, despite the fact that they were indoors and the curtain was still drawn.

Taking the medical bag from its place slung over his shoulder, he set it down by Caitlin's feet. If the sheriff was standing there, it was a safe bet that he wasn't going to contaminate any evidence if he joined her.

"I'm here. What do we have?"

At the sound of his voice, she winced, like he was speaking too loud. When she answered, though, she was as succinct and professional as he could've hoped.

"Male vic. Twenty-six years old. Caucasian, brown and brown. License in his wallet lists his stats as 5'11", 215 pounds. Identified by same ID as James Sullivan, also known as Jack. Confirmed by his wife. Both of them outsiders."

Of course, she would have to make that point. To Caitlin—and most of Hamlet—being an outsider was as much as a descriptor as age or height or weight. You couldn't change it, not really. It just was.

"How'd he die?"

From his first glance, it was fairly obvious. Lucas wanted to hear Caitlin's opinion anyway. It wouldn't change his mind—only an autopsy and further testing might—but it didn't hurt to ask someone with a practiced eye. Maybe the sheriff saw something that he hadn't.

Using the tip of her pen, she gestured at his throat.

"It's gotta be strangulation. Someone snuck up on this guy, tied him up tighter than a twine knot. From the look of him, and the level of rigor mortis, I put TOD at a couple of hours ago. You'll get a better read in the fridge."

He stiffened at her last comment. "That back room might be small, so what? It serves its purpose as a mortuary, Caity. It doesn't have to be fancy. I barely use it anyway."

Her nonplussed expression seemed out of place at a crime scene. The sunglasses didn't help. "It's a fridge, Luc. I get the chills whenever I have to go there and not just because of the bodies. Don't fool yourself."

She was goading him. Standing there, wound up tight and nearly vibrating in place from a mixture of fury and frustration, Caitlin was itching for a fight if only to let off some steam. It was how she always got whenever there was a problem she couldn't fix with a snap of her fingers or a flash of her sheriff's badge. She considered crime in her jurisdiction a personal insult.

This murder was an ultimate betrayal. Though outwardly she seemed calm and collected, inside she was spoiling to release some tension. He could oblige her, or he could get to work.

Lucas let it go. Hiking up his trousers, he crouched down low to get a better look at the victim.

Strangulation was never pretty. Jack Sullivan might have been a handsome man once but there was no sign of that in the caricature he left behind. Big brown eyes bulged, red splashing across the whites where blood vessels burst violently. Thick rope, common rope twisted around his throat. Lucas could see the purple bruises peeking out on his neck. No sign of scratches on his skin.

So he hadn't struggled. Strange.

Lucas reached behind him for his medical bag. After digging through it, he found a pair of latex gloves. "How many guests are staying at the inn right now?" he called out as he snapped them on.

The sheriff hesitated in answering. She knew where Lucas was going with this. A lifelong fan of mystery novels and true crime, her ex was *detecting*. Out of spite, she wanted to ignore his question. But since it helped her to talk out a case, she obliged him.

"Just two. Both outsiders, our vic and his wife. Bonnie was off for the night, her back aching from the storm. She was in her third floor room all night. Her daughter had the desk 'til two a.m. when she dragged Roy out of bed, made him take over until she then relieved him at eight this morning. Body was discovered at about half past nine.

"Even if I thought they had it in them, surveillance clears all three. I've already been down to see the tapes. It backs up their statements. They're not involved. Just bad luck that they own the place."

Lucas leaned in closer, peering at the dead man's hands. "Anyone else pop on the video?"

"Only the wife. Caro says she left around ten p.m. last night. Tapes confirm it. They have her coming back in at nine a.m."

"It took her half an hour to find the body?"

"She thought he was still sleeping. Took a shower first, got ready, then got the shock of her life when she went to wake him up."

"What about the room?"

Caitlin flipped through her notes. "Couple reportedly requested a private room. Caro gave them a far room on the second floor because it best fit their request. Unfortunately for us, the cameras don't reach that far. We have no visual of anyone going in and out of this room. She did say that she had cause to use the boards for Sullivan's room in the middle of the night." Using the point of her pen, Caitlin scanned her notes, circling part of Caroline's statement when she found it. "As of 1:47 a.m., we have confirmation that he was still alive. Me and my team just gotta figure out what happened to change that."

Lucas knew her well enough to know when he was being dismissed. But Caitlin knew *him* well enough to know that he wouldn't be shut down until he was ready.

"Okay, no one on the camera. But these doors all

lock. How did someone even get in here to strangle the guy?"

She snorted. "The cameras are the height of security in the inn. I'm lucky there was that much. Bonnie told me that every damn lock on the first and second floor can be opened with the same keycard. Anyone who's ever had one, or could get their paws on one, could open the guest rooms."

That made sense. Took away a bit his thrill for a locked room mystery, but still. "Not even counting the outsiders, most everyone in Hamlet has stayed over in the inn for a night out."

"Yeah." With an aggravated sniff, Caitlin nodded at the bed. "Whenever you're ready, Sherlock, I'd love for you to give me your read on our DB. I don't know about you, but the sooner we can get all the facts down, the sooner I can get to work on solving this thing. I've seen a lot over the years. Nothing like this. This one is a real piece of work, I've gotta warn you."

She wasn't kidding.

Leaning in again, he moved the vic's head so that he could get a better look at the taut rope knotted around the man's thick throat. And, okay, so that he didn't have to see the man's destroyed eyes. The way they bulged unnerved him, how eerily they stared accusingly at the ceiling even worse. Lucas preferred to focus on the marks left behind from the rope. Later, when the sheriff gave him the okay, he would remove it.

For now, though, he slipped one gloved finger underneath. Very little slack existed between the stiff flesh and the twisted rope. Abrasions left red scratches running through the mottled purple bruises of the ligatures. A classic case of homicidal strangulation.

But no fingernail marks. Not from the assailant trying to restrain a large man. Definitely none from a physically fit male in his prime trying to defend his very life. It almost seemed like Jack Sullivan laid there and allowed someone to strangle him. It made no sense.

The fact that he was murdered in Hamlet was just as incomprehensible. Who would want to kill this outsider?

His concentration was suddenly broken by a keening cry, followed by a muffled sob. When it continued, decreasing in volume if not its intensity, Lucas turned to look back up at the sheriff.

While he was studying Sullivan, Caitlin had returned to her notes. Meticulous as ever, Lucas was willing to bet that she had everything about the dead man, from his birthday to his shoe size, written down in a code that only she could decipher.

Caitlin was flipping through her pages again, adding notes and crossing things out as she tried her best to capture the crime scene on paper. Photos would come later, he knew. For now, she wanted to get down as many of her thoughts as possible.

As if she felt his gaze on her, she glanced up and asked, "You got something for me yet?"

"No. It's just... what's that noise?"

"The weeper?" Caitlin waved her hand vaguely in the direction of the closed bathroom door before jotting something else down. "It's the wife. Mason is in there trying to console her. I guess she's taking it kind of hard. Like I said before, she's the one who found the guy."

"Hmm." Standing up, he moved closer to Caitlin. "You looking at her for the murder?"

She looked up from her notepad in time to catch Lucas as he tried to get a glimpse of her scribblings. She pushed her sunglasses down her nose so that she could face him directly. Her eyes were glassy and bloodshot courtesy of her late night but there was green steel staring back at him.

"This isn't one of those mystery books you liked to read. Let's leave the detective work to the real cops. I just need you to take a look at the body and verify the cause of death. Can you do that?"

It was a slapdown, no doubt about that. He couldn't say he was surprised. A wicked hangover could turn Caity into a demon. He knew that. It was one more reason why he was glad he got out when he did.

"Calm down, kitty. No need to sharpen your claws

on me. I know my job." Wiping his hands on his slacks, Lucas stepped away, gave her space. He kept his back to the bed, knowing there was nothing more he could do for the victim until he got the corpse down to his office. But something nagged at him. "Question. Has anybody moved him?"

"Luc—"

"Doctor," he told her as the first glove came off with a snap. Two could play that petty game.

Before she shoved her sunglasses back up her nose, he could've sworn he saw her roll her eyes. "Just the witness, *Doctor* De Angelis. The vic's wife came in, found him face down on the bed and assumed he was still sleeping. Mase was first on-site and he took her statement. Husband's still lazing about in bed even after she showered and got dressed, so she grabs the blanket, tries to shake him awake. Says he's cold. Panics. Tries shoving him onto his back."

Falling easily into her role as sheriff, Caitlin brought him over to the bed. Using her pen as a pointer, she gestured to the body.

"Big guy. Gotta be what? Way more than two hundred pounds dead weight, given his stats. It was a struggle for her. You can see where the sheet got all twisted as she pulled and eventually flipped him over. Once she saw the rope, she was done for. Knew he was gone, screamed the whole house down. Caroline got

Mase on the radio, who got me. And then I buzzed you."

Lucas nodded. That would explain it. "Alright. Well, it's definitely homicide. He didn't do this to himself. I mean, I can't say anything for sure until I get him down to my office, but I'm pretty sure someone else tied this around his neck and pulled real tight."

"She might have done it," Caitlin mused. She underlined one particular bit of chicken scratch covering the page. "It's… it could be possible."

Just like how he could tell when his ex was goading him, he was well aware that she was baiting him. Like a wriggling worm on a hook, she dangled that little tidbit in front of him, waiting to see if he'd bite. He almost didn't because she so obviously expected him to. Even when they were still married, she always liked to tease him that he was a doctor by trade, and a detective at his core.

Lucas lasted five seconds.

"Okay. Tell me. Who do you think did it?" Before Caitlin answered, he guessed, "The wife?"

She shrugged. "Hey, that's Homicide 101. The husband—or, in this case, wife—is usually the prime suspect."

"So, if you ended up on the slab in my office, it would be because I was the one who put you there?"

"Don't act cute with me, Luc. You know what I mean."

He had to admit she had a point. She wasn't entirely wrong. In most murder cases, it was a safe bet that the victim was killed by someone close to them. The surviving spouse was always going to be the first one questioned, whether because they had pertinent information or because they were the perpetrator.

"What can you tell me about Sullivan's wife?"

Without even looking at her notes, Caitlin rattled of the woman's information. "Tessa Sullivan. Twenty-five. Light brown hair, hazelish eyes. I put her at 5'4", maybe 5'5", 115 pounds. Petite. Worked as a kindergarten teacher before getting married to Sullivan last September."

Lucas called up a mental image of the woman and compared it to the brute strength required to both incapacitate and then execute a man of Sullivan's size. "And you think she could do this to her husband?"

"You haven't seen her yet. I have. Ignore the stats for a minute, Luc. I'm telling you, she's got this... this *look* in her eyes. It could've been her." Slapping her notepad against her thigh, Caitlin muttered under her breath, "Damn it, it *should* be her."

He quirked an eyebrow at her heated reaction. When it came to her job, she was cold and clinical. Evidence solved cases, not her personal feelings.

The Sullivan woman had gotten under Cait's skin.

Interesting.

7

He was saved from having to respond by the soft sound of the bathroom door opening. After Caitlin's last comment, Lucas wanted to get a good look at Tessa Sullivan himself.

Except the shadow that led the way was far too big for the petite woman Caitlin described. A quiet murmur echoed in the hotel room a moment before Mason Walsh stepped out.

He raised a hand in greeting when he saw Lucas. "Hey, doc. Sheriff called you in?"

Lucas nodded. "I've done all I can here. I'm gonna call in a couple of favors, see if I can get some help moving your vic over to my place." He glanced over at Caitlin. "Are you done with him?

"Yeah. I promised Bonnie that I'd clear this room as soon as possible. We can get the DB out of here, then my guys can start processing the scene. Willie's gonna come in early and pull a double shift at the station in order to free up the fellas. I'll get Mason and Sly to help me out here. After that, I can give them a couple of hours down each and check in on you later."

Walsh cleared his throat. "Actually, boss, I thought I would see about getting our witness settled somewhere else."

"What? Why?"

"It's too hard for her to focus on giving a coherent statement when she knows her husband is lying in his bed like that. I got her to stop crying so much, but it's rough. She wants to go."

"No," Caitlin said flatly.

"Sheriff—"

"Deputy, I told you that I didn't want her leaving. Was I unclear before?"

"No, ma'am."

"Then we're done here. Let's leave the wife with Caro and Roy while we get to work on the crime scene."

Walsh puffed out his chest. "With all due respect, Sheriff, I still think I should move her first. She doesn't want to stay at the inn anymore. I get that."

Rubbing the bridge of her nose in open irritation, Caitlin snapped, "Don't be ridiculous. Bonnie has more than twelve rooms open in her place at any given time. The outsider only died in this one."

"Wow, Caity," Lucas murmured under his breath. "Wow. So sensitive."

"Zip it, Luc. You know I'm right. The inn is the only place we have in Hamlet for outsiders. I can't let her leave. Not yet. She's the best lead I got. And I doubt she'll want to stay in the cells since *someone* keeps insisting she's innocent."

With his eyes darting back to the room where he left the weeping woman, Walsh obviously didn't catch on to the fact that the sheriff was talking about him until she jabbed him in the side with her pointer finger.

"What? Wait— *that* again, Sheriff? I already told you. There's no way Tess could've killed her husband. She was locked up tight in the holding cells all night, first with me watching, then with Sly. No way she could've done it."

"Locked up?" Lucas echoed. It seemed there was way more to this than he first thought. And it was suddenly even clearer that the poor widow had nothing to do with her husband's murder. Kind of hard to strangle a man when she was behind bars for whatever reason.

"Tess?" Caitlin said at the same time. Her comment was more of a sneer. Partly because of how chummy her deputy was becoming with her witness, but mostly because it burned to know that her theory was already full of so many holes, it was basically Swiss cheese.

Walsh had the decency to flush. “Mrs. Sullivan. There was an incident outside of Thirsty’s last night. I had it under control.”

Caitlin scowled. “Is that where you found her? The bar?”

“It’s where I saw you, too,” Walsh reminded Caitlin.

Lucas wasn’t even the least bit surprised to hear that. From the way Caitlin straightened, drawing herself up to her full height though the deputy still dwarfed her, Lucas bet she never expected Walsh to throw that back in her face.

“What I do when I'm off duty is my business, Deputy, and I'll thank you to remember that when we're on. Besides, I managed to refrain from getting carted off to the holding cells, so I was better off than Sullivan’s wife.”

Walsh was walking a razor thin line. Lucas watched their match like the interested spectator he was. Caity’s color was up, her cheeks nearly the same shade as her hair. He thought about warning the younger man before deciding against it. The deputy had to learn sooner or later. Might as well get some entertainment out of it since, for once, Caitlin wasn't fighting with him.

Walsh gulped, his Adam’s apple quivering as he set his jaw. “That's true, boss. Think about it. You had plenty of friends around to keep you from getting into trouble, including me, Willie, and Sly. Poor Mrs.

Sullivan didn't have anyone but me last night. Now her husband's been taken from her. Here. In Hamlet."

"I'm aware of that. Doesn't change a thing. We still have a job to do."

"I'm trying to do right by our vic's wife. You might want to treat her like a criminal. I don't."

"Okay. That's it. Stand down, Deputy."

Walsh immediately began another retort. "But—"

Having had enough at last, Caitlin tore off her sunglasses and silenced him with one firm look. Because her team was so small and close, she tended to let her deputies get away with a lot. Sometimes she had to remind them who was in charge.

"Go to the station. Bring the witness there and leave her in Wilhelmina's custody. I want to question her myself. Then—and only if I'm satisfied in her responses—we'll discuss the witness's relocation. Do you understand?"

"Yes, but—"

She wasn't done. "I've changed my mind. I'll buzz Sly to join me here, then I'll tackle the wit. You've been on duty for more than sixteen hours. It's made you twitchy, Mase. Take a few hours down now."

"Boss—"

"Those are your orders. Go."

Walsh swallowed roughly. "Yes, Sheriff."

He wanted to continue to argue. That much was obvious. He didn't, though. When she got like this, no one disobeyed Caitlin De Angelis—except, perhaps, Lucas. However, the doctor happened to agree with Caitlin. Tessa Sullivan was the best lead that the sheriff had. She had to keep her close.

Walsh disappeared into the bathroom without another word. As Lucas gathered up his medical bag, he could just make out the deputy's muffled voice as he explained what was going to happen next. Silence followed. Either Mrs. Sullivan accepted what he said, or she spoke too softly for it to carry into the hotel room.

This time, when the bathroom door opened again, the woman exited first.

She took him completely by surprise.

If Caitlin hadn't told him that Tessa Sullivan was in her mid-twenties, he would've put her much closer to her late teens. She was small-boned and slender-framed, lost in a hooded sweatshirt that was two sizes too big. Her dirty blonde hair fell in waves to her shoulder. It stuck up in tufts from where she pulled at it in her grief.

The deputy fell in step behind her, close enough to catch her if she stumbled. Lucas didn't quite understand the fervor with which he defended this woman to Caitlin before but, watching as she moved zombie-like across the room, he got it now. Mrs. Sullivan —*Tessa*—her size and demeanor, clearly inspired protective feelings in others. Hell, he had to fight the urge himself to scoop her up in his arms and tell her that everything was going to be fine.

Caitlin flipped her notepad closed, tucked the pad in the back pocket of her uniform pants. She slipped her pen behind her ear, losing it almost immediately in the red tangle, then hooked her sunglasses on the front pocket of her uniform shirt. Her hands free, she met Walsh and Tessa in the middle of the room.

She didn't offer to shake hands, or any other sort of greeting. No surprise there, either. The woman was only an outsider, and one who had brought trouble to Hamlet. In Caitlin's opinion, Tessa was lucky not to be locked up again.

"Deputy Walsh is going to bring you back to the station. I know this is a very inconvenient time for you, Mrs. Sullivan, but the first forty-eight hours in any homicide are crucial. Anything you can tell me, anything you might remember, it could make a difference in catching your husband's killer."

The poor thing flinched, her hand flying up to muffle her sob.

"Sheriff..."

Caitlin purposely ignored her deputy's warning tone. Lucas knew exactly what she was doing. If she didn't acknowledge it, she didn't have to discipline him for it.

Instead, she loped over to Lucas and grabbed him

by the upper arm. Which, he realized the second he felt the bite of her fingers, he should've expected.

"Before you go, just one more thing." The possessive stroke that followed wasn't quite professional, and he struggled not to jerk away from her. "I want to introduce you to our doctor. Dr. De Angelis also acts as our medical examiner. He's going to be the one taking control of your husband's remains."

Dropping her hand, Tessa lost the last bit of her color in her too pale face.

Caitlin kept her hand on Lucas's arm. "I'm sure you'd prefer we wait until you've had time to process what's happened here today but, unfortunately, we don't have the time. Sorry." No, she wasn't. "I'm going to ask if you'll allow an autopsy. Because this is a homicide, we'll get approval from the county judge if we have to. I hope it won't come to that. It'll speed things along if you okay it now."

Tessa's eyes flickered from the point where Caitlin clutched him up to his face, then widened as if seeing him for the first time. Rimmed with red, with a trail of tears that tracked down her cheeks, he still thought the golden color was the most beautiful thing he had ever seen.

Hazel, Caity said. She wasn't even close. He met Tessa's stare directly. His bag slipped from his hand, landed with a *thump* at his feet.

Something shifted in that moment. He couldn't

explain it. He might have imagined it. But when she shuddered, took a deep breath, nodded, Lucas knew it was because of him.

"Yes," she whispered. "Do what you have to do."

"He's in good hands," Lucas promised.

Taking her suddenly by the elbow, Walsh murmured to the woman before leading her out of the room. Lucas traced the shape of her as the deputy hustled her away from the crime scene, purposely blocking her from seeing her husband's body. Before he knew it, he was left alone with Caitlin and the murdered outsider.

Lucas gave his head a clearing shake. It didn't work. He wasn't sure he'd get the tear-streaked cheeks or haunted golden eyes out of his head any time soon.

Realizing that Caitlin still had her fingers hooked around his bicep, he shook her off. Her point was already made, though, and she took his sudden rebuff without comment. A small smile lingered on her lips as Lucas moved away, bending down to recover his medical bag.

Tucking a loose strand of hair behind her ear, she cast her gaze around the room. The smile transformed into a grim look of determination.

"Okay, now that she's gone, we can get to work. I need a camera in here to get the photos before you move Sullivan. I need a sweeper to check for any evidence I missed my first run-through. I've got to talk to Bonnie again, see if I can get a copy of her tapes. First, though, I gotta buzz Sly, get him down here." She unclipped her radio from her belt, cursing as she did. "Why didn't I hire another deputy when the budget said I could? I could've used another guy."

Lucas shouldered his bag. "Don't think I'll help you and Collins with the processing. My job is to take care of the victim's body. You can solve the crime on your own, *detective*. And," he added, "you wouldn't be down one man if it wasn't for your knee-jerk reaction in sending Walsh home."

"Okay, look. I'm sorry about the mystery crack from before, alright? And maybe I am being too rough on the kid. Hell, this one's got me shook. Mase was right. Sly gave me a report that this guy's wife was in the holding cell overnight, and Mase already stood up and vouched for this outsider. I'd love for her to be responsible for this, but how? Damn it, she's smaller than me. Even if I didn't believe my guys, I gotta believe my own eyes. It would've taken real strength to strangle this Sullivan." Caitlin snorted. "I could snap her in half like a twig."

"You sound pissed, Caity," Lucas pointed out after a moment's silence. They both knew that an angry sheriff was a foolish sheriff. She'd overlook something if she couldn't get her head on straight. "You really want it to be her."

She almost lied. It wasn't right for the head of

Hamlet's law enforcement to wish guilt on someone just because it would be easier. But this was Luc. She couldn't lie to him.

"Okay. Yeah. Nothing against her and all, but yeah. I want it to be her." She paused for a beat and put her sunglasses back on. "You know why?"

Lucas had known Caitlin long enough to understand the way her mind worked. "Because if she did it, that means one of us didn't."

"Someone killed Jack Sullivan. That's fact. And as far as I can tell, no one's crossed out of Hamlet since the outsiders came in."

Which meant that their peaceful little village now harbored a murderer.

So this was shock.

If it wasn't for Mason's steadying hand on her arm, Tess thought she might just drop. Her limbs were heavy, though her head felt weightless. She was bobbing along some vaguely familiar hallway, her eyes seeing yet unfocused. Every part of her that counted was back in that hotel room.

Jack was dead. If she told herself that enough, would she believe it?

She saw his body. She *found* his body. And still it seemed like some horrible joke.

Her hands were trembling. She folded her fingers into her palms, tightened her hands into fists to stop the shakes. She absolutely refused to fall apart. This was when she needed to be strong.

With a shudder, she straightened, determined to stand on her own two feet. She didn't know these people. The deputy… she didn't know this man. After last night, he already certainly thought she was a lush. Now she was nothing but a fragile disaster. He knew it, too. She straightened, and he continued to rest the warmth of his palm on her chilled skin, holding tight.

Fine.

Using him as a buffer between her and the rest of the world, Tess let him lead her down another hallway and out the back entrance she would have given anything that morning to know about. Now, though, it simply meant she was that much closer to an exit to get out of the damn hotel.

She didn't argue as he guided her toward the same cruiser she'd ridden in last night. As he helped her escape from Jack's room, he explained in a hurried whisper that this was all a formality, that he had to take her down to the station. She accepted that she had no choice. But she didn't have to be carried there. Once she was outside, she pulled away from him.

He immediately reached for her again. Tess ducked away, wrapping her arms around her waist.

"No. I'm okay now," she told him. Her eyes were

dry. She felt like she'd cried all the tears she had to shed in that bathroom. Turning, she saw that Deputy Walsh's uniform was damp from where he'd held her as she sobbed. She winced. And lied again. "I'm okay."

"Are you sure?"

No. "Yes."

Tess waited until he reluctantly moved away from her before she struggled to find something else to say, something that wouldn't draw her thoughts back to what she left behind. It was impossible, so she asked, "Who was that?"

Everything that happened in the hours since she found Jack was a blur. It was like someone stuffed cotton inside her skull; she could barely think. She remembered clinging to Mason, and the way he took her into the bathroom so that she didn't have to stand in sight of her husband's body. People came and people went but only two things stood out from the haze: fiery red hair and a pair of icy blue eyes.

Mason waited until she buckled herself in and he had taken his seat beside her to say, "I suppose you're referring to the doctor." Lucas was a looker, no doubt, but he had hoped that in her grief she hadn't noticed. "He's a good guy, I guess. Does his job."

"The doctor. He's the man who's going to..." She couldn't bring herself to say it. She didn't have to. Mason nodded and she knew. "Okay. Um, what about the woman? The one with the red hair. Is she in charge? I don't know, she came off as real official but... I— I think I've seen her before. How? Is that possible?"

Mason took his time answering her question. "That would be Sheriff De Angelis. She's the head of law enforcement in Hamlet so you could say she's definitely in charge."

He draped his arm behind her headrest, turning to look behind them as he backed the cruiser out of its spot. Tess noticed that he left his arm there once they were heading away from the hotel. She scooted closer to the door, leaving a gap between them.

Tess could've sworn she felt his fingers ghosting over her hair. Leaning into the window, she struggled to remember the last two days because it was better than realizing how much he closed the gap.

Her memories were hazy at best. The alcohol and the shock hadn't helped any. Even so, she was certain she was right. And Mason had purposely avoided the part where she asked how she knew the sheriff.

Weird.

She wracked her brain. Looking back, the only two people she met at the station last night were Deputy Walsh and Deputy Collins. The sheriff never stopped in, so it wasn't there. The niggling doubt managed to shove aside some of her guilt and grief. She clung to it like a lifeline.

Tess was absolutely positive she'd seen that red hair before. And then it hit her.

"The bar. Last night. I remember now. She was dancing and you— *Oh.*" A dull color spotted her cheeks as the complete show from last night flashed in her memory. Including the way the intoxicated sheriff threw herself into Mason's arms. "You know her very well."

His hands tightened on the steering wheel. It was no use denying it. "You saw that." He could kick himself for letting Caitlin paw at him last night. "You have to understand—"

"I don't have to understand anything, Deputy." Her words spilled out in a rush. The color deepened to a rosy red. "You don't have to explain to me."

He wanted to. "The lady at the bar—she's my boss. I'm just one of her deputies, that's all. And, yeah, she might get a little... *excitable* when she's had some to drink, but she's the best sheriff we've ever had. She won't rest until we find out what happened to your husband, you can trust me on that."

Mentioning Jack was like throwing a bucket of ice water over her flaming embarrassment.

Her voice went flat. "So she's going to be the one questioning me."

"She has to do her job." He kept his tone gentle. "We all do."

"I know."

TESSA DIDN'T SAY ANOTHER WORD THE REST OF THE WAY to the station. Respecting her silence, Mason kept his thoughts to himself. So that she didn't see him peeking, he stole glances at his quiet passenger every now and then. She looked so small, so utterly breakable. He wanted to take her hand, promise her that she had nothing to worry about it. But since he didn't want to lie, he said nothing.

Her husband was dead. She might be innocent—at the moment, he was sure that meant precious little to her. And since he couldn't explain how Jack Sullivan became the first murder victim in Hamlet in Mason's lifetime, he knew there was plenty for her—and the whole village—to worry over.

As he pulled into the station and cut the engine, he decided to ease one of his own worries. Whatever happened during the interrogation Sheriff De Angelis was sure to put her through, Mason wanted Tessa to know one thing.

"Um, Tess— it's okay if I call you Tess, right?"

Her gaze flickered toward his shoulder and the damp patch that lingered there. She shrugged helplessly. "That's fine."

"Good. There's something I want to tell you, Tess. It doesn't have any bearing on the case or anything but, well... Sheriff De Angelis, she's just my boss. There's nothing going on between us. I mean, just in case you were wondering. Not that you were. It's just, after the bar last night—"

"Forget about it."

He couldn't. "It's just that the sheriff, she's—"

"You're a good man, Deputy. Mason," she corrected when he began to protest. A small, shy grin splashed across her face for an instant. "Don't worry about me. No matter how tough she is, I won't forget how kind you've been. How helpful. I promise, I won't hold you accountable for the actions of your superior. I'll be fine. I just want to answer her questions and lay down. Maybe then, when I wake up, this will all be some horrible dream."

As Tess bent to undo her seatbelt, Mason leaned back in his seat, one hand rubbing his chin.

Kind? Helpful? That wasn't it at all. But if that's what she had to tell herself, he could accept that. She'd just lost her husband. He knew that. He also knew that, technically, he was no longer poaching. He couldn't steal a man's wife when that man was dead.

It was a terrible thought. Mason was ashamed of even having it. Didn't make it any less true.

8

Lucas was sewing Sullivan back up when he heard the door behind him open. Knowing who was looming made him take his time on the final few stitches.

There was only one person who treated his office as their own and, still raw from their encounter at the inn, he wasn't sure he was ready to face Caitlin again so soon.

But that was Luc speaking. Dr. De Angelis knew that he had to be professional and do his job. And part of that job was addressing the lead investigator on the case.

Even if she was his ex-wife.

She'd gotten rid of those ridiculous sunglasses. Her hat was gone, her red hair lanky and flat against her head. She clutched a shiny maroon thermos to her chest. She sniffed, sneezed, then scowled. "God, it stinks in here. I hate this fridge."

It was a closet-sized morgue, hardly bigger than a freezer, and just as cold. He could never understand why she always seemed surprised whenever she had to meet him down here. At least she'd remembered and worn her uniform jacket this time.

He nodded at her. "You look tired, Caity. Third cup of coffee?"

Caitlin glanced at the thermos in her hand as if unsure how it got there. "I don't know. It might be my fourth at this point. I lost track."

"Be careful. Next thing I know, you'll be the one on my slab."

"Ha ha. Funny." Now that she noticed her coffee, she unscrewed the top and took a healthy gulp. "Let's focus on the one stiff we got. I've given you a couple of hours down here with him. Did you find anything new?"

He shook his head. "Nothing that contradicts my initial findings."

Quickly, he ran down a list of Jack's injuries, all of them consistent with homicidal strangulation. The only thing missing was some sign that Sullivan fought back. Though he flirted with the idea that this could possibly be suicidal strangulation, he dismissed the idea immediately. There was no evidence that anything else was used to tighten the rope. Only a pair of hands. If Sullivan did it to himself, the rope would've gone slack when he first lost consciousness. He wouldn't have died. The corpse with the fresh Y-cut proved otherwise. Which meant someone else had to be involved.

"I've already bagged and tagged the rope for you, in case you need it for a match, or maybe you can get some prints off of it. I'm also going to take samples from his body anyway, send them out for testing. As soon as all that's done, we can release the body. I don't know about you, but I always feel better when I know the freezer's empty."

She nodded. No surprise. As much as they argued, when it came to their work, she never second-guessed him. If Lucas told her there wasn't anything else he could do with Sullivan's body, she would believe him.

She proved it as when she said, "Let me know when you're finished. I'll sit down with the wife again and find out what she wants to do."

Lucas yanked off his gloves one by one, balling them up before tossing them in the hazardous waste bucket. As he went over to the sink and started to wash his hands, he turned to look over his shoulder at Caitlin. "How'd that go? How's the fair missus holding up?"

"As well as can be expected. I left her at the station with Wil. I finally had to send Sly home to get a couple hours down after he finished up in the inn. I need everyone in tiptop shape if we got some murderer on the loose." She paused, took another sip. "Mase buzzed me as I was heading over here."

"Asking about the widow?"

"Yup."

Lucas turned the sink off, grabbed a towel. "He seems very fond of Mrs. Sullivan. Are you sure this is the first time they've ever met?"

If Caitlin heard the suspicion lacing his tone, she chose to ignore it. "It's Mason Walsh. How could he? He's never stepped foot out of Hamlet. Come on, Luc. The kid's got some white knight in shining armor complex. She's the damsel in distress that he has to save. It's nothing."

"Is that so?"

She snorted. "Yeah. Trust me. I've known the kid his whole life. It's not in him to leave Hamlet, but he's always had stars in his eyes. He's too used to the girls in town. He figures his only shot at love will come with some outsider."

Lucas thought it was interesting how Caitlin kept calling Walsh a kid, like he wasn't only a couple of years younger than she was. He didn't think she was even aware she was doing it. But he didn't buy into the deputy's act. It wasn't just about being a hero to the shocked, grieving widow, or even finding true love. Tessa Sullivan was attractive and she was available. Not to mention, she was a slice of life from outside of Hamlet. He was willing to put money down that even with Jack Sullivan still breathing, Walsh would've made a play for her eventually.

"I don't know. That poor woman is married and he's sniffing around her like a dog in heat."

Caitlin pointed at him. "She *was* married. I remember you saying vows once upon a time. 'Til death—or divorce—do you part, right? She's as single as I am. Kid sees an opportunity and he's running with it. I don't blame him."

Lucas raised his eyebrow. "Don't you think that's a little inappropriate? He's one of your deputies, Cait."

"So? She doesn't seem to mind." She paused, then added casually, "He's asked me if he could offer her one of the spare rooms in his place while she's staying here."

The snort was out before he could stop himself. "I don't think so."

Too late, he realized his mistake. Already under pressure as Hamlet's sheriff, she would be looking for a reason to turn this on him. She always did. Her shoulders tensed at his snort. The casual way she asked, "Why not?", did not fool him one bit.

Still, he couldn't help himself.

"Why not?" He goggled at her. "Because I think that's *definitely* inappropriate, don't you?"

Caitlin didn't blink as she returned his stare. She did, however, narrow her eyes dangerously at him. He could almost see the gears of her wayward mind spinning. When she suddenly slammed her coffee thermos on the slab, dots of her spilled drink landing on the dead man's arm, Lucas braced himself for what was coming.

"I know what this is about. Why you keep bringing up this outsider. Why you're standing there with that disapproving look on your face at the thought that Mason wants to take her in for the night."

He crossed his arms over his lab coat, careful not to touch any of the miscellaneous fluids on it. "Okay. This I got to hear. C'mon, Caity. I'll bite. Why?"

"You have a thing for her. The Sullivan woman. That's why you don't want Mase chasing after her. Now that her husband's dead, you want her to throw you a bone."

And this, Lucas thought, was precisely why he couldn't stand being married to such a jealous shrew. Try to remind the sheriff that her deputies should have some boundaries with a civilian and, suddenly, he was panting after Tessa himself. She was being ridiculous and, despite her many insistences to the contrary, she would never change.

"Caity. *Caitlin*. Listen to yourself. I don't know that

woman. I haven't even said one word to her. Did you ever think that I feel sorry for her? She's been in our village for one day. Her husband was *murdered* and if you—the sheriff, damn it—aren't already trying to marry her off to one of your deputies, it's because you're accusing your ex-husband of taking advantage of the poor thing."

His words were calm, his actions measured. Pointedly breaking eye contact with her, he grabbed the towel from its place by the sink. After wiping the spilled coffee off of the corpse, he picked up Caitlin's thermos, placed it gently into her empty hand and headed for the closed door.

She found her voice just as he opened it. "Don't walk away from me, Lucas. Don't you dare."

"I'm not walking away from you. I just refuse to continue this pointless conversation while standing over a murder victim's remains." He held the door open, gesturing for her to join him out in the hall. "If you want, we can finish this in my office."

Shoving past him, she spat out, "I know the way."

As she stalked ahead, Lucas lingered in the morgue's doorway and closed his eyes. He took a deep breath, prayed for a single ounce of patience, and then followed the sound of her clomping boots.

She cornered him as he tried to slip by her into his office. Grabbing his sleeve, she tugged until he was looking down at her. "Okay, okay. I don't know where that came from." She let go of his sleeve, shrugging helplessly. "We're not married anymore. I know that. I'm not supposed to get jealous."

"That wasn't jealousy, Caity, it was momentary insanity. Ever since I left the inn, all I've worried about is your case. The most important thing right now is finding out who killed Jack Sullivan. Not who's next in line for his wife."

"I know. I'm sorry. I've been running all morning, checking out the crime scene, talking to everyone who worked the night shift in and around Bonnie's inn. No one saw anything, Luc." This time, she made sure the lid on her thermos was screwed on tight before she dropped it onto the edge of Lucas's desk. Frustration made her run her trembling hand through her hair. "I've got nothing so far. Tessa Sullivan is my only lead. I've gotta keep her here. She won't stay at Bonnie's. I know better than to agree with Mason, but what else am I supposed to do?"

His annoyance at Caitlin faded away as she turned imploringly to him. She always looked at him that way, like he would have the answer to any question she had. First, when they were married, then later, when they had to work side-by-side as Hamlet's sheriff and its makeshift ME.

At least, this time, her faith in him was founded. He actually had an answer for her. Taking a seat at his desk, he said one word: "Ophelia."

It was obvious from the way she seemed to deflate that she had no clue what he meant. "What?"

"Ophelia," he repeated. "She can stay there."

It clicked a moment later. "Your sister's place?"

Lucas set his jaw. The more he thought about, the better it seemed. "Why not? Maria has been trying to re-open her cozy little bed and breakfast for ages now. I know she's hesitant—"

"Of course she is! Don't you remember what happened last time?"

His stomach roiled. Underneath his desk, his hands clenched into fists. "That was different. I made sure that nothing like that would happen to my sister again."

Anger made him reckless. Lucas was usually so much better at concealing his emotions when he had to. From the way her thin eyebrows rose, he knew that Caitlin could see right through them. When she nodded, he accepted that there was no doubt in her mind that he was fully capable of doing just that.

And he was.

"Anyway, I've got to question her again. She's no use to me right now, and I can't justify keeping her overnight." Rubbing her tired eyes with the back of her hand, Caitlin finally admitted the truth to Lucas. "I don't know what I'm doing. I'm just making it up as I go along, This is the first murder we've ever had here. If we don't count Turner, that is."

Lucas's lips thinned. "Why bring up Turner? Everyone in Hamlet knows that was an accident."

"I know. And I figured that out when we found his wreck."

What else could it be called when an outsider took the wrong turn back out of town and ran his truck off the road and into the gulley that surrounded most of Hamlet? As much as she wanted to call it his comeuppance, as the head of the HSD, she settled on *accident* in all of the paperwork.

With a huff, she added, "I don't think this one's going to be that easy."

He had a feeling she was right. He was also not quite sure that it was strictly coincidence that had Caitlin jumping from the topic of Maria to Mack Turner like that. She'd always been intelligent, but she was also shrewder than he ever really gave her credit for. If anyone could figure out what happened, she would.

Lucas had to change the subject back. As far as he was concerned, Turner's case was closed. There was no reason to dredge all that ancient history up again. It would only make his sister suffer if she had to relive it. He wouldn't allow that.

Picking up his radio, he asked Caitlin, "Should I call Maria?"

"Yeah, sure. Might as well." She huffed, unscrewed her thermos and guzzled down the last of her coffee.

"Right now, I don't care where that woman goes so long as she's not at my station when I'm done tonight."

"I'll take care of it personally," Lucas promised.

And that, Caitlin admitted to herself, was exactly what she was afraid of.

9

Mason was watching her so closely, Tess felt like an insect underneath a magnifying glass. She wished he would stop. It unnerved her, her skin breaking out in tiny goosebumps as if she actually felt the touch of his continued stare.

Why wasn't he blinking? It was really beginning to creep her out.

What made it worse was that, as they sat cross-legged and facing each other on the bench stretched across the jail cell, she had no idea why he kept studying her.

Tess was pretty sure she was only one wrong word away from snapping under the day's stress. It bothered her that she couldn't understand what he was looking for. Did he think she managed to sneak out and choke her husband to death? Or was he watching, waiting to see if spontaneous strangulation was suddenly catching?

She'd already shed enough tears while clinging to him that morning, so if he was expecting another breakdown, he'd be waiting a while for *that*.

There was a hollow feeling in her chest. Her head kept spinning. The more she tried to concentrate and accept the reality of what happened, the harder it was. The words simply didn't make sense in her head. No matter how many times she made the sheriff repeat them during her questioning earlier.

Jack is dead. Dead. Jack is dead. Jack. Dead. He's—

"Tess?"

Her whole body shook at the sound of her name. In that fleeting instant, the certainty that Jack was gone slipped through her hands like grains of sand. It would be back. It was just the shock talking.

"I'm sorry." She blinked. "Did you say something?"

Concern flooded his deep brown eyes. And, she thought, it would be so, so easy to drown in them.

Mason nodded at the pile of cards set between them. "It's your turn."

"Oh. Okay." She drew her card. Ace of spades. Her hand shook. She quickly tucked that card behind the three of clubs. "Nothing."

The plodding of sensible shoes caught her attention, followed by a soft cough. A hefty shadow fell across the bench.

"How are you kids doing in there? You need me to get you anything before I start getting ready to go off shift for the evening?"

Tess shook her head.

Mason waved over at Wilhelmina. "We're doing just fine. And don't worry. If Tess needs something, I can handle it."

The other deputy pursed her lips. "Sounds fair, Mase. Let me know if you change your mind, sug, yeah? You too, Mrs. Sullivan. Take it easy. Sheriff's gotta be coming back soon."

"Thanks, Wil."

"Thank you," Tess echoed.

She liked the older woman. Wilhelmina probably had a good twenty years on the other two deputies she met. There was a matronly air about her, with her platinum-dyed hair permed into fluffy curls and a swath of blue eyeshadow that peeked over the edge of her thick eyeglasses with the cat's eye frames. She carried some fluff around the middle, though Tess would call her husky before anything else, and moved around the station like a clucking mother hen.

She was the fourth member of their four-man law enforcement team, though Wilhelmina confided that she was more of an overpaid, underworked secretary. Despite Hamlet's small population, there was always the inevitable paperwork. That was her responsibility. Mason, Deputy Collins, and Caitlin traded off on the majority of patrols.

Collins was already gone when Mason brought her back to the station. Mason went off duty right after, though she seemed to think that wasn't his idea. He returned shortly after the sheriff finally concluded her interview session, but both Wilhelmina and Mason assured her that Sheriff De Angelis left clear instructions that she had to remain in the station house for the time being.

She wasn't under arrest, so she didn't have to stay in the cell. That was one thing Tess insisted on herself.

Even she knew it was pathetic that the hard bench beneath her was the only tangible thing in her life at the moment. She couldn't help it. Part of her realized that while she'd been struggling to get comfortable on that bench last night, her husband died in a hotel bed. Alone. The discomfort in her back and legs were the only thing that reminded her that she was still alive when he wasn't.

Who knows what would have happened if she hadn't gone to the bar? That thought made her stomach retch. If she hadn't already thrown up the water Sly offered, plus the bile that burned her throat as it came up, Tess would've heaved again.

Mason tried to get her to take a seat in one of the comfortable visitor's chairs. She stubbornly refused.

Rather than leave her alone, he grabbed a deck of cards from one of the desk's drawers and joined her in the cell.

Which was how she ended up playing a half-assed game of gin rummy while everyone around her pointedly ignored the blinking neon elephant in the room. Except for her interrogation, none of the others so much as mentioned Jack. She sure as hell didn't. If she didn't acknowledge it, it didn't happen.

Or something like that.

Mason took his next card, the tip of his tongue sticking out as he concentrated. He'd already won the first two games, even though she suspected he was trying to lose to her on purpose. Feeling guilty, she tried to focus all of her attention on her cards.

In between laying down another set, he twitched as if he'd been electrocuted. She gasped and he chuckled. Unclipping his radio, he immediately showed it to Tess.

"Boss just buzzed me," he told her. He threw his cards face down on the bench before standing. "I'll go see what she wants. Wilhelmina will keep you company. Keep you honest." He winked, his attempt at humor just another subtle way to put her at ease. "No peeking at my cards."

She probably should have laughed. He was trying so hard. The silence echoed around them as Mason loomed over her. He opened his mouth as if he wanted to say something, glanced at his radio, changed his mind. Almost apologetically, he backed out of the open cell.

"I'll be right back, Willie."

"Sure thing, Mase, sugar. I'll hold the fort for you. The little sug will be just fine."

Wilhelmina liked to call people *sugar*, and Tess thought the older deputy was just as sweet. When the sheriff wasn't drilling her earlier, Wilhelmina let Tess sit with her at her desk. She had one of those portable DVD players and an entire storage case full of movies. During lunch, she let Tess pick. It was a relief to watch something as familiar as *The Wizard of Oz* and pretend that Jack wasn't lying in a morgue somewhere, being worked on by that handsome doctor.

The doctor... between flashes of Jack, the way he looked, the way she found him, Tess couldn't push the memory of the dark-haired doctor out of her mind. She felt drawn to him, though she couldn't for the life of her explain it.

It might've been because he hadn't looked at her the way that some of the others had been doing since she made that terrible discovery. Like she was either guilty as sin, a wave of trouble that rolled into their idyllic town, or so very fragile, she would simply shatter. In that one instant when they locked eyes, Tess had a feeling that he saw *her*.

That's when Mason glanced back at her as he left the room. He most certainly saw her, though Tess still couldn't figure out why. Sparing a small smile for her, he twisted the knob on his radio to set it to the proper channel before stepping out of earshot to answer the sheriff's summons.

Wilhelmina clicked her tongue, drawing Tess's attention her way. The smile that pulled her painted pink lips was indulgent.

"Mase is a good boy," she confided warmly. "If you let him, he'll take care of you. You've got nothing to worry about, sug."

Tess knew that Wilhelmina was trying to reassure her. If she thought she was in trouble last night when she first encountered the deputy, that was nothing compared to the mess she was in now. Her husband was gone, she was trapped in this place, and she had no idea what she was supposed to do. Apart from giving consent for Jack's autopsy, all she'd done was answer the sheriff's endless questions until she nearly confessed to the crime just so the insistent redhead would finally shut up.

As far as Tess was concerned, worrying was the only thing she could do. And she didn't *want* Mason's help. She'd spent the last year letting Jack take care of her. It was her turn to do some of the caring.

"I just want to go home," she said. "Will I be able to go soon?"

"'Fraid not, sugar. Can't spring you until we get the sheriff's okay."

"And you said she'd be returning soon?" Tess pleaded with Willie with her gaze. *Please* let the sheriff be almost back. If she wasn't freed from the station soon, she might actually earn a night in the cell.

"Should be. Sit tight, okay? I can't imagine you'll be here much longer."

As much as she wanted out, Tess wasn't looking forward to seeing Sheriff De Angelis again. The woman had been thorough and exhaustive with her questions. By the time she was done, Tess's head was so muddled and confused, she was seriously beginning to wonder if she *was* the one who strangled Jack.

The only thing she knew for sure was that her husband was dead and someone was responsible. It was obvious that the sheriff wanted her to be guilty. After three hours of intense questioning, she would've confessed to anything for just a moment's peace.

Hearing Judy Garland croon *Over the Rainbow* had calmed her enough that she was fairly certain she couldn't have killed her husband while she was locked in the holding cells overnight. That was now. If Sheriff De Angelis started to interrogate her again, she might crumble.

She needed to get the hell out of there.

MASON RETURNED A FEW MINUTES LATER, RUBBING THE back of his neck as he clipped his communicator on his belt. He was frowning, though he tried not to let Tess see.

After exchanging a pointed look with Wilhelmina, he announced, "Sheriff is on her way in. Wil, she says she's taking over for you. Once she's back, you can go home to your kids."

"Thanks, sugar. Bev is watching her younger brothers but I'd like to have supper with them if I can."

"Five minute warning buzz. She's almost here." Turning to look at Tess, she could see the slight strain on his face. "We'll have to save our game for later, miss. Come on out of the cell. She wants to talk to you again."

Tess's stomach dropped. She knew this was coming. At least, once the sheriff was done, she would be able to go. She wasn't quite sure where she would be going *to*—and she didn't care as long as it was far away from the Hamlet Inn.

All she had to do was get through another round of questioning. If the sheriff didn't charge her, she'd have to let her leave. Right?

After gathering the scattered cards together, she handed the deck to Wilhelmina. Mason stayed by the open cell, his back resting up against the bars, his arms crossed over his chest. His eyes were narrowed on the door at the other end of the station house.

When the sheriff finally stormed into the station a few minutes later, she wasn't alone. And Tess understood Mason's sudden shift in mood.

Tall, dark, and lean, the man with the sheriff was *beautiful.* Not how she would normally describe a man, it was the first word that popped in her head. With chiseled features, long, dark eyelashes, and a pair of lush lips, his good looks positively stunned her. He had coal-black hair, cut short on the side, longer in the front. Having parted it precisely on the left side, each strand was perfectly in place.

His eyes were like diamonds, as cold and as hard as ice. Already a pale blue color, his olive skin tone made them seem unnaturally light. She was captivated by his gaze. Tess knew she was staring. Everyone in the station could probably tell that she was entranced by his unexpected appearance. Who was this man? What was he doing here?

And then she remembered.

The eyes—she would never forget icy eyes like those. The man, the dark-haired man who stood with the sheriff over Jack's dead body. The doctor.

It was like there was no one else in the room except for the doctor and Tess. He headed straight for her, his hand outstretched. Sheriff De Angelis trailed behind him, though she didn't try to stop him as he ignored the two deputies, all of his attention entirely on Tess.

"Hello." His voice was pleasant, with only the

faintest hint of some exotic accent that she couldn't quite place. "We weren't properly introduced before. My name is Lucas."

She took his hand. "Tessa Sullivan."

"I'm sorry for your loss, Mrs. Sullivan. I very much regret that we're all meeting under such circumstances."

While Wilhelmina murmured her sympathies softly and Mason hovered protectively right behind Tess, Sheriff De Angelis stood next to the doctor and scowled at the point where Lucas still held Tess's hand. Envy flashed in her glassy green eyes, her thin lips twisted in the ugly expression she didn't bother to hide.

Her voice, however, was cordial and professional. "Mrs. Sullivan, would you mind stepping outside with me?"

Tess's shoulders slumped. She let her hand slip out of Lucas's, holding it to her chest as if it could protect her. "More questions." It was a flat statement.

"Of a more delicate matter," the sheriff confirmed. "The doctor's finished his work for the evening. I wanted to talk to you about that."

His work. On Jack. Using the same hand she just shook in greeting, this man had tended to her husband. She felt like she was going to throw up. "Okay. Yeah. Sure."

With a wide-eyed stare, she glanced at Wilhelmina,

then Mason. She felt much safer with them than she did with Sheriff De Angelis.

Except De Angelis didn't seem to want to have this conversation with an audience. It was possible she was trying to keep this as painless as she could; despite the relentlessness of her questions earlier, Tess got the impression that the sheriff, for all her barking, really only wanted to do the best job possible.

It would be an insult to Hamlet if she didn't.

ONCE THEY WERE OUT OF SIGHT, WILHELMINA SIGHED. "Poor kid. I can't imagine how hard this has gotta be for her. Stop off for a visit and end up a widow. I know I'll sleep better when our Caity figures this whole mess out. I can hardly believe it myself. A murder in Hamlet." She shook her head. "Never in all my years."

"It'll be easier on her once the boss stops treating her like a prime suspect," Walsh pointed out. "Anyone with eyes can see that she's innocent."

"Sometimes the prettiest face can hide a monster."

"That's true," Walsh said, actually agreeing with Lucas, "but that doesn't explain how she could pull off a murder job when I pulled her over for drinking and driving last night. I kept her in the holding cells until Sly sprang her this morning. No way she could've snuck out, even if I believed she had the strength to throttle her husband. Doc, you looked over the body. What do you think?"

"Whoever did that to Mr. Sullivan had to be very strong indeed."

Walsh jabbed his finger into the air. "Exactly!"

"Maybe it was a good thing you locked her up last night, Mase," Wilhelmina told him. "Can you imagine what would have happened if she was there?"

Wilhelmina's question had them all thinking about it. Maybe having two outsiders to contend with would have given whoever did this a second to pause. Or maybe Lucas would've been working on two dead bodies that morning.

With a rough shake of his head, Walsh obviously pushed the gruesome thought away. "That's why it's so important that I find her someplace solid to sleep tonight. Someplace safe. She's terrified of the inn now and I don't blame her. I asked the sheriff if I could put her up at my place. I've got the room."

Lucas didn't like the way Wilhelmina started to gush, telling Walsh what a wonderful idea that was. Was any of Caitlin's deputies concerned with how bad it would look to have their murder victim's wife shacking up with a member of the department mere hours after his body was found?

Clearing his throat, catching both of their attentions, he said, "Actually, that's why I'm here. Me and Caity came up with a better plan. We thought, since she's an outsider, it would be better if she continued to rent a room instead of becoming someone's roommate."

"She doesn't want to stay at the inn—"

"I'm not talking about the inn," Lucas cut in. "I thought she might want to stay at Ophelia. Maria's getting her a room ready right now."

"Maria's opening Ophelia back up?" Wilhelmina said. "Good for her."

Walsh slipped his hands in the back pockets of his uniform trousers. He kept his tone light, while his body language said he was anything but happy with this latest development. "And the sheriff okayed this plan?"

"She thinks it's a great idea."

"Okay. Maria's place. Sure. I know where that is. I can take Tess there in my cruiser."

Lucas expected him to offer. Didn't mean he was going to let Walsh get away with it. "That's good of you to offer, Deputy, but I don't mind driving Mrs. Sullivan over. Maria's expecting me anyway. I'm gonna take her. Caity knows."

There was no way for Walsh to argue without looking like a spoiled child. He was back on duty—he purposely put himself back on early—and Caitlin needed all hands on deck. She couldn't spare him, no matter how much she tried to persuade Lucas otherwise. She had lost that argument back at his office. Lucas wasn't going to let Walsh win one here.

Though his frown made his displeasure obvious, he didn't fight Lucas.

Smart man.

Tessa didn't even question it when Sheriff De Angelis brought her back inside and Mason announced that she would be staying at something called Ophelia. The doctor was going to drive her there and get her settled? Sure. Mason was going to stop at the Hamlet Inn and bring her her luggage now that the crime scene was processed? Why not?

It wasn't dark out yet. Despite spending countless hours trapped inside on the sheriff's orders, the sun was still shining, though it wouldn't be for much longer. As she stared, she could see that it was already starting its nightly descent, disappearing between the trees that lined the main road outside of the station house.

The sky was splashed in purples and pinks. It was pretty, she noted absently. And cold. It was getting chilly out. She glanced down and, for the first time, noticed the thin material of faded and worn sweatshirt. Where was her coat? She needed one, but must have left the inn without it.

Rubbing her arms, she glanced around the parking lot. Except for a trio of police cruisers parked together and a red car separate from the pack, the lot was empty. Where was her car? The deputy hadn't left it abandoned on the side of the road outside of Thirsty's, had he?

How the hell was she going to get home?

Tess turned to the doctor. "You don't happen to know where my car is, do you?" At his blank look, she shook her head. "Never mind. I'll worry about that later."

Maybe it was a good thing Lucas was offering to drive. She didn't think she trusted herself behind the wheel just yet anyway.

Lucas led her to the red car parked at the far end of the lot. It was a flashy car, sleek and shiny. Mustang, she realized, a candy apple red one. Wow. Using the remote on his keys, he disengaged the locks and opened the door for her. Murmuring her thanks, Tess sank against the leather seat.

It felt weird to be sitting in a car that wasn't a police cruiser. Last night, Mason helped her into the back of one. That morning, Deputy Collins insisted she sit up front when he brought her back to the Hamlet Inn. Mason did the same when he brought her back to the station. And now the doctor was giving her a ride in his fancy sports car.

Once he was sure she was comfortable, he closed

her door before going around to the driver's side. Tess watched through the windshield as Lucas spared a light caress along the front of the bumper before patting the hood and reaching the driver's side door. That done, he slipped inside.

Tess immediately stretched her seatbelt across her body. It snagged on her breasts, the fit too tight. Fiddling with the buckle, she noticed that the doctor was watching her closely. Their eyes locked for a beat, he coughed, then turned away. Without him watching, she finally managed to loosen the belt and snap it into place.

He waited until she was settled. Looking in his rearview to make sure no one else was in the lot—and, okay, to keep from ogling his passenger—Lucas strapped himself into his seat and started the car before coasting out of his parking spot.

"So, what did the sheriff want to talk to you about?" he asked, speeding down the road. It was easy to see how comfortable he was on these streets, as if he'd driven down this straightaway so many times, he could navigate it with his eyes closed. His Mustang took the curves easily.

Tess grit her teeth, grateful it wasn't raining.

Because the alternative was freaking out over just how fast he was driving, she thought about his question. Interesting way to start the conversation. It seemed as if the good doctor didn't want to acknowledge that she caught him staring at her boobs.

"She told me you released Jack's body. She wanted to know what I wanted to do." She folded her hands in her lap. There was a small bruise on her knuckle. Her thumb whispered absently over the purple mark. "I'm going to have him cremated. I don't know if that's what he wanted. He never said. I never asked. But the sheriff, she said I had to decide because I'm his next of kin." Bewildered, she added, "I'm his *only* kin."

Lucas turned off of Main, heading toward First. Out of the corner of his eye, he watched her unfold her hands as she reached to check the fit on her seatbelt. He eased off the gas a little. "No family?"

"Neither of us had any. My parents died when I was just a kid, one after the other. Jack… he never knew his. He grew up in foster care, going from house to house until the system kicked him out at eighteen. When we met, we just clicked. I guess we both knew what it was to be alone. And now—" Her voice shook, then grew thick as the fact that she was alone again slammed into her like a truck. "Oh my god, I'm so sorry. Like, I know he's dead, but I somehow manage to forget for a few minutes. And then, of course, it hurts even more when I remember. I agreed to burn my husband today, but it just doesn't seem real. I don't think I really understand he's gone, you know?"

"You will," Lucas told her. His eye slid over to her as

he blew past an intersection without a single streetlight. Tess swallowed back her gasp, white-knuckling the edge of the leather seat. "Let me tell you something. Nothing can bring your husband back. It's hard to wrap your head around that now because I bet you're willing to do anything to prove me wrong. But I'm not wrong. And when you accept that he's gone, it'll be even *worse*."

At the slap in his no-nonsense words, Tess stopped focusing on the road ahead of her. Instead, she recoiled, feeling like he'd reached out and given her a needed shake.

"It'll suck, trust me," he told her. His icy eyes darted back over to her, getting a glimpse of her shellshocked expression. He gentled his voice. "But, hey, that's how you start to heal. And you go on because, as much as the world seemed to end for you this morning, it hasn't. Not really. Sun comes up, sun goes down. World turns. It's just turning without Jack Sullivan now."

"Wow." Tess blinked, stunned. He wasn't wrong. Sure, he could have put it a little gentler, a little nicer. Didn't make him any less right. And because it sounded like the doctor was intimately familiar with the cycle of numbness, disbelief, bargaining and denial she'd been drowning in since she found Jack murdered, she didn't say another word.

He slanted a look to his right. "Ah, jeez, I didn't mean half of that. Okay, no, I did—but I didn't mean to be so harsh. My patients knock me for my bedside manner all the time. I guess, if you're looking for someone to pretty this whole tragedy up for you, you should've gone with the deputy."

"No."

"No?" His lip curled. "What's the matter, Tessa? Not a fan of the deputy?"

"It's not that— I mean, he was nice enough. But I had to get out of there. The sheriff, the deputies... the questions. My head was so full before. Hazy. I couldn't think. They wouldn't let me."

She also didn't think she could spend another second with Deputy Walsh right now. As kind as he was, the man hovered, like she was two seconds away from a breakdown. She wasn't an idiot. She knew she was teetering on the edge. If she didn't get the chance to process this all in her own way, if she couldn't get a moment to freaking *breathe*, then that might be the push it took to send her spiraling into the abyss.

Tess took in a deep breath, shuddering it out on the next exhale. She bowed her head, tucking her chin into her chest as she admitted, "Your honesty is kind of refreshing. I think I needed to hear all that. It still hurts so, so bad, but my head feels a little lighter now. The sheriff couldn't get through to me. Mason, neither. But now... I'm starting to understand what happened."

His lips curled slightly when she mentioned

Mason. She noticed and pretended not to when Lucas pointedly didn't say anything about the deputy.

Instead, he asked, "And what happened?"

"Jack's dead." Tess said the words with conviction. And, this time, she thought she might believe them. "So, thanks."

Lucas blinked. "Oh. Well, in that case, I'm happy to help."

10

The only indication that the house Lucas drove up to was a cozy bed & breakfast was the decorative *O Maria* painted on her door when she first opened two summers ago.

There used to be a matching sign. That was gone now. Lucas pulled it out personally after what happened to her.

The way he looked at it, without a sign advertising the place, no outsider could find it and cause his sister any more trouble. He tried not to acknowledge the hypocrisy in the fact that he was actually driving one over himself.

With Caitlin breathing down his neck at the office earlier, he barely had any time to prepare Maria for the trouble he was bringing with him. His sister, always willing to help, agreed without any questions.

He was sure she had some now. Wonderful. It should definitely be interesting.

Maria was waiting for them at the front door. He could read the puzzlement in her friendly expression, the slight droop to her welcoming smile, the confusion that darkened her light blue eyes as he parked his car, then went around to open the passenger side door for his sister's guest.

Tess thanked the doctor, but shook her head when he offered to help her climb out of the car. Ever since escaping the station house, she had started to feel a little more awake, a little more like herself. She kept telling herself that the shock would fade; the grief continued to overwhelm.

At least she was still breathing.

Before this, she never would've fallen apart the way she had at the hotel. Tess allowed herself some slack because of the very extreme circumstances, but it was beginning to bother her that everyone she encountered expected her to simply shatter. Tess was built much stronger than that.

She could get through this. She'd been through worse before and survived. All she had to do was get out of Hamlet in one piece. She'd be fine after that.

One step at a time.

The step that took her away from Lucas's car brought her face to face with a Victorian-style house, a wall of red brick with a white decorative trim. She could see turrets and towers, plus a bay window that reminded her of the one in the Hamlet Inn. It wasn't as large as the inn had been, and it only had two floors rather than three, but, on the outside, it appeared as cozy and inviting.

Plus, it had a porch swing. She'd lived her entire life in apartment buildings. She would do anything to own a house with a porch swing.

A woman stood on the top step, her hands wrapped securely around the white railing that surrounded the porch. She waved when she saw them, though she made no move to meet them on the manicured lawn or the cobbled walkway that led to the front of the house.

Tess paused at the foot of the stairs. Lucas brushed her arm as he passed her, greeting the smiling woman with a crushing hug. When he finished squeezing her, he placed one of his arms around her shoulders.

And, once again, Tess felt like the outsider.

Lucas nodded at her. "Tessa, I'd like to introduce you to my sister. Maria, this is Tessa Sullivan."

Even without the introduction, Tess would've thought the woman was related to the doctor. Her long hair, hanging straight and shiny to the middle of her back, was the same dark shade. A fringe of bangs fell into a pair of eyes that were just as stunning, even if there was a warmth that kept them from seeming as arctic and remote as Lucas's own peepers. Maria was tall and willowy; standing side-by-side with her brother, she could see there was barely an inch difference in their height.

"Nice to meet you—" A small pause. "—Miss Sullivan."

Maria's throaty voice was more heavily accented than her brother's. It carried the lilt of Italian, and a hint of a question.

A pang shot right through Tess. Her stomach dropped. She knew she had to correct the other woman. "It's Mrs. Sullivan, actually."

"Of course. And your husband will be joining us, yes?"

The assumption was innocent enough. How could Maria know? That didn't stop Tess from letting out a short gasp, her breath catching in her throat.

Would her husband be joining her? No. He wouldn't.

"I... oh, God." She wrapped her arms around her middle, desperate to hold herself together. Everything was spinning. She backed away from the front porch, her steps unsteady as she shook her head. "No... no."

Golden eyes were wild in fear, in despair. Her eyelashes fluttered as she swallowed back the bile that rose in her throat.

Jack was dead.

Dead.

Her husband was gone, and she would never see him again.

Ever a doctor, Lucas's instincts immediately kicked in.

Leaving Maria behind on the porch, he hurried over to Mrs. Sullivan, jumping down the three steps in one leap. The outsider's reaction—the way she suddenly paled, her tremors, the soft sob she let out as she tried to run away—was a huge concern. Maria leaned forward, grasping the porch rail with her hand.

Moving behind Mrs. Sullivan, Lucas grabbed her by her upper arms, steadying her while, at the same time, stopping her from continuing her quick retreat.

"Take a deep breath," he instructed. "In and out, 'atta girl. You'll be fine."

"Luc? *Sta bene*?" Maria had a habit of breaking into Italian when she panicked or was unsure. She rubbed her neck with her other hand, dipping low to touch her fingers to the cross that rested at the hollow of her throat. Letting go of the banister, she started for the steps, though she didn't leave the porch. "What's wrong?"

When Mrs. Sullivan shuddered out another breath, her color returning, he reluctantly stepped away from her. Turning to back toward the porch, he called out,

"Maria, do you think we can show Tessa her room? And then I'd like to see you in the kitchen. There are a few things we have to discuss."

She looked from Lucas to the shaky outsider, her curiosity a tangible thing. But she didn't question her brother's request. After taking a moment to compose herself, she nodded. "Come with me. I turned down the bed in the Lavender Room." She smiled indulgently in Mrs. Sullivan's direction. "I'm sure you'll love it."

Lucas leaned down to whisper something to the outsider. She shook her head. He offered her his arm. She refused it. As Mrs. Sullivan gained some of her composure back, she dropped her trembling hands to her side, moving further away from him. Lucas let her go but, as she started toward the front steps, he followed barely an arm's length behind her.

Maria watched the scene in avid interest. She only realized she'd been caught staring when Lucas, a touch of annoyance to his tone, said, "Maria? Which room is the Lavender Room?"

"Oh. Sorry. It's right this way."

Lucas reached to take Mrs. Sullivan's elbow, pulling his hand back before he made contact. A muffled *mmm* ripped his attention from the outsider woman as she carefully climbed up the porch and slipped inside of Ophelia. A quick glance toward Maria revealed that she'd seen everything and had already made her own assumptions.

He bit back his scowl.

She was so looking forward to this.

"She's pretty," Maria noted as the two of them walked into the kitchen. Having set the outsider up in the Lavender Room—one of her biggest, but also the furthest from the center of Ophelia—she didn't bother to keep her voice down.

"And you're fishing," Lucas told her. There was no heat in his accusation because, well, he'd been expecting this ever since he heard Maria's *mmm*. He could hide a lot from everyone else, including his ex, but not his sister. "Besides, she's married." He hesitated, then realized that he'd have to tell Maria the truth eventually. "Or she was. Her husband's one of mine now."

A spark of recognition lit up her pale eyes. "Wait... that's her? The outsider whose husband was found throttled in Bonnie's inn?"

"How did you— no. Don't tell me. I don't want to know."

Ever since her attack, Maria rarely left the house she'd spent years painstakingly turning into a bed and breakfast. She had a radio—Lucas insisted on it—so it wasn't unusual for her to be involved in Hamlet's gossip mill. He just never expected her to learn about Sullivan's murder so quickly. The last thing he wanted was for Maria to have a setback because another outsider had died in Hamlet.

Lucas gave her a quick once-over, taking her in with his practiced doctor's eye. His younger sister actually seemed excited at the news. Since Sullivan's murder meant that she had Tessa Sullivan as her first guest in more than a year, he guessed she was allowed a little excitement.

It was his fault, too. He'd point-blank refused to allow her to open Ophelia's doors after what Turner put her through. And, there he was, insisting that she look after this new outsider.

He had to. Otherwise, Tessa would be staying with Deputy Walsh and, well, that was just not going to happen.

Reaching out, he gave Maria a one-armed squeeze. "Thanks for doing this for me. You sure you don't mind?"

"Not at all, Luc. It gets lonely here in this big house. You don't stay hardly enough—"

Lucas snorted. Drawing his arm back, he moved around Maria, opening the cabinet above the rangehood. He took out a half-eaten box of cookies and shook it. "If I stayed here instead of at my place, you'd have to find a better hiding spot."

Maria watched as Lucas opened the box and grabbed as many cookies as he could. She held out her hand. He obediently placed two cookies against her waiting palm.

She laughed, taking a nibble off the edge. "You're lucky I love you enough to share my chocolate chip."

Because his mouth was stuffed, he only managed a nod in response. Her suave older brother tried to blow her a kiss and ended up spraying chewed up cookie crumbs on his shirt.

She kept a stack of napkins on the small two-seater table in the kitchen. "Here," she said, handing him one. As Lucas knocked the crumbs to the floor—and she made a mental note to mop later—Maria brought the conversation back to Tessa Sullivan. "Tell me about the outsider. You only said to get one room ready, nothing else. How long will she be here?"

His hand clenched reflexively, his dirty napkin crumpling in his fist. "I'm not sure. Caity wants her to stick around. No surprise, she didn't want to stay at the inn after what happened to her husband—*no*," he said, cutting her off as she began to ask. "I won't tell you what happened to him so don't even start."

"You're no fun."

Older brothers rarely were. He gave her another one of her cookies as a peace offering. Then he grabbed two more to munch on himself. "I don't want you to worry, Maria. Caity might disregard it, but this

Tessa, she has an alibi. She's just another victim. I wouldn't bring her here if I thought there was any danger in it. Trust me."

"I'm not worried. Honest," she insisted when her brother's skeptical expression judged her without a word. "Besides, she's such a small thing. She could never hurt me. I don't have to be afraid that she'll—never mind that."

"Turner should've suffered more for what he did to you," Lucas muttered darkly.

"*Tried* to do. I fought him off, didn't I?"

That didn't make him feel any better. "That won't ever happen again."

"Of course not, Luc. You made sure of it."

Lucas froze, the last of the cookies halfway to his mouth. "I did? How?"

"The locks," Maria reminded him.

He thought about that, chewed on his cookie, nodded. "You're right. Those locks were worth every penny I paid that outsider to install them. He ripped me off royally, but it was still worth it. Hey, you got some milk?"

"In the fridge. Cups are—"

"I know where they are. I'll pour us each a glass. You take a seat."

Though she immediately grabbed one of the two chairs, pulling it out in order to sit down at the table, Maria couldn't keep back her protest.

"I have a guest, Lucas. I have to check on her, start supper, and make sure she has everything she needs. If I'm starting over with Ophelia, everything has to be perfect. She's an outsider. What if she tells her friends about my place? I could rent out the rest of the rooms, run my B&B again. This is what I've been waiting for."

Lucas let his sister's voice wash over him as he poured out the milk and brought the two glasses over to the table. She had a point. Though she never made any indication that Hamlet was too small for her, he knew that Maria's dream was to run a successful boarding house. She loved her community and wanted to share it with the world.

It was Maria's one downfall that she actually welcomed outsiders; apart from having a sudden desire to keep Deputy Walsh away from Tessa, he knew that Ophelia was probably the best place for her to stay. No one else in Hamlet would treat her as graciously as Maria De Angelis.

The vulnerable Tessa needed security. The lonely Maria needed guests, yes, but Lucas knew she also needed a friend.

He put one glass in front of his sister. "Drink your milk."

Maria stuck her tongue out at him. It didn't matter that they were both adults. When Lucas got high-handed with her, Maria couldn't help but act like a toddler. One stern look later and she was sipping at her milk. She'd learned years ago not to argue with her brother when he got like this.

Lucas sat down opposite of her, draining his glass in three large gulps. If Maria felt coddled, he at least was content. Nothing like milk and cookies and the bone-deep assuredness that his loved ones were safe to make a man feel at peace. Sure, there was a murderer loose in Hamlet—as Caitlin pointed out in the hotel room—but behind the best locks money could buy, he could provide protection.

Still, he also knew that Maria's kind heart and a touch of naivety could render the best security measures unreliable. Look at what happened with Mack Turner.

He refused to allow anything like that to happen again.

"Just because you have a guest here, I want you to still be careful. And I don't mean just the locks, Maria. There's no reason to let anyone else in Ophelia right now. Do you still have that paper for the front window? If you do, please use it."

Lucas had printed a sign that read **NO VACANCIES** right after Turner abruptly checked out of Ophelia. In case anyone tried to rent a room at the bed and breakfast, that one sheet would turn them away. She never really needed it. Word traveled so quickly in Hamlet, everyone knew about what that damn outsider pulled. If he hadn't gotten into that accident on the way out of town, some of her neighbors would've caught up to him eventually. Either way, when Lucas decided Ophelia was closed, that was it. No one even tried to rent a room.

Not until Lucas brought this outsider to her home.

She knew her brother, knew how he cared for those he considered his. By bringing Tessa Sullivan into Maria's B&B, he was wordlessly promising to watch out for the shaken widow. Maria wondered if the grief-stricken woman realized it.

Tapping her nails against the half-empty milk glass, Maria thought about how pale Tessa was, how they'd left her sitting on the lavender bed, staring blankly at the room around her. From her buzz earlier, she knew that someone had strangled the woman's husband. It couldn't have been Mrs. Sullivan—Lucas had to be sure of her innocence or there was no way in hell he would've brought her to Ophelia to hide out.

Which begged a very interesting question.

"Luc, do you think she's in trouble?"

It wasn't so far of a leap. A married couple of outsiders find their way into Hamlet only for one of them to wind up dead a few hours later. What did that mean for the survivor?

Lucas shrugged, though the way his lips thinned revealed him to be more concerned than he let on. "It doesn't matter. I'm not taking any chances. I already have one body in my freezer. I don't want another one."

11

Tess wasn't sure how much time passed between Lucas and Maria shuffling her into the room and when she heard the gentle knock muffled against the thick wooden door.

The whisper of a never-ending *tick-tock-tick-tock* told her there was a clock somewhere nearby. She didn't bother searching for it. Until someone told her she could get the hell out of Hamlet, time didn't mean anything to her. If she started measuring at all, it would be in the minutes, the hours since she found Jack.

Jack.

She shoved the pain aside. Lying curled up in a ball, she found she didn't have the strength or the desire to go answer the door. So she didn't.

"Mrs. Sullivan?"

Tess felt the punch straight to her gut.

"Are you awake? I've brought supper."

She hadn't had anything since the rest stop yesterday afternoon. The idea of eating turned her stomach. Her shaky hands and lightheadedness told her not to be stupid, though. No matter what, Jack would've hated to know that she was taking such bad care of herself. Grief was one thing. Guilt another. But she wasn't dead. She had to remember that—and start acting like it.

So though she would have much rather closed her eyes and pretend to be asleep, she called out a reply. "The door's unlocked."

The rattle of the doorknob was followed by the clanking of cutlery. Maria bumped the door in with her hip, struggling to right the tray she held out in front of her with both hands. She listed to one direction, taking careful steps not to slosh the glass of water or spill the heavy plate of food she carried.

Tess immediately started to rise. "I'm sorry. I should've—"

"No, no, no. You're my guest. Stay there, stay comfortable. I've got this."

It didn't matter that Maria told her to stay put. Tess's first instinct was to jump up and help and while she still wanted to, she also didn't want to insult her hostess. Moving so that she was on the edge of the bed, she readied her body to move quickly in case it looked like Maria was going to stumble and drop the tray.

And then she saw the familiar grey strap crossing Maria's body and understood exactly why the other woman was having a hard time managing her tray. Tess's bag had to weigh at least thirty pounds.

"My luggage!"

At the sight of the grey and pink oversized, overstuffed duffel bag slung over Maria's slender frame, she felt her heart lighten for the first time since she left home. She didn't realize how little she had until something that was hers before was in front of her, back in her possession.

Even better? Hanging off of Maria's wrist, Tess caught sight of her purse. She had left that behind in the inn, too, and very nearly decided to write it off as a loss since she never wanted to go inside that room again.

It was tough, but she resisted the urge to reach out and snatch it off of Maria's arm. "My purse, too! Oh my god, thank you. I didn't know how I was going to get it back."

Maria placed her tray down on the nightstand beside the bed. "Don't thank me. Deputy Walsh dropped it by. He wanted to make sure you were doing fine."

"Oh." Some of her happiness died away at Maria's admission. She vaguely remembered that the deputy said he'd bring her her luggage. Checking up on her so soon, though? Tess wasn't sure what to make of that. "How... *nice* of him."

Nice nothing, Maria bet. She had known Mason her whole life. That man might seem like the perfect deputy. She never fully bought into his act. From the time he was a ten-year-old brat who insisted on claiming the best-looking cupcake in the lunchroom as his due, she watched as Mason did whatever he had to to get whatever he wanted.

She recognized the gleam in his dark eyes when he asked about the outsider. He wanted her. Unfortunately for him, she also knew her brother very well. She didn't understand it, wouldn't question it, but Maria knew who she was pulling for. No matter what, she would always stand in Lucas's corner.

"Sure. He also wanted to remind you to have something to eat. I managed to shoo him out when I showed him I was on my way up with your supper." She gestured to the plate on the tray. "I make homemade chicken pot pies on Sundays. It's my favorite stick-to-your-ribs, comfort food. I thought you might like one. Anyone needs some comfort, sweetie, it's you."

"You're bringing me dinner?"

"I know Ophelia's supposed to be a bed and breakfast but, hey, I like to cook. Eat what you can and I'll come back to pick up the dishes in a bit. Anything else I can get for you?"

Tessa glanced at the tray. Maria had provided utensils, napkins and a glass of ice water along with the crispy, golden-brown pot pie. It looked amazing and, though her stomach was queasy, she had to admit it smelled delicious.

She shook her head. "I think I have everything already. That was really nice of you."

"Don't mention it. I'm just doing my job. Eat up. I'll knock when I come back." With a wave, Maria started to head back through the open door. Just as she stepped over the threshold, though, she paused, then turned back around. "Oh, I almost forgot to tell you. Locks automatically engage at nine. The doors open again at seven. If you need to get in or out during those hours, please let me know in advance so that I can take care of it."

"Locks?" Tess repeated. She knew her head was heavy, and she'd had a terrible shock, but she didn't know what the other woman meant. "What kind of locks? I don't understand."

Maria looked uneasy. She tucked her hair behind her ears, staring at a point on the wall about two feet to the left of Tessa as she entered the room again. "Ophelia's doors have a dual lock system. You can lock the door on the inside yourself if you want privacy. But, for the safety of me and my guests, there's an outer lock. Once it goes on, it's like the whole house is on lockdown. I can't change it once it's set."

"Don't you— I mean, isn't that a little much?"

"It was Luc's idea. He insisted. It was the only way he'd let me even think about letting guests stay again."

"And you're sure that's..."

Tess didn't want to accuse Maria of anything, but she couldn't think of a nice way of saying *legal* without implying that what she was doing was *illegal*. Which, she was pretty sure, locking the whole house down without giving her guests a choice had to be. This was supposed to be a bed and breakfast, not a jail.

She let her words hang in the air.

"I know what you're saying," Maria replied, "but I gave up fighting with Lucas years ago. Let's just say, when your brother has an in with the sheriff and an overprotective streak a mile wide, little things like 'should he do it' don't really matter as much as you'd think."

From what Tess knew of the doctor, he was level-headed, the type of man to keep cool during a crisis. To go so far as to install a lockdown system in a rural bed and breakfast that would rival one in an institution seemed at odds with the image Lucas tried to project. It didn't make any sense to her.

"Why would he insist on locks? It seems so—" Again, Tess had to choose her words carefully. Her first instinct was to use dangerous. Instead, she settled on: "—so extreme."

"Well, it might've been because of Mack Turner."

Maria thought about it for a second before nodding. "No, that's not right. It's *definitely* because of Turner."

Tess wasn't sure if she was supposed to know anything about a Mack Turner. A lot of the last day and a half was a blur for her. Some parts remained crystal clear, while others had a cottony haze surrounding them. Perhaps she met this Turner guy, or someone told her about someone with that name. It sort of sounded familiar. Maybe. She wasn't ready to swear that she knew who Maria was talking about.

Her confusion was obvious. "Nobody told you about Turner?" Maria guessed.

"I don't think so. Were they supposed to?"

"Maybe not. I mean, it was a bit of a secret when it happened, but there's no such thing as a secret in Hamlet. You'll see. You can't take a crap here without at least three people knowing when you flush."

Tess couldn't stop the snort of laughter. She would've thought it was too soon to find anything funny. That was before she met Lucas's sister. Maria was the first person in Hamlet that didn't look at her as a conquest, a victim, or a suspect.

It was obvious that the doctor had filled her in on Tessa's story the second they met in the kitchen but Maria wasn't treating her any different; the comment about comfort food was the closest she'd come to even touching on the effects of Jack's murder.

She got the feeling that Maria was the sort of woman

who often ran with what life gave her, no questions asked. Her brother dumped the prime lead in a man's murder into her care and she served her a handmade chicken pot pie while talking about bathroom habits in a small town.

"Don't mind me. Sometimes my mouth gets ahead of my brain. What was I saying before?" She reached up, fingering the beautiful silver cross she wore on a delicate chain around her neck. "Sorry, I was talking about Turner. No wonder my mind wanders."

"Turner," echoed Tess. "Who's that?"

"That *cretino* was a guest of mine last summer who chose not to follow Hamlet's rules of hospitality."

Tess remembered her conversation with Deputy Collins only that morning. Though it felt like a million years separated the Tess from before she found Jack and after, the deputy's deep, resonant voice stuck in her brain. "'Hamlet helps'," she said.

"In Turner's case, it was more like help yourself. Ugh. Like I said, *cretino*. An outsider. Not too bad looking, and, I admit, that's how he fooled me. That, and he insisted on paying up front, renting the biggest room in all of Ophelia. I gave him the Blue Room—except he mustn't have liked it much since he didn't stay inside."

Her whole expression darkened as if remembering something unpleasant. Something that made her furious.

"You don't have to—"

Maria refused to take Tess's offer of an out. She waved the other woman's concerns away. "Everyone knows. You might as well, sweetie, and I'm not ashamed. You see, I woke up when Turner tried to climb in my bed. I might've thought it was an accident if he hadn't tried to cover my mouth so I couldn't scream. I didn't have locks then, but there was one thing I *did* have. I've always kept a baseball bat by my nightstand. When a woman with nothing to lose starts swinging like she's Babe Ruth, most men don't linger. Turner didn't.

"Lucas insisted I close up my B&B, and I went along with it." Maria's eyes lit up. "I missed running this place. Ophelia, she's my heart, *mia cuore.*" She paused, seeing something in Tess's sudden surprise that caught her attention. "What did I say?"

"Nothing. I just... never mind. Just listening. Please, go on."

Maria nodded. "Yes, well, what happened with Turner... it spooked me, not going to lie. Getting the locks helped. The year off helped. Now it's time to bring life back to my Ophelia. I'm so very glad you're my guest, Mrs. Sullivan."

So busy trying to pay attention to what Maria was telling her, the pang at being called by Jack's name was more of a sting this time. It obviously took a lot out of her hostess to share her tale. Though her head was fuzzy, terrible images and horrible guilt trying to sneak back in, Tess was determined to understand.

When she did, she recoiled.

"You're telling me that this guy... this Turner guy... he snuck into your room?" Tess covered her mouth with her hands, breathing out strangled words around her fingers. A chill skittered up her spine.

Sneaking into a room, rope in hand, a dead man in bed—

"When you were *sleeping*?" Her voice rose. Her face paled. "*Here*?"

Maria, realizing her mistake moments too late, quickly waved her arms in front of her. "No, no, it's not like that. You don't have to worry about him coming back. They found him the next morning. His truck, it flipped over into the gulley on his way out of town and, *dio mio*, I'm not helping, am I?" She cringed when she saw the look of horror on Tessa's colorless face. "Whoopsie. *Scusa*. I'm so sorry."

It took her a second to push past the memories. Then, after another moment, one where she vividly remembered the bottomless valley Jack nearly drove them into when they first arrived in Hamlet, Tess finally recovered enough from her shock to say weakly, "Well, I'm definitely onboard with the locks now."

Four hours later, after dinner had been cleared away and the locks engaged at nine on the dot like Maria promised, Tess hadn't changed her mind. Though it bothered her that she was basically locked in a pretty, pretty cage, she felt a lot better knowing that the bars served to keep others out far more than to trap her in.

To be fair, her room in Ophelia was gorgeous. Maria called it the Lavender Room. She wasn't wrong. The walls were painted with the pale purple color, trimmed with a white border. The bedspread was lavender. The lampshade was lavender. The shag carpet was cream-colored, the wooden furniture a deep mahogany; the neutral colors made the purple pop all the more. A purple, white and grey vase was centered on the matching mahogany nightstand. Plastic flowers were artistically arranged inside the vase. They were, of course, lavenders.

An oversized window took up one wall and peered out onto the street in front of Ophelia. A pale purple scalloped valance stretched across the top, with a cream-colored window blind covering the rest of the wide length.

On the other side of the room, a closed door with the same matching ornamental L painted on it caught her attention. The design was lovely, simple at first glance until Tess got closer and realized it was drawn by hand in paint the same shade as the wall. Behind the door, a pristine white bathroom beckoned her.

The only spot of color she saw in the bathroom was the lavender shower curtain pulled taut across the tub. When Tess carried her duffel bag into the cozy room and yanked the curtain back, she let out a soft chuckle. Maria had placed purple anti-slip discs cut in the shape of flowers on the floor of the tub.

No matter her mood, Tess had to appreciate the level of dedication and attention to detail in Ophelia's master.

Despite the fact that she was obviously the first guest in some time, the water fell from the square-shaped shower head fast and hot. The pounding on her back gave her some relief. For a few stolen minutes, she let all of her worries and fears flow off of her with the shower spray. She imagined the day's horrors swirling down the drain with the bubbles of her body wash.

When the water went from soothing to chilly, Tess realized it was time to focus on what was next. She couldn't stay in the shower unless she wanted to drown herself. Even in her thoughts, that wasn't any kind of legitimate option. She'd come too far to give up so easily now.

Instead, she got out of the shower and dressed in a pair of comfortable sweats that still carried the scent of home on them. Breathing in deep, it was a fierce ache that made her press her hands to her chest. She wished like hell that she *was* home.

But she wasn't. Everything in the room, from the precise decorations to the soft feel of the full bed, was a constant reminder that she was far from the cramped bedroom she had shared with Jack in their tiny apartment.

Maybe that was a good thing, she realized as she slipped beneath the lavender and cream-colored quilt. Lying next to his empty place, reaching out for a sleeping body she could no longer touch, surrounded by his things… she wouldn't have been able to stand it.

She could never have gone back to the hotel room where he died, either. She was so grateful that Lucas brought her to this place, that Maria was cheerfully putting her up in her bed and breakfast.

And maybe, when she woke up the next morning, this would all have been a terrible dream.

THERE IT WAS AGAIN.

At first, when sleep continued to elude her no matter how late it got, she thought she had imagined it. As a super small town, she already noticed that there wasn't much traffic in Hamlet. After Maria went to bed, Tess was stifled by the silence. It was so quiet. Except for the nagging tick of the clock in her room, she didn't hear anything until the first time the car passed.

It didn't bother her. The revving of the engine, the hum as the car passed by the front of the house, it caught her attention because it was a momentary break in the heavy silence. Back home, the apartment where she and Jack lived overlooked a busy throughway. Constant traffic sped past her window all hours of the night.

But then it happened a second time. She froze in place, her fingers gripping the edge of her quilt as she held her breath. The rev, the hum. It sounded exactly the same. There was the smallest of pauses between the two sounds, almost as if the driver idled nearby before taking off again.

Half an hour later, she heard it again. The pause lasted longer this time. She counted it in her head. *Sixty, sixty-one, sixty-two, sixty-three…* More than a minute ticked by before the car revved up and sped away. The roar of the engine echoed through the night. Her head turned so that she was watching the closed window blinds opposite of her bed. The car had lingered in front of Ophelia. She was almost sure of it.

She waited for close to an hour. Wound tight and breathing shallowly, her heart thumping in her ears, every single noise seemed magnified. She moved her leg, the whisper of her sweats against the satin sheets sounding like sandpaper against steel.

Just when she started to relax, just when she thought she was overreacting, she heard it again.

Throwing her quilt back, Tess clambered out of the bed. Her toes sank into the thick shag of the carpet, muffling her steps as she ran for her window. She didn't stop to lift the blinds, choosing instead to shove her jittering fingers through the slats, leaving her a peephole wide enough to get a good look at the street.

Luck was on her side. Though there were only a handful of streetlights out there, leaving most of the road in inky blackness, there was one tall post not too far from Ophelia. Enough light fell in front of the house for her to see the car parked across the street. She squinted. No use. She couldn't make out the driver's face, hidden in the shadows.

She didn't have to. There were only a few people it could be. The Hamlet Sheriff Department only had four current employees. Who else would be driving around in one of their cruisers?

Her fingers slipped off of the blinds, closing the gap she created. She turned away from the window, pressing her back against the wall. As her heart raced, Tess couldn't stop thinking about Jack, how he'd been sleeping alone in an unfamiliar bed when someone snuck in and strangled him.

Though she already checked three times, Tess tiptoed across the room and tugged on the door. Double bolted. Even if the outer lock was undone, she kept the one inside her room engaged. True, she couldn't get out, but no one else could get in either. Not even a cop.

Climbing back into bed, she froze when she heard the purr of the car's engine whisper through her window. It happened so quickly, she wondered if the driver had circled the street and come right back around. Had he seen her looking out at him? If not, she didn't want to peek through the blinds a second time.

Let it be the cruiser again. She couldn't stop it.

Maybe it would be a good thing. With what happened to her husband last night, she should feel more at peace knowing that the sheriff's team was keeping a close eye on her.

She should. She sure as hell didn't, though. Not when the sheriff made it perfectly clear that—alibi be damned—she thought Tess had something to do with Jack's murder.

Feeling helpless and alone, she recognized that she was at the mercy of everyone in Hamlet. The sheriff, her deputies, the doctor... even the woman who ran this bed and breakfast. She currently had no car, very little cash, and Sheriff De Angelis's order that she stay in town until further notice.

Even if she wanted to disobey the sheriff, she had no idea where Deputy Walsh impounded her car or how to get it back. And, of course, she couldn't go anywhere without Jack. She owed him that much.

The endless tick of the clock mocked her. She pounded her pillow, tried sleeping on her side, even got up again to get a glass of water from the bathroom. Nothing helped. Tess couldn't turn off her brain. The events of the day wouldn't let her be. She couldn't sleep and didn't expect to. The only plus was that the rest of the night passed by in silence. If the cruiser came back again, she was too exhausted to notice.

As the sun began to rise, sending golden rays of light streaming in through the slats of the blinds, Tess was still awake, staring unblinkingly up at the ceiling.

She didn't see the flat white expanse above her, though. Just a length of rope twisted tightly around a man's neck. The dead eyes, splashed with red. The waxy, white skin. It didn't matter if she closed her eyes. She saw it regardless.

The image of Jack's corpse was burned in her memory.

12

She must have fallen asleep after all. The momentary escape took her almost by surprise.

It felt like Tessa had only closed her eyes for a single second when she was blinking her lids open to a blank ceiling and an ache that had nothing to do with the firm mattress beneath her.

The purple room was bathed in shadows, the sun having moved across the sky as she slumbered. She could tell that she hadn't slept too long—perhaps a couple of hours—but it was enough. Shoving the quilt away from her, she climbed out of bed.

It's a new day, she thought, followed by the absolute certainty that Jack was still dead.

It staggered her. Stumbling, she reached out

blindly, grasping the edge of her bed with a flailing hand. Her legs folded and she dropped down.

Jack was *gone*.

She didn't know why she expected anything different. Tess was neither a child, nor that naive. Having suffered the loss of both her parents at a young age, she understood the concept of death and just how permanent it was. You could beg, borrow, and steal. Nothing brought the dead back to life.

The doctor, in his no-nonsense way, had been absolutely right. The sooner she accepted that, the better it would be. Yes, the first few days would be the hardest. She'd get past it.

She always did.

Her mother dying from cancer? Tess overcame it. Hospitals still made her nervous and the scent of a strong disinfectant left her stomach queasy, but she accepted that cancer was a bitch. Though you could fight it like the battle it was, cancer was never fair. Sometimes you just lost the damn war.

Her father, the victim of an automobile accident one short year later? She didn't let her childhood fear keep her from buying her first car, or later driving across the country on vacation in a beater even older than she was. She habitually checked her seatbelt, sure, but her father's death taught her a very valuable lesson. You could be as cautious in life as possible. Didn't mean a thing if only one person was careless.

Jack's death would be harder to take in. She had no illusions about that. It was sudden and traumatic and so very, very violent. The nightmares hadn't followed her when she finally fell asleep—but that was only because she'd been too exhausted to dream.

Tonight would be another night, with thousands more to follow. She wouldn't always get that lucky.

Wonderful. Something to look forward to.

In a bid to drown out her nagging thoughts, Tess got up and decided to keep herself busy. She finally found the clock in a far corner; a quick glance revealed that she had slept through breakfast *and* lunch. She was okay with that. Though she got down close to half of Maria's delicious dinner last night, her stomach was still tight. She couldn't imagine eating ever again. So, rather than find her hostess, Tess took a quick shower, changed her clothes, and started to tidy up her room.

Once her bed was made, Tess tackled her luggage. She had the sinking suspicion that Sheriff De Angelis would require her to stay in Hamlet for much longer than she wanted to. Since she had no choice in the matter, the least she could do was make herself comfortable. There was an empty dresser in her room. After unpacking her duffel bag and putting all of her toiletries in the bathroom, Tess folded her clothes before placing them neatly in the dresser drawers.

Just when she was closing the last drawer, a burst of static filled the room.

"Hello? Mrs. Sullivan? Are you there?"

"Hello?" Tess felt silly responding to the disembodied voice. She recognized it by the huskiness and the Italian lilt to be Maria, even if she had no idea where she could be calling from. "Yes, I'm here."

"If you can hear me, I'm talking to you through the intercom. Lucas wired them in every room since phones don't work this side of town. I don't have a radio to offer you, so this is the best we have. Your intercom should be near the bed. If you're getting this, all you have to do is push the button on the top and you can talk back."

Following Maria's instructions, Tess turned to look at the bed. For the first time, she noticed a square box posted a foot above the headboard. It was plastic, about the size of an index card, and colored the same cream shade as the other accents in the Lavender Room.

She found the button on the top and pressed it.

"Hello?"

"Oh, good. You figured out how to make it work. Did I wake you?"

She shook her head, realized that Maria couldn't see her, then pressed the button again. "No, I was up. Did you need me for something?"

"I'm just finishing up tonight's supper and I wanted to know how you preferred to be served. Did you want me to bring it to your room now or should I wait?"

Tess's stomach protested. She still wasn't up for a heavy meal. But sitting down with Lucas's sister, talking to another woman, getting a chance to spend some time out of her own head? *That* sounded perfect.

"Actually," Tess told the intercom, "do you think I could come join you in the kitchen? If I'd be in the way, or if you have other plans, I totally understand. It'd be nice to have the company, though."

There was a pause, then Maria answered, sounding surprised yet pleased. "Of course you can." After giving Tess directions on how to find the kitchen, she added, "I can serve us both in the kitchen. That's usually where I eat my dinner anyway."

"Okay. I'll be right there."

The kitchen was on the same level as her room. Tess passed the spiral staircase that would lead up to the second floor and made a left through the next doorway. The dining room she arrived at was as lavish and painstakingly decorated as the Lavender Room, only the color scheme was a mix of cyan and pale gold. There was even an unlit candelabra in the center of the long table.

A second doorway led off from the dining room. Following Maria's directions, she went through that door and found herself in a homey kitchen that impressed her far more than the dining room simply because it wasn't trying to be anything except a kitchen. The appliances were stainless steel and cutting edge, everything neat and clean, but the battered round table looked so much like the one at her apartment, she immediately felt at ease.

Red gingham napkins were folded in front of the two place settings. They were a perfect match to the dish towels by the sink, and the hand towels hanging over the oven door handle. As Maria set two plates of food on the table, Tess saw that the dishes had an apple design dancing around the rim of the dinnerware. It was adorable.

"I wasn't sure what you'd like for dinner and you didn't answer when I knocked for breakfast so I couldn't ask. I figured, why not make something easy and delicious, something that settles the stomach and eases the soul." With a flourish, she gestured at the steaming plates. "*Ecco!* Tomatoes and shrimp over polenta."

Tess blinked. The thick, yellow meal that served as a bed for the tomatoes and shrimp looked familiar, even though she had no idea what polenta was. She pointed. "Is that the polenta?"

Maria nodded. "Yes. It's kind of like grits. Have you had those before?"

"I actually love shrimp and grits."

"Good. Then you'll love this more. Now dig in."

Tess took a deep breath, wary of the way her stomach had rebelled all afternoon. One sniff of the spices and the buttery shrimp, though, and she was surprised to find that she was kind of hungry after all. "This smells really, really good."

"I know." Maria beamed. "My brother says I make the best polenta in Hamlet. I tell him, it's because we're the only Italians in the whole village so of course mine is the best." Nudging a fork toward Tess, she nodded. "Go on. Eat."

MARIA WAITED UNTIL THE OTHER WOMAN PICKED UP HER fork and stuffed the first tomato slice into her mouth before taking up her own fork and sitting down across from the outsider.

There was something different about her today, Maria decided. The dark circles under Mrs. Sullivan's eyes were more pronounced, though her golden eyes seemed vivid and bright; no longer glazed and dull, like they had been when Maria brought her the chicken pot pie last night. After she showered, Mrs. Sullivan had braided her hair out of her face and changed into a t-shirt and jeans that accentuated her tiny frame. She hadn't put on any make-up.

This close, Maria thought she looked like a girl rather than a woman. At twenty-eight, she was barely older than Mrs. Sullivan, but she felt like she should take care of her.

Someone had to.

From Lucas, she knew that Tessa Sullivan was twenty-five, and that she'd been married to her husband Jack for a year before this tragedy struck. She couldn't imagine how the newly made widow was handling all of this; Maria thought, if she was in her place, she wouldn't have the strength to leave her bed.

And here was the poor woman, obviously distraught, terribly alone, and she was putting on a brave face to sit and eat with her hostess.

That was why Maria chose to make the polenta. The poor thing looked like she was skin and bones. It hadn't escaped Maria's notice that she barely touched the pot pie last night. It did her heart good to see half of the polenta finished before her guest started to pick at it with her fork.

She kept the conversation light, careful not to mention the dreadful circumstances that had the woman staying at Ophelia. Maria did most of the talking, in between eating her own supper and then clearing the dishes. She waved off Mrs. Sullivan's offer of help, instead telling her another anecdote about living in Hamlet while she loaded the dishwasher.

It also didn't get by her that the stories that intrigued the other woman the most all featured Lucas.

Maria was still chatting when she heard the dishwasher signal the end of the cycle. Startled, she looked over at the clock hanging next to the rangehood. Where in the world did the last two hours go?

She pushed away from the table. "I didn't realize it was so late. Not that I don't want to talk more, but I've got to be heading out to the market. I need to pick up a couple things for breakfast tomorrow."

Maria hesitated. It had been so long since she had a conversation with another woman. Caitlin, she decided, didn't count. Lucas's ex was more of a sister than a former sister-in-law, and Maria knew perfectly well that Cait would rather eat her hat than engage in "chick chat".

Mrs. Sullivan hadn't seemed to mind. So, with an impish shrug, Maria offered, "If you want, you can take the ride with me."

"To the market?" Mrs. Sullivan couldn't quite hide her surprise. "There's one in Hamlet?"

The laugh that escaped Maria was reminiscent of a twittering bird. It was a high-pitched trill, both sweet and a trifle annoying at the same time, and it seemed at odds with Maria's normally throaty voice. "Yes, we have a market. It's probably nothing that you're used to, but it suits us. I'm not actually going to visit Jefferson's market tonight, though. I'd planned to take the ride into town, hit the big grocery store they have. There's more variety there."

"I—I shouldn't. I appreciate the offer, but I don't

want to piss off the sheriff anymore than I already have."

Maria had to admit she had a point. Caitlin could be both demanding and particular. "I see. Maybe next time, then, after Caity's cleared this whole mess up."

"That sounds great. For now, I think I'm gonna take another shower, maybe get some more rest. I, uh, I didn't get much rest last night and I think I need a little more."

"Um... well, there's more polenta in the fridge if you want it. And I don't mind if you want to help yourself to a snack later. I'll be back well before nine o'clock in case you need me."

"Okay. Thanks."

Maria started to leave the kitchen before stopping by the refrigerator. She was torn. She'd promised Lucas she would keep an eye on the outsider. Then again, she was also the proprietor of a bed and breakfast struggling to find its legs after a short break. As much as she thought she should stay behind, it was kind of hard to honor the breakfast part of the agreement when she was fresh out of bread and eggs.

She lingered in the kitchen. "Mrs. Sullivan—"

"Tessa, please. Or Tess."

Maria caught the woman's small flinch, the same tiny frown pulling on her lips whenever Maria directly addressed her. It finally hit her. Of course she wouldn't want to be called by her husband's name. It had to be a stark reminder, a sharp stab every time she heard it.

She had thought it odd that Lucas seemed so comfortable with Tessa, calling her by her first name so soon after they met. It was a Hamlet custom, keeping outsiders on the outs by always using their last name when they addressed them. In this one case, she would follow Luc's lead and buck tradition.

"Tess, then... would you mind if I ask you a favor?"

"You're putting me up in your house, feeding me, helping me, and you think I'd mind doing anything you asked? Whatever you want, it's yours."

"If you happen to see my brother... maybe you could, um, *not* mention that I took the drive into town? He usually makes the trip himself every Monday, buying all the groceries we both need, but sometimes I just have to get away. Out of Hamlet for just a moment. He'd lose it if he knew but..." She shrugged impishly. "Maybe he doesn't have to know?"

Tess knew exactly what Maria meant. Even though she had spent only three days in Hamlet, she already itched to leave. A ghost of a smile flashed across her face. First the locks, now this. "He's that overprotective, huh?" she guessed.

"You have no idea."

It was her fourth shower in two days. She didn't care if she stripped all the oils from her skin or if she ended up a wrinkly prune. There was something about standing underneath the steady stream of water, doing the same routine as she did every day that gave her some sense of calm.

And the towels that Maria provided were so soft and fluffy, it was like drying off with a piece of cloud. After the last few days, she needed that comfort.

Once done, she changed into a pair of comfortable sweats before sliding her feet into her favorite pair of slippers. Even though she had packed for a romantic getaway with Jack, her husband knew she got cold easily in bed. She preferred to sleep in sweatpants and t-shirts; her duffel was packed with them. That wouldn't last. She was quickly running through all of her clothes. If the sheriff didn't give her the okay to go home soon, she would have to figure out a way to get her laundry done.

Something told her that while Hamlet had its own market, it wasn't big enough to boast its own laundromat.

Tess brushed her hair, decided against going to sleep with it wet, and hurriedly dried it before throwing it up in a high ponytail. Yawning, she left the bedroom.

No surprise that she felt battered and bruised and just *beat*. All she wanted to do was go back to sleep. So long as the nightmares stayed away, she might find some peace. Jack wasn't dead when she slept. She wasn't trapped in some backwater little town, with suspicion hanging over her like a black raincloud.

When she was asleep, the bed didn't seem so empty.

Closing her eyes, Tess took a deep breath, exhaled roughly. She couldn't afford to have those thoughts because, if she did, she would *never* sleep.

What a shame that there didn't seem to be a single television in the bed and breakfast. She could've used the mindless entertainment. Something to help her turn her brain off at last. Since she couldn't do that, heading back to her bed was the best bet she had.

Her mouth was dry. As delicious as Maria's polenta had been, Tess secretly thought she might've been a bit too heavy-handed with the salt. She'd grabbed a glass from the kitchen and filled it with water from the tap before she took her latest shower. Suddenly thirsty again, she shuffled over to the nightstand where she had left her glass.

Tess took a healthy gulp, her gaze falling on a piece of paper lying facedown on her made bed. She set the glass back down, confused. She didn't remember seeing that there earlier. Had Maria come in and left her a bill? She'd never stayed in a B&B by herself before. Maybe that's how it was done, getting billed for every day that she stayed. It made sense to her, though it seemed odd that Maria would deliver it to her room while she showered instead of giving it to her in the kitchen before she left for the market.

Tess picked up the paper, turned it over, and blinked. One thing was immediately clear: it wasn't a bill.

It took her a second to read the message. Someone had cut letters out of a magazine, differing shapes and styles and fonts. Once she read it, it took her another second before she comprehended the threat.

Jack be nimble, Jack be quick
The noose I tied was just too thick

You can cry, you can weep
but, I warn you, never sleep

One outsider down. Who's next?

The note slipped out of her hand. Strangling her scream, Tess didn't even stop to think. She immediately ran for the door.

Who's next?

Not me.

13

Locked.

The damn thing was locked.

Tessa gripped the knob, rattled it, pulled. It didn't budge. With frantic fingers, she yanked on the bolt, in case that was the reason why the door was stuck. No. The bolt slid easy, back and forth, while the door stubbornly stayed closed.

Okay. Okay. Don't panic, she told herself, already lost in the throes of extreme panic. *Okay*.

The door was locked. Maria must have returned from the market and locked Ophelia down early. And then she had time to leave a twisted nursery rhyme—

No, not Maria.

But *who*?

Didn't matter. She had to get out, and if Maria

locked down Ophelia for whatever reason, there was no way she could escape through the door. With the threat running through her mind on repeat—*never sleep*—she wasn't staying in this room, either.

That left one option.

"Please, please, please," she chanted under her breath as she ran over to the window.

She didn't know what she was doing or where she would go. The only thing that mattered was following the threat written in the note and getting the hell out. Adrenaline coursed through her as she fumbled with the blinds' controls. It didn't go up smoothly, the blinds jerking awkwardly as she twisted the controls with as much force as she could.

Once she had a clear enough shot to the window, Tess said a silent prayer and tugged.

"Yes!"

The window slid right up. It wasn't part of the lock-down. No screen, either. She took one quick look to gauge the distance between the window and the front porch, decided it was worth the risk of twisting her ankle, and clambered out of the window. She landed with a soft cry, falling forward on her palms, only to pop back up a heartbeat later.

Run. She had to run.

Pure instinct drove her. She headed straight down the steps, her path taking her to the street that stretched in front of Ophelia. Except, just as she took the last step, she heard the same damn rev and hum of the car that haunted her all last night. She wasn't thinking as a clear-headed, intelligent individual; at that moment, she was a cornered animal, more likely to lash out than accept aid.

Fear made her reckless. Stupid. Even as she knew there was a good chance it was a cop turning onto the street, she threw up her hands to block the headlights shining in her face before turning around and sprinting away in the opposite direction.

The nearest house was more than twenty feet away. Tess didn't even think to go there for help. Instead, she ran behind Maria's bed and breakfast. A copse of trees bordered Ophelia's backyard. No one would ever think she'd purposely take to the woods.

It was dark, a sudden chill in the air that warned of another incoming storm, and she was wearing a thin t-shirt and loose sweatpants. She had slippers on, so she wasn't ruining the bottoms of her feet as she stumbled over rocks and sticks and tangled weeds. She still had to slow her pace more than once to keep from losing one of her shoes.

Tess was lost the instant she entered the trees. She never had any reliable sense of direction. Add that to the dark night and the fear that led her to run into the woods in the first place, and she knew that there was no way she was getting out again without some help. What she thought was a small gathering of trees proved to be far more vast than the single peek out of Ophelia's kitchen had led her to believe.

Once she realized that she had no idea where she was, she stopped running. Her breath came in big gulps as she struggled to get in enough air. Every time she tried, she wheezed, as the air whooshed out again before she managed to swallow it. Her heart raced and her pulse thundered. With her hand clutching a stitch in her side, Tess tried to straighten. She'd barely moved before she froze suddenly in a hunched position the instant she heard the snapping of a stick.

The quick break filled the quiet night. It wasn't too far from where she was.

She let out a soft moan as the broken stick was soon joined by another. The thud of heavy footsteps matched the thud of her heart as she realized her fatalistic mistake. So worried about the threat left on a piece of paper, she listened and ran. The person who wrote the note didn't have to do anything. In her panicked flight away from trouble, she might've killed herself anyway.

Who was out there? *What* was out there?

An animal?

Worse?

Tess squinted, desperate to see. No good. Her eyes

hadn't adjusted enough; she was basically blind. Leaning down, she scraped her hands across the earth, searching for something she could use as a weapon. Her fingers mashed into the side of a heavy rock. Smaller than a bowling ball yet twice as heavy, she hefted it up in her arms, prepared to bash someone's head in if she had to.

"Mrs. Sullivan? Tessa? Is that you? Are you out here?"

Relief made her weak. She dropped the rock, barely missing the toe of her slipper. "Deputy? I'm over here."

The footsteps stopped. There was a *click* as he turned his flashlight on. The bright yellow beam made her eyes shutter. She lifted her hand to her face, shielding her gaze as she searched for Mason. Once she found him, standing there in his uniform, radio in one hand and flashlight in the other, she flung herself at him. He could've been an ax murderer after her and, right then, she would have clung tightly to him like a barnacle. She wasn't alone anymore.

Mason opened his arms at the last second. As soon as she was pressed up against his chest, he held her close, rubbing his forearm up and down her back in a comforting gesture. "My god, I thought it was you. What are you doing out here?"

She could ask him the same thing. How *did* he

know to find her? Did he follow her from the cruiser? Or was he waiting for her to do something so stupid as take off into the woods after dark?

Did he know about the note?

Did he *send* it?

Her heart continued to beat so fast, she thought it was trying to escape. Suddenly, that seemed like a good idea to Tess. "I… I have to go."

He tightened his arms around her. "Tess, wait—"

"No!" Tess's head was spinning. Panicking, terrified, she had to make him understand. Because, if he wasn't responsible for the threat, someone was.

Jack be nimble, Jack be quick—

She shoved against his chest. "Listen, there was this note, right? I have to go… it said—"

—the noose I tied was just too thick...

Hands clammy, pulse racing, her stomach finally rebelled. Pushing away from the deputy, she covered her mouth with her hands, speaking through muddy fingers. "Move!"

Mason blinked, lowering the flashlight. In its reflection, her eyes looked wild, afraid. He softened his voice. "Tess, honey, you're scaring me. What—?"

He moved closer to her. Tess shoved him away again the instant before she dropped to her knees in the dirt. Her queasy stomach pitched. She fell forward onto her hands and heaved.

Crouching down beside her, Mason rubbed her back in soothing circles. "Are you okay? What's wrong? Talk to me."

Her skin crawled. Wiping her mouth with the back of her filthy hand, she rested on her knees. The deputy was trying to be helpful. She knew that. It wasn't his fault she was running scared. And that was the only reason why she didn't push his outstretched hand away when he crouched in front of her and offered to help her up.

She didn't take his hand, either.

It took her a minute before she felt steady enough to climb back to her feet. Right away, Mason put his arm around her shoulder, trapping her to his side. She was too weary to do more than protest weakly. He pointedly ignored her objections, holding her close as he started to lead her through the woods. Tess stopped fighting. As long as he was taking her back to civilization, she'd go with him gladly.

When he sensed that she'd given in, Mason clicked his tongue. "You shouldn't be out here by yourself. It's dangerous, Tess, heading out in the trees at night. You were running for the gulley. Did you know that? If you got that far, it could've swallowed you up before you knew it. Thank goodness I found you before you hurt yourself."

Tess imagined running into the gaping maw of the

valley that bordered Hamlet on one side. She liked to think she'd stop before she tumbled headfirst into the gap. Panic was a funny thing, though. Before she discovered that note, she would've thought she'd have enough sense not to hide in an unfamiliar woods wearing nothing but her night clothes and a pair of slippers.

She shivered, as if just feeling the night's chill. Mason rubbed his hand along her arm, comforting and warming her at the same time. "Here, let me take you back to my cruiser. I've got water in the car. You can sit down, settle your stomach, and then tell me what it is that's got you upset. How's that sound?"

Tess's throat burned. She could still taste the bile in her mouth from when her stomach turned. Water sounded amazing, the deputy's protection and care even better. As her shivers turned to full body trembles, she buried her nose in his uniform jacket and nodded. Mason smelled woodsy, a mix of fresh air and pine.

It calmed her. Her pulse went from a rapid drumbeat to a dull throb. The adrenaline fading at last, she sagged against him.

Though it felt like she ran forever, she hadn't actually gone that far. Within minutes, Mason was leading her out of the trees, half carrying her to where his cruiser waited for him on the opposite side of the street. She tried not to notice it was parked in the same spot as the car that circled past Ophelia all last night.

Once at the cruiser, Mason insisted on wrapping her in the fleece blanket he had stowed in the trunk of his cruiser. It was fluffy and warm and, though it carried a weird mix of his scent and something she thought might be gun oil, Tess was feeling a lot more settled as he helped her sit in the passenger seat.

He left the door open as he retrieved two bottles of water from his trunk. He handed one to Tess, then set the other on the ground. Hiking up his uniform trousers, he crouched down so that they were eye to eye.

He waited for Tess to take a few tentative sips from her bottle before he said, "Okay. Start at the beginning. What happened?"

It hit her then that she was talking to a deputy. The law. If anyone could help her, he could. So, with a shaky voice and a hint of tears, she did what he asked. And she watched as his handsome face grew grim and grimmer as she spoke.

"Do you have the note with you?" he asked when she was finished.

She shook her head. "I must've dropped it on the floor when I ran for the door. It was locked, so I went for the window. I wasn't thinking clearly. I mean obviously, right? I… I just lost my head for a second."

"I don't blame you."

"It's just—" Tess shuddered, a quick shake that had water sloshing out of the top of her bottle. She could still see the threat, knew she wasn't exaggerating. "Those cut-out letters scared the crap out of me. It was like I *had* to run. I didn't want to end up like Jack. I *don't*."

He didn't want that, either. "No. Of course not."

"I never thought to bring the paper with me when I went."

"It's okay." Mason patted her knee. "We can get it later. It's more important that you're safe now."

Tess sat a little straighter in her seat. She didn't realize how worried she'd been that he wouldn't believe her outlandish story until he accepted it so easily. "I wasn't before you found me. Thank you."

"Hey, I got you. Don't worry." The pat became a tender caress. "You can trust me."

She wasn't so sure she should. The heat from his palm seemed to go through her sweatpants. Why was he touching her? Why did he *keep* touching her? She didn't want to offend the deputy, but if his hand traveled any further north, she was going to scream again.

Mason must have sensed it in her silence. Drawing his hand back, he swiveled his body, pointing at the dark, looming shape of the house in front of them. Tess followed his point, relieved at the space he carefully manufactured between them.

Ophelia was quiet, empty. She couldn't see a single

light on, which was weird considering she hadn't turned her light off before she escaped through the window.

"You're staying there, right?" Mason asked. "At Maria's place?"

"Yes. The doctor brought me here yesterday."

Tess glanced at Mason's profile in time to see his jaw tighten.

"I have to go check this out. I have to check on her."

Her stomach dropped straight down to her slippers. In her fright, she'd forgotten all about Maria. "Oh my god. I didn't think—"

"Shh. It's gonna be okay, Tess. Promise."

She nodded. She'd have to trust the word of an almost stranger. There was no other choice.

Mason straightened up, his hands running down the crease of his slacks as he knocked his jacket away from his hip. A stray beam from the street lamp glanced off of something metallic at his side. It caught her eye, and then she stared. She only just noticed that he had a gun strapped into a holder on his belt.

And she had to wonder if that was always there.

"I'm going in now. You can stay here in the cruiser and wait," he offered. "I'll come get you after I make sure the house is clear."

"No." She had to go back in there with him. She had to make sure Maria was safe inside otherwise she would never forgive herself. Besides, she hated the idea of being left alone outside. “I’ll come with you.”

He chucked her chin, a devastating smile at ease on his boyish face. He didn't look the least bit worried.

Tess had to wonder about that.

“That’s my girl,” he said. There was an excited gleam in his eye that matched his grin. “Come on. Let’s go.”

14

The front door was open.

Mason gestured for Tess to stay on the porch as he pushed the door in and peered into the house. Her hands over her mouth, she leaned on her tiptoes, looking around his body, searching for a threat she couldn't see.

It was impossible. Ophelia was pitch dark. This close, they both confirmed that all of the lights were off. It was eerily quiet in there.

"Maria?"

No answer.

Mason glanced behind him at Tess, saw the stark terror on her face, and held up his hand. She nodded, her golden eyes too wide in her lovely face. It took everything he had to turn back and take the step over the threshold.

"Maria? It's Deputy Walsh. Are you home?"

Nothing.

He slipped his gun out of its holster. The cocking of the trigger as he readied the gun echoed in the foyer.

"Maria?" he called one last time. "I'm coming in."

He took three steps into the dark room when, suddenly, a light flicked on, momentarily blinding him. Blinking rapidly to get his sight back, he braced himself to shoot, freezing in place as Maria appeared in the doorway.

She had a dishtowel in her wet hands, wiping the soap suds off as she dried them.

"Mase? I thought I heard you—" She caught sight of Mason across the foyer, pointing his gun right at her. The towel slipped from her hand. "*Dio mio*! What do you think you are doing with that gun?"

The gun clicked as he re-engaged the safety before tucking his firearm back into its holster. "I'm doing a routine wellness check," he explained. "When you didn't respond, I got worried."

Maria's whole expression darkened.

Narrowing her gaze at Mason, she swooped down and picked up the fallen dishtowel. "Lucas," she snapped before launching into a heated stream of Italian under her breath.

Mason didn't correct her. Instead, he went out the open door. When he came back a moment later, he had Tess Sullivan with him.

Mud covered her slippers, dotted the hem of her sweats. The outsider was shivering, arms hanging at her sides. She was so pale, it looked like she'd seen a ghost.

"Tess?" Maria didn't think she'd be more surprised if Lucas came by and told her he was remarrying Caitlin. When she left Ophelia, Tess was in the kitchen. The room was empty when she got back, so she assumed her guest was already tucked in for the night. "What in the world—"

Mason cleared his throat. "Maria, I'd like to escort Mrs. Sullivan back to her room. Do you think you can shut down the locks for me?"

Maria looked from Mason to Tess and back. She didn't know what to say, or what she should do. On the one hand, Lucas warned her not to let anyone else into the house. He'd been very clear on that point, worried that something might happen to her or Tess.

But this wasn't *anyone*. This was Mason Walsh. He was one of Caity's deputies. He didn't count... did he?

She decided he didn't. He couldn't. This was a man she'd known her entire life. The same age as Mason, they'd been together in the same class all through school. He worked with her ex-sister-in-law. His mother had even helped her come up with the name

Ophelia for her bed and breakfast, as a nod to the name of their village. Mase was safe. If she couldn't trust him, who could she trust?

"No need. It's only half past eight. I haven't engaged any of Ophelia's locks yet."

Tess's whole frame gave a jolt. Maria opened her mouth to say something more, but he held out his hand, silently asking her for a moment.

MASON TOOK ANOTHER OPPORTUNITY TO TAKE HOLD OF Tess. She trembled under his grasp when he gently laid his hand on her shoulder.

"You okay?"

"It was locked," Tess murmured. "I had to go out the window."

"Window?" echoed Maria. "*Che*?"

"Where's your room, Tess?" Mason asked gently.

"I... I don't want to go back there. What if it's not safe for me anymore?"

"Mason—*Mase*. Ophelia, she is the safest place in all of Hamlet. What's going on?"

Mason kept his attention on Tess. "See? You heard Maria. With the security here, Ophelia is practically a fortress. No one can get inside once it's in lockdown. It'll be alright. Promise."

Even as he said that, Mason wasn't too sure he wasn't making a promise he wouldn't be able to keep. There was too much at play. On the one hand, he couldn't understand why someone would leave such a cruel taunt for Tess; on the other, he couldn't bring himself to think she was lying for whatever reason. He saw the terror in her eyes, watched her get sick out of fear. Her reaction was genuine. She really believed she was in danger.

And, unless he went and checked it for himself, he couldn't help her as much as he longed to.

"I'm not going to ask you to do anything you don't want to," he said soothingly. Under his hand, Tess had tensed up again. He wanted nothing more than to calm her. "Maria can bring me to your room."

"No." Tess shook her head. Just like how she refused to let him approach Ophelia on his own, she was showing her strength as she said, "I can do it. It's... it'll be fine. I just have to tell myself it's better than going back to the Hamlet Inn. It's okay. My room is this way."

Easily keeping pace with her, Mason took hold of Tess's arm again, helping her as she shuffled down the hallway in her muddy slippers. She led him to a closed door with an oversized purple L painted in the center. Standing in front of it, staring at the design with a wary expression, she gestured at the door handle—then made no move to open it.

Mason did. Grasping the handle, it turned under his hand. The door eased inward.

She slumped against him. “It’s not locked anymore,” she whispered. “But I know it was.”

“Don’t worry, Tess. We’ll straighten this out. Stay out here. I’ll let you know when it’s clear.”

“Can I go with you? I think I’ll feel better if we’re in there together.”

It might be the most inopportune moment but Mason felt his heart skip a beat—and that wasn’t the only part of his body to react at the way she latched onto his side, clutching him as if afraid to let him go.

Tess wanted to invite him into her room? Nothing was going to stop him. And if he could be her hero, banishing the demons and shedding some light on the monster terrorizing the innocent outsider? He might even earn another invitation.

Mason guided Tess over to her bed. He settled her on the edge, feeling the pang of loss when he eased her grip off of his uniform jacket, then did a quick sweep of the room with his practiced gaze.

The first thing he noticed was that the window was still open, just like she said. Nothing else seemed out of place. Her purse was sitting on the desk. A half-empty glass was on the nightstand. He definitely didn’t see a slip of paper lying anywhere.

So where was the note?

He walked around the bed, moving purposely

while Tess continued to rest, head in her hands. Picking up the glass, he made sure Tess wasn't looking back at him before lifting it to his nose. He took a sniff. Water. He hadn't smelled any alcohol on Tess, either, but after the way they met, it was worth checking.

After setting the glass back down, he lowered himself to his hands and knees, peering under the bed. It was too dark to see anything. He took his flashlight from its place on his belt, clicked it on and looked. Nothing except a pair of sneakers lying haphazardly on their sides.

Just in case, he crossed the room and went into the bathroom. A folded towel was perched on the toilet lid. Tess's toothbrush was on the side of the sink. It smelled like her in the bathroom, a hint of cinnamon and spice lingering in the air. He breathed in deep, then yanked the shower curtain back to see if anyone was hiding inside the stall.

Having cleared the bathroom and the shower, he went back in the room. Tess hadn't moved an inch from where he placed her. Maria, neither.

She lingered in the doorway, confused and unsure. When she saw him again, she waved him over. "Deputy Walsh, may I speak to you?"

"Sure." Mason held up one finger, then turned toward Tess. He couldn't help himself. Crouching down again, he rested one hand possessively on her knee. "Sit tight. I'll be right back."

Even though she kept her face buried in her hands, he saw it when she nodded. Her shoulders were shaking, though she didn't make a sound. Mason's heart broke for her. This wasn't supposed to happen. Not in Hamlet.

He watched her for a second, listening for tears, before rising and joining Maria out in the hall. With a nod, he gestured for her to move further from Tess's room.

"Mason, *cosa sta succedendo*?" Maria rattled off a string of Italian before clutching his arm. "What's going on? Is she okay? Why would she think my Ophelia isn't safe for her?"

He patted her hand. The last thing he wanted to do was upset Maria De Angelis. She deserved the peace.

"She's had a little bit of a fright, but she'll be fine. It's nothing like what happened to you," he added quickly when Maria's grip tightened. "I have to ask you something, off the record. You didn't mess with her room, did you? Lock her in earlier tonight, or go in there when she was in the shower?"

If he didn't want to upset Maria, he failed miserably.

"What? No!" She looked horrified at the accusation. "I honor my guests so long as they respect me and my rules. Why would you even ask me that?"

Because his inexplicable yet undeniable attraction to that pretty little outsider made him do stupid, stupid things. Sticking his hands in his pockets, he ducked his head in a bid to avoid her insulted glare. "Ah, jeez, Maria. I'm a deputy. I had to ask, even if I knew you had nothing to do with it."

"With what? *Dimmi*! What's going on? I go out for groceries and, when I come back, Mason Walsh is aiming a gun in my Ophelia. I don't understand."

Mason hesitated. Never one to gossip, he wasn't sure that it was his place to tell Maria about what happened to Tess. An instant later, he corrected himself. He had to tell her. As deputy, it was his responsibility to make sure that everyone in Hamlet was safe. One outsider was already dead, and another threatened. Who's to say that the culprit would stop at outsiders?

Keeping his voice low, he quickly explained to Maria the events of the evening, starting with the locked door and ending with the fact that the threatening note was now missing.

He made the right choice in telling her. Instead of being angry and hurt, Maria was concerned. But not, like he sort of expected, for herself. She was worried about her guest.

As devoted to her bed and breakfast as she was, Mason should've realized that.

Maria shook her head royally, her long dark hair cascading down her back. "That's awful! She's such a sweetheart. She doesn't deserve someone upsetting her like that, especially not in my Ophelia. Is there anything I can do for her?"

Mason had been thinking the same thing ever since he had to help her find her way out of the woods. He almost offered to take Tess back home with him—but even he realized that taking advantage of her after her scare would be kind of sleazy. Having her stay with Maria was the best thing for her, especially since the sheriff was still harping on her being the only suspect in Sullivan's murder. He dreaded what Caitlin would say when she found out about this twist in the case.

No, he needed to keep his distance as best he could. Didn't mean that he couldn't still take care of Tess.

"She needs a good night's sleep. I don't know if she'll manage it on her own. You wouldn't happen to have anything that might help her relax, would you? Like a sleeping pill?"

Maria pursed her lips, thinking. She shook her head. "All I have is aspirin. But I know where I can get something."

Mason immediately knew he made a mistake. "Ah, no. I don't want to bother—"

"Hush, Mase," Maria said, swatting him in the arm. "Luc is up all hours of the night. Come. I'll get my radio. He's used to weird buzzes, especially from me. He won't mind."

Yes, but Mason might.

He took two steps after her, prepared to tell her that

he changed his mind, before he realized that he was just being selfish. As much as he wanted to keep Tess to himself, he couldn't deny her something that might help her. It wasn't her fault that the only one who could offer her a peaceful sleep was Lucas. And it made complete sense that Maria's response to his request was to call on her brother. He was the only doctor in town and, since Hamlet didn't have a real pharmacy, he was in control of any and all medications. Tess needed a sleeping pill? Lucas would have one.

Damn it.

Maria returned a few moments later, her radio in one hand, a wooden Louisville Slugger clutched tightly in the other. She beamed over at Mason. "I got Luc on the radio. He says he's gonna stop at his office first for the medicine, then he'll be right over."

"That's great." It wasn't great. If Tess needed someone to save her, he wanted it to be him, not the doctor. Since he couldn't tell Maria that, he focused on something else instead. He pointed at the bat. "Going out for some batting practice?"

She hefted the bat up, a wicked and fierce glimmer in her pale eyes. "If someone else thinks they can sneak around Ophelia, then *si*. Most definitely."

15

Mason rubbed his jaw, stifling a yawn. Stubble pricked the tips of his fingers. It had been a long night. Once the sheriff gave him the all clear to go off duty, he'd have to make sure he shaved before he went to see Tess again.

The sun was up by the time his rounds brought him back to the station house. He was feeling it. In the years that he'd been a deputy, Mason worked his fair share of overnight patrols but never so many shifts back to back. His eyes were dry, itchy, like he got sand in them. The yawns kept coming. He fought to hold them back. The sheriff had ordered him to take short breaks for rest. He was the idiot who kept cutting them even shorter.

The scent of freshly brewed coffee slapped him awake as he dragged himself into the station. It was empty, though that didn't mean he was the only one there. Station coffee couldn't brew itself; somebody had to be nearby. After helping himself to a styrofoam cup of the stuff, only pausing to splash some milk in to cool it down, he went off in search of whoever was on duty with him so early.

Bang.

Crash.

The slow, steady whine of a dying beep.

“Are you fucking kidding me?”

Mason’s lips curved around the rim of his cup. Caitlin. Of course. He should have known. The woman was like a robot. She'd been going nonstop since they found Jack Sullivan’s body, living on coffee and a steely determination to solve the outsider’s murder in record time.

He thought about it for a second, realized that her cussing while on duty meant she was real riled up, and went to prepare a second cup of coffee. Mood she was in, he might need a peace offering. Then, a cup in each hand, he crossed the station.

The main station house was a wide open floor, with two desks, a handful of visitor’s chairs, a battered old fridge, and a tray table next to it that held the department’s microwave and coffee pot. Hamlet’s single holding cell was toward the back. Off to the right, there were two doors. One was the bathroom. The other, a closed-in office that the sheriff rarely used.

It was that room where Caitlin had brought Tess to do her interviews on Sunday. And it was that room where Caitlin's angry cry had just come from.

He knocked with his elbow, then carefully let himself in.

"Morning, Sheriff. I brought you some coffee."

She already had an empty styrofoam cup on her desk. He placed his offering next to it in time to dodge Caitlin's arm as she reared back and swung her open palm right at the side of her ancient desktop monitor.

Thwack!

Shaking out her stinging palm, she growled at the monitor. At least the beeping stopped.

"Feel better?"

"Damn it, Mase, the stupid internet went out again. Blasted cables were up all morning but the second the e-mail I was waiting for comes in, internet goes out. It's messing with me on purpose. I know it is."

He nodded in sympathy. While all of Hamlet had a love-hate relationship with technology, Caitlin took it to the extremes. Mason long ago gave up on telling her that beating the machine wouldn't fix it.

"You really should look into getting one of those fancy cellphones. Pay for the right plan, you're supposed to be able to get internet on it whenever you want."

"Then I'd have to drive out of Hamlet anytime I wanted to use the thing. And I'll be damned if they try putting up another cell tower around here. That first one never took and, hell, we just don't need it enough." She knew some of the younger kids, like Addy's Sally, made a big fuss out of having no cell service. It didn't bother Caitlin. She sniffed. "Give me my radio any day."

Hamlet communicators were reliable. The channels were always open. It was bad enough she had to go to the county's big municipal center on the rare occasions she needed help with one of her investigations. If she didn't have to take that narrow one-way strait, she wouldn't.

Caitlin hated leaving Hamlet. When they were still married, Lucas was always going, taking a couple of hours to visit the bigger shops, or even week-long trips when he went away for his job. To keep up to date in his practice, Lucas was forever attending classes, seminars, even hosting lectures of his own. It used to drive her insane with jealousy.

Now she paid her neighbor to get her anything Jefferson didn't have in his store, and she watched from a distance as Lucas sped his Mustang out of town. It still drove her nuts, yeah. As long as he didn't bring anyone back with him, she managed.

She had to.

"Speaking of heading out of Hamlet," Caitlin said, accepting the coffee with a nod, "I've got to take a trip today." She made a face. She couldn't help it. "It's for the Sullivan case or else I'd be out with the rest of you guys. I shouldn't be gone long. Now, go on. Report. How was your patrol last night?"

"Oh. Um. Good, I guess."

"Really? And Ophelia? How was that?"

Mason froze. "What do you mean?"

Caitlin let out a laugh. He didn't find any humor in it and, he realized after a beat, neither did she. "Come on, Mase. We both know you took a spin by Maria's place at least once last night."

He couldn't really deny it. And it wasn't like he did anything wrong. Hamlet was small. If his patrol took him past Ophelia, he was only doing his duty.

It struck him that no one had radioed Caitlin and told her about the threat left for Tess. If Caitlin knew, she would've said something. No doubt. In her way, the sheriff was being playful. If she knew another crime had gone down, she'd be furious.

Last night was rough. He stood guard over Tess, watching as Lucas checked her out, took her measure, assured her that she was safe if she stayed *inside* of her room, regardless of what any faceless boogeyman left in a note. Mason longed to jump in, but the doctor never gave him the chance. So he tried instead to charm Maria into letting him stay the night, renting one of the rooms so he'd be close by if either of the women needed him. That hadn't worked, either. She obviously had more faith in a baseball bat than in Mason's gun.

Probably didn't help that he'd pointed it at her, he admitted to himself.

In the end, he waited until Tess took the medicine Lucas brought before purposely walking the doctor out. If he couldn't stay, he'd make damn sure Lucas didn't.

Not that it mattered. It was already too late. Seeing the way Lucas eyed her when he didn't think anyone was looking, Mason knew the other man was only going to stand in the way of him and Tess.

Just like he was sure that Lucas wouldn't tell his ex-wife anything about what happened at Ophelia. He would do his best to protect the outsider.

And so would Mason.

"You're right, boss. It was quiet. No trouble at all."

"That's what I want to hear. We need more trouble like we need another outsider in town."

He could never understand why she hated outsiders so much. They brought excitement, possibility. Everything was always so stagnant in Hamlet. A fresh face could inject a little life in their sleepy village.

Except for Jack Sullivan, he amended. That man had only brought death.

Mason shook his head, clearing that thought as quickly as it came. "Yeah, well, since it's quiet, I was wondering if I could go off duty now. Take a couple personal hours since I just came off a double."

Caitlin didn't answer him right away. Clicking angrily on the computer's mouse, she peered at her screen, scowling at whatever she saw. She wore her long red hair tied back, the tail resting over the shoulder of her crisp beige uniform shirt. She flipped it out of her face before taking her seat, her fingers tapping rhythmically against the desk.

Tap, tap, tap. Tap, tap, tap.

Mason suspected his boss had a pretty good guess what he wanted the personal for.

"We have a murderer out there in our village. Anyone could be the next victim. You haven't forgotten that, have you, Deputy?"

Tap, tap, tap.

"No, ma'am."

"Didn't think so." She leaned back in her chair, sipping the coffee Mason brought her. "We're all on duty until further notice. No approved personal. Doesn't mean you can't get some sleep. When I get back from town, I'll buzz you and you can take a couple more hours down. I mean it this time. Take them. You look like hell, Mase. Rest. Take the time when you can."

He ran his hand over his stubble. It felt thicker. "I will."

"Good. I'm gonna need you patrolling again

tonight, trading off with Sly. These hours are a killer, yeah, but that's because we're trying to *beat* a killer. We can't let her win."

Her. It might have been a slip. He doubted that very much. Caitlin still believed Tess was involved in her husband's death. Wonderful. More than ever, Mason thought he made the right decision in keeping the threatening riddle from the sheriff. She would only find some way to pin it on Tess.

Tess didn't deserve that. Caitlin wasn't there. She hadn't seen how badly shook Tess was. He was a deputy, more than eight years under his belt on the job. If that woman was faking, he'd turn in his gun and his badge.

He itched to get back to her, to make sure she was okay. And he hated the idea that the doc might manage to do so before he could.

No approved personal. He got that. But what about—

Mason cleared his threat. "Sheriff, I was just wondering. Tomorrow night is my scheduled off time—"

"There is no scheduled off time either when we have an open investigation. You *know* that. No pretty face or sob story should turn your head so much that you forget who you are and what you've sworn to do. Hamlet is your home, Deputy. And it's your priority."

Mason took her slap at him with a wince and a

gulp before he straightened, his hands folded behind his back.

"You're right, Sheriff. I'm sorry. Forget I brought it up."

CAITLIN STUDIED HER DEPUTY, RAMROD STRAIGHT AS HE stood at attention. Lord help her, she could almost swear she saw the little hearts fluttering over his head. Mason had it bad. As much as she hated to admit it, there was a slight chance Sullivan's wife was innocent. If she ended up proving it, what did it hurt to let Mason work this little crush out of his system?

And, she realized, if the outsider hooked up with Mason, that left Lucas wide open for her.

"Okay. Fine." She threw her hands up in the air, making a show of giving in. "Take tomorrow night for yourself. Just make sure to keep your radio on in case I need you."

"I always do," he promised. Then, deciding to make his escape before she changed her mind, he added, "Good luck with the internet."

"Yeah, yeah."

Mason started to back out of the office, paused as if remembering something, and hesitated. Hands in his pockets he turned to face Caitlin again.

"Hey, Sheriff? Quick question. You... you, uh, don't still think that Tess killed her husband? Right?"

Tess again, Caitlin thought. Someone ought to warn the kid not to wear his heart on his sleeve. It was a dangerous place to keep it. She knew that better than anyone. Lucas broke hers so many times over the years, all she had left were shards.

She drank her coffee, taking a second to compose herself so that she didn't snap out her answer—or a warning.

"Mase, I have to follow that lead all the way to the end."

"But... *why*?"

"Because once I'm done looking at Tessa Sullivan, I'll have to start looking for one of us."

ON THE WAY TO HIS OFFICE THAT MORNING, LUCAS purposely made a right instead of a left when he hit the main fork in the road. He was supposed to go to work. He didn't. His Mustang brought him back to Ophelia instead.

As he let himself into his sister's house, he flashed back to the night before. It had spooked him to get a buzz from Maria so late, and he almost lost it when she admitted that someone had snuck into the bed and breakfast last night to terrorize her guest. The only thing that kept him from insisting she shut Ophelia down again was that Maria hadn't been in any danger

—and, if she had been, she still slept with her trusty bat underneath her bed.

It worried him that Tessa Sullivan seemed to be a target, though. And that, when she was in danger, Mason Walsh had been there to take care of her. If it wasn't for Maria catching the look on his face and telling Walsh no, the deputy would've booked a room at Ophelia to keep his eye on the outsider.

He couldn't have that.

Telling himself that, as the doctor, it was up to him to follow up with his new patient, Lucas decided to make a house call to the bed and breakfast rather than returning to his office to catch up on his patients and reports. A house call still counted as work. He wouldn't let anyone tell him otherwise.

He checked in on his sister, finding her in her bedroom. He told her his plan, trying not let it embarrass him too much when Maria squealed in excitement and rushed him out of her room so that he could go see Tessa. Her girlish advice ringing in his ears—or maybe that was her high-pitched shrieks—Lucas headed for the Lavender Room. He rapped his knuckles gently against the door, then pressed in close.

The rustle of sheets, the soft shuffle of dainty steps across the carpet, and then, "Yes? Hello?"

"It's me. Lucas."

It was already after ten; the outer locks had been

disengaged three hours ago. He heard the click as Tessa unlocked the door on her side.

A moment later, she swung the door inward. Wearing a plush pink robe and a pair of muddy slippers, Tessa kept her hand on the door handle. She made no move to invite him in.

Her hair was sleep-tousled in a most appealing way. It made Lucas wonder what it would be like to see those soft curls spilled across his own pillow.

Tessa looked up at him in honest confusion. Her expression seemed softer this morning, more open and far less wary. She lost some of the pinched look of fear she'd worn when Lucas brought over the medication last night.

Good.

"Morning, Tessa."

With her free hand, she anxiously tightened the belt on her robe. "Um—hi."

"I hope I didn't wake you."

"No, no. I was already up." She couldn't quite meet his eyes. "Is there something I can do for you?"

Lucas offered her a rakish grin, bowing his head so that she had no choice but to look at him. Tess could feel her cheeks heat up. "Since I was in the neighborhood, I thought I would stop in and check up on you.

How are you feeling? Did you take the pills I brought you?"

"They worked. First real sleep I've gotten in days." And because they knocked her out, she didn't experience any of the nightmares she'd been afraid to have. Ten hours of dreamless sleep, it was the best gift anyone could've given her last night. "I appreciate it."

"Don't mention it. I'm the doctor. It's my responsibility to take care of my patients. And since you're here, for however long the sheriff wants you to stay, I'll do my best to take care of you."

"Oh, wow. I— I don't know what to say."

It seemed like Lucas did. "Have you had breakfast yet?" he asked.

That was the last thing she expected from him. Except for when Maria was forcibly reminding her that she had to eat, she didn't think about food. Her stomach went from queasy to settled to angry, depending on her mood. Her appetite was long gone. She shook her head.

"Great. Tell me you'll come with me to have some."

Was he serious? Tess dared to look up at him, her gaze drawn to his chiseled jaw and the way his expression both enticed her and warned her not to refuse.

Oh, yes. He was dead serious.

But *why*?

"Oh, I... um, I'm sure Maria will be expecting me to

eat with her. Your sister's very kind. She's been feeding me every chance she gets."

"She must think you're too skinny."

"She might have implied that once or twice," Tess admitted. "I like her. I don't want her to waste her work if she's already started breakfast."

Lucas waved away her concerns. "I stopped by Maria's room before I came to check on you. Don't worry about her. I already told her that we were going to go to the coffeehouse together. She just asked me to bring home one of Addy's scones. My sister is an amazing cook," he confided, lowering his voice as he leaned in, "but she can't bake to save her life."

The handsome doctor was close. Super close. Tess's heart skipped a beat. Her mouth was suddenly as dry as the Sahara. Swallowing roughly, she found herself nodding. "Okay. I'll go with you. Just let me get changed."

"I'll be waiting on the porch. Come outside when you're ready."

"Give me five minutes."

"No rush," Lucas said, reaching out to tap her nose. She felt that casual touch all the way down to her toes. Even when he backed away, her skin still burned. "I'll wait as long as you need me to."

Jack never wanted to wait for her. If she wasn't ready when he was, he would threaten to leave her behind—and, sometimes, it wasn't just a threat. She lost count of the times that they went somewhere in separate cars because he couldn't stand waiting around for her to finish getting dressed. Lucas's patience was so foreign to her that she stood, stunned, as he walked away, whistling.

Giving her head a quick shake, she shut the door behind him and, stripping as she went, ran right to the bathroom. One year being married to a stickler with time had long since turned her into a quick-change artist when the situation called for it.

So even though Lucas told her that he was content to wait, the two of them were pulling up to another Victorian-style house barely twenty minutes later.

When Lucas said he was taking her to a coffee-house, she was expecting a Starbucks or maybe a local café. The narrow, spindly house—a *house* house—was unlike anything she imagined. It had the turrets and the railings like Ophelia, but it was a third of the size with at least one extra floor. And, she felt the need to point out again, it was a house.

"Is this it?"

Lucas killed the engine. Opening his door, he climbed out of the car. "Sort of."

Sort of? What did that mean? Tess unbuckled her seatbelt, reaching for the door handle.

She saw what he meant a minute later. He guided her around the side of the house, surprising Tess with another building similar in style to the first, only much smaller. It reminded her of a greenhouse, with the same weathered facade as the Victorian in front of it.

Another wooden sign, eerily reminiscent of the sign welcoming visitors to Hamlet, hung over a pale blue door.

In a looping, swirling script, it read: ***the coffeehouse***.

"This is one of Hamlet's many treasures," Lucas told her. "Not only does Addy do the best baking in town, but the coffee is to die for. And if Gus is cooking, there's no better meal. Except for when Maria is in charge of the kitchen," he added loyally. "They do all the baking and cooking in the main house. The coffeehouse is where you can go to sit with your coffee and just relax."

Tess didn't think she remembered how to relax. With Lucas as her breakfast companion, she figured it was worth a try.

Lucas slipped his arm around her shoulder before opening the door for them. "Come with me. There's a table in the back where we can talk without too many people staring."

As Tess walked beside the doctor, she couldn't help but notice that he wasn't kidding. There were at least nine other people being served inside and each one was watching in avid interest as Lucas led her to an empty table against the far wall. She tucked herself close to his side, more than willing to use his bigger body as a shield.

He pulled out her seat, waited for her to take it before he moved to sit opposite of her. The instant his ass hit the chair, the waitress appeared.

She was a perky little thing, all of maybe fourteen years old. On the tall and gangly side, she wore a burgundy apron that slipped off her slim shoulders. Her hair was cut short, her face too feminine for the cut to seem boyish. When she smiled in a warm greeting, Tess saw the most endearing gap between her two front teeth.

"Doctor De Angelis, hi! Mom was just talking about you and here you are. I swear, it's like she's psychic or something."

"Good morning, Sally."

Cordial yet frosty, Tess decided. He was a local, sure, but one who kept himself on the fringe. She wondered if it had something to do with his being the only doctor in Hamlet.

The teen's cheeks turned a rosy sort of pink. Tess didn't blame her. Whenever Lucas turned his stunning good looks in her direction, she felt herself getting warm, too.

LUCAS WANTED TO RETURN HIS ATTENTION BACK TO HIS lovely brunch companion—but he knew he couldn't. Not yet. Even as he smiled up at the local girl, he was aware that nearly every other villager was watching their table in open interest.

It was a calculated risk. He wanted to take Tessa out, even though he knew they'd be on full display. In fact, he was almost counting on it.

He offered Sally one of his professional grins. His *I'm the doctor and you can trust me* smile.

"What can I do for your lovely mother?"

Sally giggled. "Well, she was only just wondering this morning if you're gonna be opening up your office soon for seeing patients. She's got that patch thing going on with her foot again. I know she wants you to check it out but Aunt Cait says you've been busy with sheriff stuff."

Sally's mother, Adrianna, was a close friend of Caitlin's, close enough that Sally referred to the sheriff as her aunt. Addy was also, with her husband Gus, the owner of the coffeehouse.

Originally called *The Danish Coffee & Cake Shop*—because most shop owners in town took pride in Hamlet and it showed—nearly all of the locals simply referred to their shop as the coffeehouse. The only nod to the original name was the small *DC&C* stamps printed on the coffee mugs. Even Addy eventually gave up the fight and had Maria paint her a new sign to overhang the front door.

"You tell her that anytime she needs me, give me a

buzz. I'll be starting regular hours in the next couple of days, but I'm never too busy for her."

"I'll tell her, doc. So, what can I get you two? Mom's got a fresh crumb cake coming out in the next ten minutes."

"How's coffee to start?" Tessa nodded, so he told Sally, "Two coffees, please. And is Gus on the grill?"

While Sally was the server and Adrianna did all of the baking, Gus stayed in the main kitchen in their house, preparing any of the hot meals ordered and sending Sally across the grass to deliver them.

Like its original name, the plan that the coffeehouse was only a coffeehouse changed shortly after Addy and Gus opened the place. Hamlet had been in need of a homestyle diner-type joint, with breakfast and lunch served for any of the locals who were tired of the only other two restaurants in town. The coffeehouse filled the void. And despite being a haven for Hamlet locals, it was always crowded.

"Yeah, Dad's working straight through the lunch rush like usual."

"Perfect. If you could bring us a list of what he's cooking up today, that would be great. My guest and I will be having brunch following our coffee. We'll choose from his specials."

Even after he gave their order, she didn't move away from their table. He could tell that it was on the tip of

Sally's tongue to ask about Tessa. Considering how rare it was for outsiders to find their way into Hamlet, especially in such a scandalous way as Tessa had, there was no doubt in his mind that the teen knew exactly who she was. But gossip was currency in such a small village. By bringing Tessa to the coffeehouse, Lucas had just made Sally rich.

He leaned back into the uncomfortable seat. "Thank you, Sally. The coffee, if you could. We'll go with the house special. The Danish, please."

Sally nodded, tucking her pad into her apron. She certainly knew a dismissal when she heard one, immediately retreating from their table.

Lucas had a good idea what she would do—and what she would say to her mother—as soon as she scurried back through the **Employees Only** door that led into the smaller kitchen.

Lucas watched the teen go, accepting that any peace they would have at brunch would be short-lived. He turned to Tessa, prepared to warn her that even this table hadn't managed to hide her. He cocked his head, though, when he saw that she was looking at him strangely.

"What?"

16

"Your name is De Angelis."

"Yes."

"And the sheriff... that's her name, too."

He knew where she was going with this. To be honest, Lucas was surprised it took her this long to say something about it. It wasn't like he had ever hidden it. "That's right."

"Maria is your only sister, but Caitlin has your name. So you two—"

"We were. A long time ago." It was important to him that she understood that point. "Stupid kids got married before they realized it would be work. We got divorced years ago but she always says that my name is one more thing she got in the divorce." He shrugged. "It wasn't worth the argument. You've met Caity, you know what she's like. If she wanted it, she could keep it."

The young waitress came back with their coffees. Lucas took his black, watching curiously as Tessa dumped in three creamers and two sugars before stirring it all up with the flat of her knife. She took a sip, added one more sugar, then sipped again.

Satisfied, she remarked, "I don't know why she would bother."

"Bother what? In keeping my name? I've always liked it."

Tessa grinned. It was about time he finally saw such a light-hearted expression cross her face. Lucas was struck by the simple beauty of it. He knew she was more than seven years younger than he was but, at that moment, she seemed soft. Youthful. *Innocent*. He found himself grinning back.

She flicked the discarded lid from one of her creamers at him. "I didn't mean it like that. It's just..." Her grin lost some of its shine. "It feels so weird to think of myself as Tessa Sullivan now that Jack's gone."

"Were you married long?" Lucas tested his coffee. Finding it too hot, he set it to the side.

"Just a year. Actually, this was supposed to be a second honeymoon thing and—I'm sorry. Talking about him seems to help, but then I... I don't know. Just. Sorry. You probably don't want to hear about him after what happened and... yeah."

"Don't apologize."

Her brow furrowed. "Did I?"

"You did. And it wasn't the first time. Seems like that's all you do, saying the word *sorry* over and over again."

Tessa took another sip. If it was a nervous tactic to stall the conversation, it didn't work. Lucas watched her closely, waiting for her answer. He didn't say anything. The silence eventually forced her to continue.

"It's still really hard for me to get it, to get that he's gone. I mean, I know I signed that form for the cremation. I didn't want any ceremony and maybe that was a mistake. Without seeing it, there wasn't any closure for me. Then again, I think I saw enough in that hotel room, right? I don't know. I guess it didn't hit me that he was... that he was actually *murdered* until I got that note last night.

"I was so stupid, too. I mean, what was I thinking? Running out into the night like that, nearly getting myself killed, all because somebody thought it would be funny to mess with the... what do you guys call it?"

His lip curled. The smile didn't quite reach his eyes. "Outsider."

"Right. I'm an outsider who brought death to Hamlet, whether I meant to or not. Of course they would want me gone. The note, while over the top, almost did the job." Her laugh was forced. "I don't think I've ever ran so fast in my life, and all because someone tried to turn my own husband's murder against me."

Lucas had come to the same conclusions himself. Nobody ever locked their doors in Hamlet which was what had gotten his sister into so much trouble last year. That was why he insisted so strongly on the dual system on the rooms in Ophelia. The front door might be open. The rest of them wouldn't be.

Except the note had appeared in the Lavender Room before Ophelia's lockdown. That meant that anyone could have snuck into the bed and breakfast and left the note—if, in fact, there was a note.

No, he decided. There had to be one. Tessa was too good, too *sweet*. She would never lie to him.

"You don't think they meant it?" he asked her. "The threat?"

She shook her head. "Looking back, I know that it had to be a prank. Some sick person's idea of a joke. I only wish you and Maria and the deputy didn't have to see me fall apart like that last night. I feel like such an idiot. Just because Jack's gone, it doesn't mean I'm next."

He wasn't sure if she really believed what she was saying, or if she was trying to convince herself that it was a joke so that she didn't have to be afraid. Taking a sip of his coffee, he studied her over the rim of his mug. That was what was missing today, he realized. She didn't seem so afraid.

"I didn't want to say anything before but, now that you say that, there's something different about you now." Lucas set his mug down, absently rearranged the cutlery so that the fork and knife were parallel to the mug's handle. "That must be why. I told you. It had to get worse before it got better. I never expected someone to play such a mean-spirited prank, it's not what we do here, but maybe it helped a little if it made you accept Sullivan's death at last. Twisted closure, yeah, is closure all the same."

"Yeah. I guess. Hey, thanks," she said to the young waitress as Sally refilled her empty mug.

Sally wordlessly offered the carafe to Lucas. He shook his head and she moved on to her next table.

Three creamers, three sugars. He took three pink packets from the ceramic holder, palmed three half & half containers from the chilled bowl, and slid them across the table to Tessa. She beamed at him. With a gracious nod, she prepared her second cup of coffee with all the precision of a chemist working at her station.

Lucas leaned back in his seat, taking the time to really observe her. The sleeping pills were a big help. The dark circles under her eyes no longer looked like puffy purple bruises. A soft smile lingered on her lips more often than the sad frown he'd become accustomed to seeing. There was steel in her spine. Her husband's death had bent her, tied this woman in all sorts of knots, but it hadn't broken her.

"It's something else," he observed.

Tessa stopped, her mug halfway to her lips. "Excuse me?"

"It's not just because someone tried to scare you."

"Try nothing," she muttered darkly. "They sure as hell succeeded. I about convinced myself that I was going to die in the woods behind your sister's house."

Lucas raised his eyebrows. "And then Deputy Walsh rode in and saved the day."

"Yes, well..." Tess let her sentence trail to a close. She filled the silence by taking a big gulp of her coffee. The creamers hadn't cooled it entirely. As the heat scalded her tongue and the back of her throat, she choked and forced it down.

Okay, she decided. That was enough for now.

Something warned her against allowing Lucas to bring Mason into their discussion. She cast around for an idea of something else to talk about before settling on the truth. Besides, she didn't think he would let her get away with anything less. She couldn't understand how, but he was far too good at reading her.

"I've been thinking about Jack a lot," she admitted.

"That's not a surprise. You lost your husband suddenly in a very brutal way."

"Yes, but..." Tess exhaled roughly. The confession was a hard one, but if there was one person in Hamlet who wouldn't judge her for it, she was betting that would be the doctor. "I guess I'm kind of glad he's gone. Is that terrible of me?"

"I can't say."

She felt compelled to explain. "He wasn't a bad man. He just wasn't the man I wanted. Don't get me wrong, I loved him, but I think I stopped being *in love* with him a long time ago. I still tried to make it work, though. He was so good to me in the beginning, but he could tell... we just drifted apart. There never was that sort of *ah-ha* moment. I didn't love him one day, then resent him the next. It's just... he kept me caged, Dr. De Angelis. The pretty little bird expected to sing on command. And all I wanted was to be free. Maybe not the way it happened, but I can spread my wings now, can't I? And because I'm happy, it makes me feel even worse that I am."

Lucas reached out, placing one of his hands over her slender one. "Some beauties were meant to fly," he told her. "I would never clip your wings."

No, he thought. But that didn't mean he wouldn't want to clasp a chain around her ankle and keep her close.

That was dangerous. To imagine owning this woman. He tensed slightly, caressing the top of her hand with his palm before pulling his arm back to his side of the table. Busying himself, he picked up his mug and took a deep drink.

Tessa seemed to remember herself at the same moment. Clearing her throat, she looked around the busy coffeehouse, staring at anything and everything except the flash of lust and heat of desire in his icy blue eyes.

He was sure she recognized it all the same.

WHEN LUCAS DROVE HER BACK TO OPHELIA AN HOUR later, there were two cars parked nearby. One was a mint green two-door coupe that had Maria written all over it. She had parked it in the driveway rather than the garage which made Tess wonder if she had taken another market trip or something else while Tess was at brunch with her brother.

The other was parked on the opposite side of the street, directly across from the bed and breakfast.

It was a police cruiser.

Of course, it was.

"The sheriff?" she asked when she saw it. Great. Just great. After their discussion at the coffee shop, Caitlin De Angelis was the last person she wanted to see.

Lucas shook his head. "No, that's not Caity."

And then he said, "It's Walsh," and Tess found

herself sinking into her seat. She should've expected this and been more prepared.

Jesus. That guy was never going to take a hint.

It wasn't that she didn't appreciate everything he did for her last night. She did. Mason was a lifesaver. He'd been right there, willing to lend a helping hand ever since he pulled her over. Which was why, when Lucas raised an eyebrow at her, wordlessly asking if she wanted him to continue driving right past the house, she shook her head.

"You sure?"

Tess nodded. "He's probably just taking the time to come and check up on me after last night. I know I acted like a moron. He's like you, pulling the good guy routine because you feel bad for me. Don't worry. I think I can handle him."

"Oh?" His eyebrow rose infinitesimally higher. "Like you handled me?"

A small smile was her only reply as she unsnapped her seatbelt.

Lucas reached over her to pop open the door for Tess. His hand brushed against her thigh as he drew his arm back slowly. "I'm heading down to my office to do some work. If you need me for any reason at all, get Maria. She knows how to get in touch with me."

"Thanks for brunch," she said, climbing easily out of the car.

"My pleasure. Oh," he added as she closed the door

behind her and stepped away from the Mustang, "and Tessa?"

She paused, turning to look at him through the open window. He still had his arm slung around the headrest where she'd been sitting, leaning in so that she could hear him without him having to raise his voice.

"Walsh isn't *anything* like me."

She barely had time to wonder what he meant before he peeled away from the curb. Giving her head a shake, she started for the walkway that led up to Ophelia. She believed Lucas when he said that the cruiser belonged to Mason. How could anyone else expect her to know that? If she got lucky, she could slip inside her borrowed sanctuary without having to talk to him at all—

The slam of a car door. Heavy boots falling in a steady rhythm as someone jogged up to her. She didn't need to turn around to know it was the deputy.

"Hey, Tess. I was hoping to catch you."

Pasting a pleasantly fake smile on her face, she turned to greet him. "Mason, I didn't see you there. How are you?"

"I'm doing alright." Mason pulled his thumb in the direction Lucas had just gone. His expression was carefully blank. "Was that the doc?"

"Oh. Yes. He was kind enough to offer me a ride

back to the bed and breakfast." Which reminded her. She still needed her car and here was the one person who might know where it was. "So, um, do you think—"

"Why were you with the doc?" he interrupted. It wasn't a casual question, either. It was a demand. "Where were you?"

Tess was so surprised by the venom in his voice, she stopped mid-sentence. The car could damn well wait. She had a much bigger problem standing right in front of her to worry about.

A six foot tall, blond-haired, brown-eyed problem.

"We went to get something to eat. Why?"

His jaw ticked. "We? You went *with* him?"

She wasn't going to let him intimidate her. Shaking her head royally, she asked, "Why not? I thought it was nice of him to offer."

"If you need something, you come to me. Not him."

Tess was so tired of letting everyone walk all over her. Jack had, and she hated it, but they'd dated for many years before they got married. After all that time together, he knew how to manage her and she... well, she just gave up a long time ago.

Talking to Lucas at the coffeehouse had been a revelation for Tess. Now that she was free from him at last, she wasn't about to let anyone put her down again.

"You're the one who called the doctor over last

night. I didn't need him seeing me like that. You told me he would help. Why are you so mad that I let him?"

Mason's scowl was a flash across his handsome features, there and gone again as he struggled to maintain his control. "Maria is the one who buzzed the doc," he told Tess. "I didn't want him coming around you. Seems like I was right."

"Mason, I don't belong to you. We just met, for god's sake."

That didn't seem to faze him. "Lucas De Angelis belongs to the sheriff. He always has, and he always will. Remember that. You're wasting your time with him."

"It was just breakfast—"

"With *him*." Mason lashed out, striking like a snake. He had his hand wrapped around her slender wrist, yanking her until they were nearly nose to nose. "I would've taken you anywhere you wanted to go. You didn't have to go to Lucas."

Tess struggled against his hold. She never expected him to grab her and it spooked her, how fast he had turned on her like that. But the more she struggled and tried to pull away, the tighter his clasp became until it was a vice clamped around her wrist. Fingers digging into her skin, his hand squeezing so tightly it was like he was mashing her bones together.

It *hurt*.

Panting softly, she tried one more time to break

free. When it didn't work, she whimpered. "Deputy, please. You're hurting me."

Mason blinked. The dark look in his eyes disappeared from one second to the next, almost as if he had been in a trance and only now realized what he was doing. With a sharp breath, he let go of Tess's hand so quickly, you would've thought he was burned.

"Ah, jeez. I'm sorry." He took one step away from her, and another. He held up his hand, staring at it as if it wasn't his. "Tess, I didn't mean to—"

He was moving away from her. That's all she wanted. If she managed to put enough space between them, she could bolt for the door and, if she was lucky, she might even make it before he overpowered her.

"It's fine," she lied. "Just... let's forget it happened, okay?"

Tess wasn't stupid. Mason was a member of the law enforcement team in a town that wasn't too keen on the idea of outsiders. Even if she wanted to complain about his sudden mood swing, she didn't think it would do any good. When it was his word against hers, she knew damn well who Sheriff De Angelis would believe. That woman was looking for one tiny excuse to toss Tess in the cells again and, this time, she would throw away the key.

No, she amended. The sheriff would drag Tess out of Hamlet by the hair and throw her into the county lock-up the next town over just so she would never have to look at her again.

Glancing down, she saw the red ring forming around her wrist. Compared to her pale skin, the blemish was extremely noticeable.

Mason saw it the same time she did. He reached for her. "Your wrist—"

Tess moved her hand out of his grasp, tucking it behind her back so that he couldn't touch her again. "Is fine," she repeated. "It's fine. Don't worry about it."

"Don't worry about it? I hurt you, Tess! I never should've—"

Mason's radio buzzed.

"I can't ignore that." He looked pained. "I'm still on duty."

Tess never believed in the old adage "saved by the bell" more than at that moment. She was desperate to get out of this conversation, no matter what. Taking the opportunity to continue to back away from Mason, she gestured at his belt. "Go on. Answer your radio."

He picked up on her retreat. "Don't go anywhere yet. Please, Tess. We're not done."

Oh, yes, they were. She took another step away, sliding her hand to cover the red mark on her wrist. Maybe, if he didn't see it, he would forget and *go*.

Engaging his radio, Mason said, "This is Deputy Walsh."

Static, followed by Willie's pleasant voice. "Mase,

sug, I need you to take a spin out to North Woodbridge, gulleyside. I've got those two neighbors fighting over that damn rosebush again. Sheriff's going out of Hamlet and Sly's just gone off duty after pulling another double. I need you to break it up before Jerry turns the hose on Christopher again."

"Got it, Wil. Don't worry. I'll threaten Chris with his wife. That usually stops his complaining. I'll check in when I got it under control."

"Thanks, sugar."

Clipping his radio back to his belt, Mason offered Tess a crooked half smile that was wavering. Despite her wishes, he obviously hadn't forgotten their discussion. "See, that's what crime in Hamlet is usually like, two old coots fighting over a rosebush. Murders make us all jumpy. It's no excuse..."

"Like I said, don't worry about it." She jerked her chin at his radio. "Don't you have to go?"

"I do," he admitted, "but I promise I'll come back to see you as soon as I can." The worry and apology that had been in his expression transformed into sudden certainty, as if he'd had an epiphany. His jaw set, a cutting edge as he gritted his teeth together and pointed at her. "Tomorrow."

"What?" Her nerves got the better of her. The one word came out like a screech.

"Tomorrow," he said again. "It's my night off. Sheriff said. Let me make it up to you. I'll show you

Hamlet. The doc took you to brunch, right? Coffee? Give me a chance. I can take you to dinner, show you what I have to offer. It's only fair."

Fair? What was he thinking? This wasn't a contest, and she wasn't a prize. There weren't any rules. What the hell did he mean, *fair*? Just because Lucas showed up to take her to the coffeehouse, it didn't mean that she had to agree to go out with Mason. She was only a few days removed from being married to Jack Sullivan — why was she the only one who remembered that her husband had *just* been killed?

Regardless of her confession to Lucas earlier, that didn't change the truth. She wasn't even sure she'd really understood what his murder meant. She certainly wasn't looking to replace him.

Especially not with a man who thought it was okay to grab her arm like she was his property.

"I don't know—"

He clasped his hands together. "Please, Tess. Please."

If Mason wasn't begging, it was close enough to make Tess feel like she had to give in. He'd been nothing but kind before his jealousy took over. She'd done her best not to lead him on, knowing that there was no way she could give him what he was obviously after, but she also wasn't cruel. Mason had been considerate and thoughtful and kind to a stranger in need. Now he was inviting her out. Maybe she was reading too much into it. She doubted it, but maybe.

And, well, if she turned him down, it would be like kicking a puppy in his face. She just couldn't do it.

"I guess so."

"Great." He moved toward her as if he was going to touch her again. Tess froze in place, expecting another rough grab. Either he caught her reaction or he thought better of it, because Mason suddenly pulled back. He pointed at her, repeated solemnly, "Tomorrow," then moved to return to his cruiser.

Tess watched him go. Once he stepped off the curb, she remembered what she had started to ask him before he distracted her with his resentful reaction to seeing her with Lucas.

"Wait!" she called after him. "I need you to tell me where my car is!"

Mason acted like he hadn't heard her. Rubbing his hand against the back of his neck, unable to hide the flush that crept up the sides of his throat, he crossed the street to where he had parked. His boots thudded against the gravel, the handcuffs on his belt clanking with the force of each step.

Just before he climbed into his cruiser, Mason waved back at her. "I'll be back tomorrow. Seven o'clock. See you, Tess."

It was a promise, Tess knew. But she took it as a threat.

As he sped off, she gave herself a small shake. The hairs on the back of her neck were standing straight up. Underneath her jacket, she could feel the goosebumps as they erupted over her flesh. The same fear that overwhelmed her last night with the note came back with a vengeance. Her wrist ached where he yanked, the skin on fire from his hard touch.

Her first instinct was to go see Lucas again. The force of her response was so strong that it staggered her. It had to be because Mason had basically warned her against seeing him again. As a child, she'd always been contrary. Her grandmother used to tell her the opposite of what she expected a teenaged Tess to do, knowing that she would always do the reverse.

She was an adult now. Tess could do what she wanted—but she would do what was best for her. And right then? Hunting down the gorgeous doctor when she was already rattled wasn't the best answer for her. Maybe later. Maybe when she was thinking more clearly. For now, the best thing for her to do was go inside and pretend that Mason hadn't been waiting for her.

Turning toward the walkway, Tess took two steps up the winding cobblestone path before she stopped dead in her tracks. Standing with her arms crossed, and her hip propping the screen door open, Maria looked like she'd been waiting a while for the other woman to notice her.

Tess knew she was caught. Her shoulders slumped. “How much of that did you see?”

Maria gestured inside the open doorway. “Enough that I think a good cup of hot cocoa is in order. Come in, sweetie. Let's have a chat.”

17

Maria didn't say anything until she'd boiled the milk, added the chocolate, and poured them each a generous portion of the steaming liquid in an oversized mug. Tess vaguely thought Maria was using soup bowls. Even better. Right now, as unsettled as she was, hot cocoa sounded like just what the doctor—well, doctor's sister—ordered.

Small wisps of smoke danced above the mug. Wary of the temperature, Maria took a tiny sip, smacking her lips in satisfaction when it passed her muster. "Ah, that's good."

Tess's tongue was still sensitive from where she burned it on coffee that morning. She pushed her mug to the side, letting her cocoa sit until it was cool enough to drink without causing more damage.

Without even realizing it, she started to rub her wrist. The red mark was fading, though the ache from his rough tug lingered.

Maria *tsk*-ed. "He did that to you?"

"He didn't mean to yank," she said, dropping her hand into her lap. "I wasn't expecting him to grab so I pulled away from him. It was an accident."

"Mm-hmm."

"What's that mean?"

Maria pursed her lips, her mug rattling against the tabletop as she placed it down. "Hamlet is a small town. Real small. I mean, it's so small that Hamlet's not even the name—it doesn't *have* a name. Do you know what a hamlet is?"

Tess had no idea where Maria was going with this. Because she liked Lucas's sister, she decided to play along. She thought about it. The most she could say she knew about *Hamlet* was that it was a Shakespeare play she'd never had to read.

Was it the one with the whole "To be or not to be?" speech? Maybe. Probably not what Maria meant, though.

She shook her head.

"A hamlet is another name for a small village. Perfect for us, right? For years, we were the no-name hamlet where the local kooks chose to build their homes between the rocky ridge of the mountains and a deep valley. We have no reliable phones. Internet works sometimes, not always. Some of the houses on the gulleyside of town have televisions but it wasn't worth it to lay cable all over so that's hit or miss. And, yet, we stay. In a good year, there's maybe two hundred of us. I see you, *bellisima*, so lost, so confused. Do you know why I tell you this?"

Tess reached for her hot chocolate, took a tentative sip. Still warm, but cool enough to drink. After she took another gulp, she met Maria's friendly smile. And she understood. "It's like you told me before. Small town, everyone knows your business. But it also means you know about them." When Maria nodded behind her mug, Tess guessed, "You know something about the deputy."

"I'm not a gossip, Tess, but I watch. My brother, he always says to me, 'Maria, keep your nose in your own home' and I try. Except you're in my home now. While you stay in Ophelia, I'll watch out for you. You've only been here for a handful of days. How well do you know Mason Walsh?"

It wasn't hard to be honest. "Not well at all. He pulled me over when I had a little too much to drink, and he made me spend the night in the holding cells. That was supposed to be it. But then... with Jack..." Tess gave a helpless shrug before grabbing her mug if only to have something to do with her hands. "I'm not a complete moron and, hell, he hasn't been exactly subtle. I know he's attracted to me, but I can't figure out why he turned like that. He was so sweet before and now… it's like he's changed. He's so…" She couldn't find the word.

"Intense?" Maria suggested.

That was it. "Yes!"

Maria nodded, her long dark hair spilling over her chest as she leaned in conspiratorially, both elbows on the kitchen table. "Oh, yes, Mason can be very intense at times. Ever since he was a kid. We went to school together and, I remember, when we were in elementary school…" She let out a sharp whistle. "You never wanted to get between baby Mase and his pudding cup."

Tess appreciated Maria's attempt at lightening the mood. It didn't necessarily work—talking about the deputy just brought back how unsettled his confrontation made her—but she appreciated it anyway.

Maria must have realized that her light-hearted tone wasn't helping. In the next moment, she traded it in favor of being completely honest and open with her guest. She kept her voice soft, almost hypnotic, as she coaxed Tess's attention on what she was saying rather than the slap of her cocoa against the mug as she swirled it.

"I don't think it's so much that he's attracted to you. With Mase, it's never that simple. I think he's convinced himself that you're the one for him."

"I barely know him—"

"Doesn't matter, sweetie. Trust me. I haven't seen him so far gone over a girl since Lindalee Murphy."

"Have I met her?" Tess asked.

Who knows? She'd been hidden away in the bed and breakfast since Sunday so she knew it wouldn't have been in the last few days. The morning she discovered Jack's body was still mainly a blur; as a defense mechanism to keep her from breaking down, she approved of the curtain in her mind, though it made moments like these awkward. She could've stumbled into Bigfoot and she wouldn't have remembered that.

"Oh, no. At least, not in Hamlet. Lindalee was an outsider—"

"Like me," she interrupted.

"Yes, like you, only she moved with her family here when me and Mase were taking high school classes. I guess you could call them sweethearts. They dated for, oh, close to two years, but I was there the day they met. Mason claimed her as his girl from day one. She never stood a chance. They were inseparable."

Were. A pit formed in her stomach. The idea of drinking any more cocoa made her sick. She placed the mug down, nudged it away from her. Don't ask, she ordered herself. Something told her she didn't want to know.

Don't ask. Don't do it. Don't—

She had to. The words blurted out: "What happened to her?"

"Don't know. After graduation, she told him she couldn't do it anymore. She left Hamlet to go to college and, well, she never came back."

"Never came back," Tess echoed, her tone curiously flat. Yup, she admitted, definitely shouldn't have asked.

Maria's big blue eyes widened. "I didn't mean it like that. Sometimes people actually make it out of Hamlet," she explained. "I mean, *I* won't, no. She must have." A pause. "He might be intense and all, but Mase is totally harmless."

Tess thought of the way he cornered her, grabbed her, questioned her about spending her time with another man. She thought of the pain in her wrist, and his assertion that they would go out tomorrow night when he never asked, but only demanded.

And she thought of the way he treated her like he owned her, how the support he gave her following the shock of her husband's death and the help he offered when she found that threatening note somehow put her in his debt.

She worried how he would react the next time she somehow managed to set him off. She didn't know him well enough to predict him and, after this little chat, she was quite sure she didn't want to.

"Yeah." She swallowed weakly. No matter what,

Tess refused to trade one overbearing man for another. "Harmless."

After he tagged Caitlin on the radio, Lucas figured that he'd see her within a couple of hours. She'd been on her way out of town to meet with her counterpart the next county over when he buzzed her. The courthouse was forty minutes from Hamlet. Adding the time of the meet, he didn't expect to see her anytime soon.

He had to keep himself busy. Idle hands and all that. His thoughts kept straying back to Tessa's pale face and the fear that glazed her pretty golden eyes. It was bad enough that her husband was killed and she found his body. Now someone was terrorizing her. He promised Tess she would be safe in Ophelia. He damn well *needed* to make sure that Maria was safe.

It had been too, too easy for someone to slip that threatening note under Tess's door. Lucas couldn't stop thinking about that.

So he found something to do. Remembering Sally's request at the coffeehouse that morning, he turned the **closed** sign on his office door to **open** before picking up his radio. There were plenty of patients he could tend to and finally time to do so.

Caitlin ended up surprising him. About a half hour

after their conversation, the telltale *clack-clack* of her boots echoed in the corridor outside of his examination room. It never ceased to amaze him how she always seemed to zero right in on his location. He would put money down that the exam room was the first place she checked for him. It was one of her quirks.

It drove him nuts when they were married. One time, he had to ask if she had a tracker on him. She laughed him off. All these years later, he still wondered.

"What do you got there?" Caitlin rarely wasted time on pleasantries when she was wrapped up in work. Marching into the office, she came over to where Lucas was working with Phil's samples. "Something for my case?"

"Not right now. I'm still the doc. I've had to turn away a few of my patients to focus on the Sullivan case. Autopsies take time, and so does all the paperwork. I'm trying to catch up with some of my regulars now that that's done." He finished labeling the first vial, started on the second. "You can wait in my office. I'll be right there."

"Why don't I keep you company here instead?" Her breath tickled the back of his neck. He hadn't realized she'd gotten so close. Before he could ask her to give him space to work, she placed her hand on his shoulder. "What are you doing anyway?"

Lucas fought the urge to shake her off. "Phil Granger came in for some bloodwork. I'm prepping his samples to send out to the lab."

"Mm-hmm." It was a noncommittal sound as Caitlin trailed her hand down his side. Lucas stiffened at the first brush of her fingers. That didn't dissuade her. She walked behind him, letting her hand make its own path as she ran her palm across his ass.

When she made the move to cross over to the front, he grabbed her hand. He gave it a warning squeeze and then didn't let go. Who knows what she'd make a grab for next if he did?

"Sheriff. Don't."

"Why not?" she purred. "Come on, baby. Can't we ever just take a minute for us? Do we always have to be on the job?"

"I can't let myself forget you're the sheriff," he told her honestly.

"Sure you can. It's easy."

"I can't. And you don't want me to."

"Yes, I do."

"If I forget you're the sheriff, I'm only gonna remember that you're my ex."

"Wow." She recoiled as if he'd slapped her. Yanking her hand back, she stormed away, placing the exam table between them. "I guess that settles that, then."

Maybe he'd been too harsh. "Caity—"

"Forget it. Moment's passed." She waved him off. "If

you didn't call me here because you wanted to see me, what was it? I'm busy, Luc. I won't always drop everything I'm doing just because you buzzed me."

He sincerely doubted that. In the years since the divorce, Caitlin had shown him on countless occasions that she would take him back in a heartbeat. She never could grasp the concept of *it's over* and *move on* the way that Lucas did. If their respective professions didn't keep them in contact, he'd be more than happy to keep his distance. After all, she was his ex for a reason. He accepted that, even if Caitlin never would.

Lucas finished handling Phil's bloodwork. Once the samples were properly labeled and stored in the refrigerator, he returned to his place on his side of the exam table. Then, as clearly and concisely as he could, he told Caitlin about his visit to Ophelia last night.

It was obvious that this was the first she heard about the threatening note left for Tessa Sullivan. Halfway through his story, she pulled her notepad out and started jotting down everything Lucas told her. She even made him repeat the twisted rhyme twice, then said nothing. Her thin lips pulled down in a nasty frown, the only sign that she was aggravated that no one told her this before. Other than that, she was strictly professional.

"Do you have the note?" she asked. "I'd like to see it."

"It was gone when she went back. I wanted to see it, too, but no one could find it."

She couldn't swallow her snort. "Of course it was."

"Caity, please."

"I'm sorry. It's just... it's so convenient. Right? Her husband gets killed. Now someone is warning her about being next. Jeez, I know there are a few of us who aren't fond of outsiders. This is a little crazy, though."

"You still think she did it."

Caitlin huffed, snapping her notepad shut with a flick of her wrist. "No one said cop work was easy. I'd be bored out of my skull if it was. But, just this once, I wish it was. I *wish* she did it."

He pointed at her. "How could she have gotten out of the holding cells?"

"I know, I know. That's the thing I keep getting back to." She tucked her notepad back into its pouch on her belt. "Maybe I should rethink keeping her in town. I want to have her nearby until I close her husband's case, but what good would it be if she ends up joining him on your slab? Good business for you, sure. Bad press for Hamlet. What?" She caught Lucas rolling his eyes. "Tell me I'm wrong."

He shook his head. "I told you enough."

That was true. And he was willing to bet that she was currently asking herself why her own deputy hadn't filled her in. Or why the victim hadn't made the report herself.

If he knew Caitlin, she'd be on her way to find the answers to those question as soon as possible. That was why Lucas wasn't *too* surprised when she nodded and said, "Okay. If that's how it is, I appreciate your help. Thank you."

She started to head away from the table, stopped as if struck suddenly by a thought, then spun around. Her hands in her pocket, her green eyes innocent and wide.

"One more thing, Luc."

He raised his eyebrows at her. He'd been expecting this. The only surprise was that it took Caitlin until now to say something. After their visit to the coffeehouse that morning, he was banking on the gossip mill getting to her before he had to buzz her himself.

It felt good, knowing he was right.

"Yeah?"

"I got a buzz from Addy today. Sally told her she saw you at the coffeehouse this morning. You weren't alone." She waited for him to deny it, her mouth tightening when he kept his silence. "I haven't seen you since Sunday," she added. "It's Tuesday now. It wasn't me."

"No." Picking up his clipboard, he started to make notes on Phil's patient chart. He hoped the blatant brush-off would be enough of a hint for Caity to drop it but, yeah, *that* was wishful thinking. He'd set this thing up. He knew he'd have to deal with it sooner or later.

"Sally said she was an outsider."

"Sally should be paying more attention to making the coffee. It was a little burnt."

"Luc. Lucas. Just tell me one thing. Tell me the outsider wasn't Sullivan's wife."

"We're not married anymore," Lucas reminded her. He was going for gentle but her incessant questions always got the better of him and his temper. From the way Caitlin's guileless expression turned stormy, he missed gentle by a mile. "If I want to take someone out for a cup of coffee, I can. I don't answer to you, Caity. What I do when I'm off duty is my business, not yours."

He'd expected open jealousy. The nasty hiss caught him off guard.

"You're wrong, Lucas." With a vicious stab, Caitlin jabbed her finger in his direction. "It's my town," she sneered. "*Everything* here is my business."

CAITLIN WAS JUST ABOUT TO OPEN THE DOOR TO HER cruiser when the soft rustling of leaves made her whip her head around. She turned in time to see Tessa Sullivan tiptoe out of the copse of trees. The woman's head was down, watching each careful step as she slid down the small slope that bordered the cobbled road.

She stepped away from her car. Raising her voice, she called out, "Mrs. Sullivan. I didn't expect to see you here."

Sullivan jumped, skittish as ever. Her head popped up, wide eyes narrowing right on Caitlin. The sheriff searched for guilt there. All she found was honest surprise.

What a shame.

"Sheriff De Angelis. Nice to see you."

"What are you doing here?"

Her question more of a demand laced with suspicion, Tess wondered if she should answer the other woman. Something told her that if she did, she wouldn't be addressing the sheriff but Doctor De Angelis's ex-wife instead.

That made her smile. "I thought I would take a walk, get some fresh air. The weather's beautiful." Her smile wavered. "Jack would've loved it. Autumn was his favorite time of year."

"A walk? All the way to the mountain side of town? Convenient."

"Not really. The doctor told me to stop by during office hours if I needed something to help me sleep. Maria brought me most of the way. I decided to walk the rest."

"What were you doing in the trees? I'd thought you'd know it wasn't safe by now."

"I couldn't help myself, Sheriff. I thought I heard a

cat when I was passing by. I couldn't just keep walking. I had to see if I could find it."

"Did you?"

Tess shook her head slowly. "There was nothing there."

"'Course not. We don't have any strays in Hamlet, you understand. Just pets. You won't find anything in the woods except for trouble."

With a small nod and a tight smile, Tess conceded the point. Sheriff De Angelis's subtle dig managed to go straight to the bone. Oh, yeah. She understood. If you were a part of Hamlet, you belonged. But they wouldn't tolerate any outsiders who begged to survive.

Strays. Right.

"Now that I think of it," De Angelis continued, "I have to ask: where's your shadow?" At Tess's blank look, she explained, "Mason."

"I'm not sure," she hedged. "I thought he was on duty."

"Didn't stop him last night."

Tess heard enough in the sheriff's short answer to guess, "You heard what happened to me."

De Angelis jerked her thumb over her shoulder, gesturing back at Lucas's office. "From the doctor, actually. And you know what? That worries me, Mrs. Sullivan. Crime goes down in my town, I've got to know about it. I *will* know about it. But I should've heard about it from my deputy. Or the civilian claiming to be harassed."

Tess's brow wrinkled, thin lines marring her forehead. She pursed her lips, started to argue. "I never—"

De Angelis held up her hand, cutting Tess off. "Don't. I've heard enough from Luc, and you can bet I'll be taking Mase to task for keeping this from me. You want to make a formal complaint, meet me at the station house.

"For now, I'll tell you this just once, Mrs. Sullivan... consider it a fair warning: don't make the mistake of thinking his loyalty is to anyone outside of town. No matter what, Hamlet always comes first."

Tess didn't know if the sheriff meant Mason or Lucas. Both, she decided. Caitlin De Angelis was just that proprietary.

She tilted back her head, jutting out her chin. If the sheriff saw it as a dare, so be it. "'Hamlet helps'," she said. "Am I right?"

Caitlin ran her gaze over Sullivan's guileless face. She sniffed. "Yeah, well, I voted against that slogan."

Without another word, she turned her back on the other woman. She was halfway around the rear of her cruiser when she realized that she was on her way back to Lucas.

Freezing in place, Caitlin pulled the thick rope of her braid over her shoulder. If she went back inside, she'd have to hear it all over again how she shouldn't be jealous. That she no longer had the right.

Too bad she couldn't turn her feelings off as easily as Lucas seemed to. To hear from Adrianna that Lucas was having brunch with an outsider had been a stab. Then to have him shrug off her attentions as easily as he had was an absolute insult.

It took every ounce of her considerable willpower to return to the driver's side of the cruiser. From the weight of the Sullivan woman's curious stare, she knew her every action was studied, dissected. That bothered her. And the fact that she cared what some outsider thought just made her more pissed off.

Once she was sat behind the wheel, Caitlin rolled down her window. "Good day, Mrs. Sullivan," she said before peeling away.

And if she got a little pleasure from causing the outsider to stumble back onto the path, well, she was only human.

18

Tess waited until the rear bumper of Sheriff De Angelis's cruiser faded from sight. Only then, when she was sure she was alone, did she wipe her sweaty hands on the side of her jeans. That was too close for comfort.

Exhaust lingered in the thick autumn air. She coughed, hoping that she didn't carry the acrid stench with her as she hurriedly crossed the street. Pausing only to run her trembling fingers through the soft waves of her hair, she forced herself to head straight for the front door.

Though she knew she shouldn't and every impulse screamed at her to run back to Ophelia and hide, she braced herself and knocked.

When no one answered, she told herself that she would knock one more time; if the door stayed shut, she would leave. She knocked, and was just stepping down when she heard the soft creak of the door pulling in. Looking over her shoulder, she saw Lucas De Angelis leaning against the doorjamb, a small smile flirting on his lips.

"Tessa, what a pleasant surprise."

At least someone was glad to see her.

Concern flashed across his flawless features in the next instant. Stepping out of the doorway, he leaned over Tess, bracing her with his hand on her shoulder. "You look shaky. Something wrong?"

She probably should've calmed down some more before she went to the door. How could she expect a doctor not to notice her nerves?

"I'm alright. It's just... I had a run-in with the sheriff a few seconds ago."

Lucas let her words sink in. Because Hamlet was Hamlet, it was inevitable that their breakfast at the coffeehouse would get back to Caity eventually. He'd been prepared for her reaction. It never occurred to him that he should probably warn Tessa what she was getting into by speaking to him in plain sight.

He closed his eyes, shook his head. That woman would be the death of him. Resigned, he asked, "She say something out of line?"

Tessa's shrug was an answer in itself. "What was she doing here?"

"She's working tirelessly on your husband's case,"

Lucas said, and it was the truth. Well, *a* truth. "She had some more follow-up on it for me."

"She's looking at me. She thinks I'm responsible. I know it."

His hand was still on her shoulder. He gave her a reassuring squeeze. "You have nothing to worry about."

She opened her mouth to tell him that he was wrong, then closed her jaw with a snap. No worries? Yeah, right. Jack was dead and his murderer was still at large.

Whatever their intentions, someone took the time to create a threatening note and leave it for her to find.

The sheriff thought she was guilty.

The doctor's ex wouldn't let him go.

And the formerly sweet deputy had left bruises on her skin.

Pulling on her sleeve, hiding the marks from Lucas, Tess wondered if she should warn him about Mason's strange visit. She ultimately decided against it. She could handle him. She could handle the sheriff, too. So long as she held onto the fact that she didn't strangle her husband, no one could accuse her of anything.

They would never be able to prove otherwise for the simple fact that *she didn't do it*.

Lucas watched as Tessa's expression went from concerned to defiant before her eyes shuttered, closing for a moment. When she opened them again, her golden eyes seemed dull. The bright spark in her gaze, the vibrant humor from brunch was eerily missing.

And it was all his ex-wife's fault.

"Look, let's not talk about Caity. Let's talk about you. What are you doing here?"

Left unsaid was how he had dropped her off outside of Ophelia less than six hours ago. What could she have to say to him that couldn't have been said earlier? Especially now that Caity had caught on to the fact that was some sort of... *relationship* budding between the two of them, the doctor and the outsider.

First brunch, now Tessa was visiting him at his office. It was like waving a red flag before a bull. It was dangerous to antagonize the sheriff. Even Lucas had to admit that.

Tessa already believed Caitlin had it out for her. If she wasn't careful, that might turn out to be truer than she expected.

"It's been three days," she said imploringly. "After last night... I just want to know what's going on. When will I be able to leave? Is she any closer to finding out what happened to Jack? No one will tell me anything."

Lucas didn't blame her for using any method she could to get information. If he were in her shoes, he'd be doing the same thing. Still, he found it interesting that, rather than Deputy Walsh, she was coming to see him.

He tried not to sound too pleased as he noted, "So you thought you'd track me down here and I would?"

He would. He definitely would. There was something about Tessa Sullivan. Whether it was her pretty face, the way she refused to let life break her, or even the innocence he sensed deep within her that made him feel so protective toward her, he'd had the urge to look out for Tessa since the instant their eyes first locked. Caitlin never needed him to protect her, not really, and he found that it felt good to be so important to another person.

The jut of Tessa's chin dared him to refuse her. "I thought— wait." She spun around, took a step away from the building. "Did you hear that?"

"Hear what?"

"I thought I heard a cat in the woods before," she explained as she started down his driveway. She pointed at the trees. "The sheriff told me there aren't any strays, but I know what I heard. That sounded different."

Lucas started to go after her. "What did it sound like?"

"I don't know. I thought I heard a click or something. Like maybe—"

At first, he thought it was a firework going off. A loud pop, the whizzing sound of the bullet streaking through the air, the slam when it struck the facade, chips of brick flying everywhere. But no one aimed fireworks at other people, and there wasn't an impact if they did, more of a contained explosion. Lucas understood all of that in the split second after the shot rang out.

An instant later, he realized that someone in the woods had just fired a gun at them.

Like a deer caught in a hunter's crosshairs, Tessa froze at the end of the driveway. She threw her hands up in the air, as if that would do something to ward off the gunshots.

Lucas was already moving. Before his brain fully grasped what the hell was going on, his arms were pumping, his legs flying as he ran to her, shouting, "Tessa, no!"

He grabbed her, tucking her under his chin as he wrapped his arms around her. He covered her entire body with his, making it impossible for her to be hit. The first shot was wild, striking the front of his office building. If the erratic shooter fired again, odds were that neither one of them would be struck. Lucas wasn't a gambler. Zero odds were the best odds. He wouldn't let her get hurt.

And that's when the second shot went off.

Aim was better that time. The bullet came within centimeters of burying itself in Lucas's upper arm. Heat flared across the skin where the bullet tagged him, followed by the warm rain of blood as it started to spill. He wasn't shot, but he was definitely hit. Cursing under his breath, he tightened his hold on Tessa in case the gunman fired a third time.

Seconds turned to minutes without another *pop*. Lucas's labored breathing filled the air, mingled with Tessa's panicked mews. She clawed at his arms, trying desperately to escape the cage they made.

The tinny buzz in his ears cleared enough for him to begin to make out her words. She was talking to him, saying something. His arm stung like hell. It took everything he had to ignore the sudden excruciating pain and focus on Tessa instead.

"Let me go! Let go of me! You shouldn't have shielded me. You've been hit, you moron!"

Not the thanks he'd been expecting, Lucas thought. Gingerly moving his sore arm, testing it, he kept her hidden in his embrace. "I know, but it's better than you being shot. It was just a graze, I promise."

"How do you know?" she demanded.

"Because I can feel it." And it fucking *hurt*. "I won't let you go until I'm sure there won't be any more stray bullets coming at us."

Tessa stomped on Lucas's shoe. *That* didn't hurt—she was barely more than a hundred pounds, his boots were reinforced, and, besides, the heat and pain radiating from his injured arm meant nothing less than a broken bone was going to distract him from it.

Still, the shock he felt at her attempt to disable him was enough for him to drop his arms in surprise.

Taking advantage of his lapse, Tessa ducked out of his embrace.

"Where did you get hit? I want to make sure you're okay."

Leaving his bad arm hanging at his side, Lucas looped his good arm around Tessa. He hugged her close, tightening his grip when she struggled to get free. "I'll show you," he promised, "after we get inside. We're sitting ducks out here. I don't want either of us getting shot at again."

Tessa wrapped her arm around his waist. Considering he was more than a head taller than her, he thought it was sweet that she was trying to help support him as they zig-zagged their way back inside the safety of his office. Once they were in, Tessa pushed the front door closed and locked it.

"The wound. Let me see."

Lucas was already peeling off his lab coat. He had on a short-sleeved t-shirt underneath which meant that he only had one layer of fabric protecting him against the bullet. The graze burned through the white coat before taking a chunk out of his arm. He watched the blood drip down his skin with a professional eye. It felt a lot worse than the injury was.

He'd gotten very lucky.

Tessa didn't think so. Reaching out, she stopped when there was a two-inch gap between her fingers and his bloody flesh. It was like she couldn't bring herself to actually touch him. That bothered him way more than the cut did.

"You've been shot," she whispered.

"I know—"

"Shot shot," she echoed. "The bullet hit you and everything. Oh my god."

"It's fine, I—"

"It's not fine. There's no reason for you to have been hit. It should've been me."

Lucas's fist tightened reflexively. A fresh spurt of blood bubbled and started to trickle. "Don't say that, Tessa. Don't."

Ignoring him, she pulled away. She looked around the office, only just realizing that it was the front room, the place where patients waited to see the doctor. There wasn't anything there to help her. "Where are your supplies? I've got to clean that out now."

That caught him by surprise. "What? No. I'm the doctor. Even one-handed, I'm sure I can fix this myself."

"Let me do it."

"Tessa—"

"Listen to me. When I first started college, before I became a teacher, I took nursing classes. Let me take care of you."

Her jaw was set. He can see she was feeling responsible for his injury. If it gave her some peace to play nurse, fine. It couldn't hurt. Besides, as the only doctor in town, there was never anyone left to take care of him. It might be nice to be the patient for once.

"I'll get the supplies," he told her. "You can bandage me up when I get back."

"No. Tell me where. I'll go."

Maybe it was the blood loss making him weak, but he decided not to continue arguing with her. Even though it would've been faster to get them himself, Lucas gave her instructions on how to find his examination room. Everything they would need to do a quick bandaging would be in there.

Tessa disappeared. He used the sleeve of his lab coat to try to staunch some of the blood. She returned a few minutes later with an armful of supplies that she dropped down on one of the waiting room chairs.

Her pale complexion had turned a sickly shade of green in the time she was gone. He expected her to hurl any second. To his surprise, she managed to keep it together. Gritting her teeth, she picked up the disinfectant first and tore the lid off.

Though he expected the sting, the disinfectant burned worse than actually getting shot had. Tessa chanted apologies under her breath as she dabbed the wound with a freshly soaked cotton ball.

It didn't look so bad once all of the blood was washed away. The cut was about three inches long, the length of the side of his bicep, and it was way shallower than she initially thought.

The bullet had taken off quite a few layers of skin, though, and while it *was* shallower, that didn't mean it wasn't just a little deep.

"Do you think we should stitch this up?"

He kept his voice mild. "You're the one with the nursing classes. What do you think?"

"I think I should let you get sepsis," she muttered, peering closely at the depth of his wound. Then, as if she just heard what she said, she gasped. Covering her face with her gloved hands, she hurriedly apologized. "I'm so sorry. I didn't mean that."

"Apology accepted," Lucas said solemnly. He let a small, inappropriate grin tug at his lips only because her face was covered and she wouldn't know he was teasing. To be honest, he liked that spark of temper she showed. It was way better than watching her take another headfirst dive into a pool of guilt. "So... stitches? Yay or nay?"

Scrunching her nose as she squinted, Tessa got a good look at the cut. She shook her head. "I think I should put on some antibiotic cream, then either gauze or some plaster."

"And I think those nursing classes paid off." When Tessa's golden eyes widened in surprise, he let out a small chuckle. "If it was a flesh wound, I'd need stitches. I'm lucky it was just a graze. Sometimes they bleed too much, but nothing important was hit."

"You were."

"What?"

Tessa was dabbing the deep abrasion with some of the white ointment she found in his supplies. "You said nothing important was hit. You're wrong. You were."

Lucas didn't know what to say in response to that so he didn't say anything. He waited until she had finished applying the gauze pad and wrapping his arm with the bandage to speak up. Though it was the last thing he wanted to do, he also knew he had no choice. "We have to tell Caity."

Tess cleaned up the wrappers before pulling off her bloody gloves and adding it to the pile of blood-soaked cotton balls. She would get rid of the medical waste in a second. First, they had to have this conversation. "Do you really think we should?"

"She's the sheriff. Last time I checked, shooting at someone was a crime. She has to know that I was hit."

He had a point. "Let me ask you a question. Hamlet has a population of under two hundred, but it's a rural area. It's got a big mountain on one side, that deathtrap gulch at the entrance, and tons of trees. Maybe guns are common here, maybe not, I don't know. Do you?"

Lucas's lips thinned. "We don't hunt here. Not too many of us carry guns because there's never any crime in Hamlet. If I had to guess, I'd say it's just anyone who is—or was—in law enforcement."

"That's what I thought."

"Tessa, what are you saying?"

Clasping her hands in front of her, Tess looked at the way her fingers interlocked. It was something to stare at that wasn't the accusation in Lucas's icy blue stare. She felt that chill all the way down to her bones.

When he continued to stare, waiting for her answer, she looked up at him with worry written in every premature line in her face. "What if she—"

"Caitlin would never take a shot at me."

"No," she agreed wholeheartedly. "But would she take a shot at me?"

And that, right there, was the elephant in the room she'd been trying to pretend didn't exist. Lucas was the one who got hit.

Was he the target?

She thought of the note no one could find, the implied threat about what would happen to her if she didn't disappear, and had her answer.

"Shit."

Tessa had to agree with that sentiment, too.

19

"I hate that you got shot." Leaning into Lucas, her fingers ghosted over the bandage, a feathered caress.

"It wasn't your fault."

Tessa didn't answer. She didn't have to. Her sad smile told him she disagreed. The guilt tugging on her lips made him wish that he had managed to dodge the bullet.

They were parked outside of Ophelia, sitting in his idling Mustang, both of them unwilling to leave the other after the scare they experienced together. Lucas was behind the wheel, running his palms anxiously along the leather rim.

Tessa had wanted to drive but, as she discovered, the man was stubborn to a fault—even after being shot. No matter how hard she tried to charm him, he refused to let anyone else get into the driver's seat. Even with the dull ache throbbing his fresh wound, he insisted on it. And if his arm ached every time he made a left turn? Oh well. It wasn't like they could stay at the office.

Lucas didn't even bother taking out his communicator. After wrestling his keys away from Tess, he loaded her up in his car and headed straight over to his sister's place instead. His office was in a more secluded part of Hamlet, tucked near the foot of the mountain that acted as one of its natural borders. No one was around for miles. He usually liked the solitude when he was at work. Now he couldn't get away fast enough.

And if he wanted to make sure no one was coming near Maria, who could blame him for looking out for her? She was his precious younger sister, Tessa a vulnerable outsider. Ophelia's security was the best money could buy. Knowing they were safe inside would make him feel a lot better when he had to leave them behind.

Using his good arm, he moved his hand to rest against the buckle of his seatbelt. "Do you want me to walk you in?"

"I'd rather go to see the sheriff with you," she retorted.

They'd had the same argument the whole way back to Ophelia. Tessa couldn't understand why he was going to see Sheriff De Angelis on his own when they were both there when the shots were fired. Just because Lucas was the one who was hit, it didn't mean that Tessa didn't have anything to add. She was the one who heard the fateful sound of something in the woods the second before the first shot rang out. She could help.

Besides, Tess hated the idea that he would be alone with Sheriff De Angelis when he told her about the shooting. She didn't know how she'd pull it off, but the sheriff would probably find some way to blame her for Lucas getting shot.

Lucas was adamant. Though he didn't come out and say it, it was obvious that he believed she was the one they were aiming at. It couldn't possibly be a coincidence that, days after Jack Sullivan was murdered, someone fired a gun at the exact spot his wife was standing at.

No matter how much she tried to convince him otherwise, Lucas refused to budge and let her go with him. He wanted her back in Ophelia, secure behind locked doors.

"I need you to stay here. It'll go a lot better if I talk to her on my own, trust me."

Those were the magic words. Exhaling softly, it was like all the fight left her. Tess nodded. Trust him. Okay. It wasn't like he hadn't already taken a bullet for her. It didn't matter that it was a graze, or that she bandaged it up as best she could. If it wasn't for her, he wouldn't have been hurt.

"I can make it on my own," she said. She clicked her seatbelt open, let it *whoosh* behind her. "Good luck with the sheriff, Doctor."

There was such defeat in her voice, he almost followed her out of the car. Only the fact that she glanced back at him as she reached the steps kept him in his seat. Lucas couldn't let her see how much she affected him. She gave him a tiny wave that he returned with a nod, then entered Ophelia.

He waited two minutes after she closed the door behind her before he pulled away from the curb.

LUCAS MET CAITLIN AS SHE WAS STORMING OUT OF HER house. Having parked behind her cruiser, he climbed out of his car in time to intercept her before she got into her own vehicle.

She was still dressed in her uniform. The bottom two buttons were undone, though, like she'd been in a rush to put her shirt back on and fasten them back up. Given the amount of time that passed since her visit to his office, he figured she'd already been home and changed out of her uniform before something enticed her to get dressed again.

Lucas's gaze strayed to her belt. Her holster was

there, her pistol secured in its place. Interesting. If only he could remember if she'd been carrying earlier when she was in his office. Crime was so low in Hamlet, the members of the HSD rarely wore them as part of their standard uniform. He could count the number of times he'd seen her wear her gun out on a routine call on one hand. This wasn't usual.

Then again, he didn't routinely get shot at either. As far as he was concerned, "usual" flew out the window a couple of days ago.

She saw him waiting by her car, barely sparing him a second glance as she snapped at him to step away from the cruiser.

"Caity—"

"No, Luc. I don't have time for you right now. Willie just buzzed me. There's been reports of something sounding like gunshots on the mountain side of town. I've got to check it out."

"But—"

"Wait." Pushing off the cruiser's window, she whirled on Lucas. "Your office is mountainside. Did you hear anything? Maybe like an hour ago?"

This was going to be bad. He already knew it. It was why he angled his body so that most of the gauze bandage was shadowed. He covered the rest with his hand, purposely hiding the injury. Though he crossed his hands over his chest, he kept his stance light, relaxed. When Caitlin found out he'd been tagged, shit was gonna hit the fan.

"Actually, yes. That's why I'm here. I want you to promise me something first, though. Promise you won't freak out no matter what I tell you, alright?"

She waved her hand anxiously, indicating he should get on with it. "Yeah, yeah. Sure. But hurry up. I've got be to be going. If you heard something down by your office, I really gotta go check it out."

"Okay." Slowly, dreading her reaction, he lifted his hand from his arm, revealing the gauze wrapped around his bicep.

She sucked in her breath through tightly gritted teeth the second she realized what he was showing her. And he knew that he'd been right.

"You promised you wouldn't freak out," he reminded her.

Her eyes flashed angrily as she glared at him. "I lied."

Lucas started to unwrap the bandage. Maybe if she saw that he'd been barely nicked—

"Look, it's just a graze. I'm fine."

She never took her unblinking gaze off his face. "Who. Did this. To you?"

He was used to Caitlin's explosive temper. Throwing a temper tantrum, yelling, crying… that was her normal. He would never admit it, but when she shut down like this, her voice barely a whisper, it scared him. He never knew quite what his ex was capable of.

"I don't know."

"Lucas."

"Honest, Cait, I have no idea. Shots came out of the trees, I ducked and covered." Lucas tightened his gauze, tucking the tail under the bandage so that it stayed secure. "I was more concerned with getting out of there in one piece. Getting the identity of the shooter was the last thing on my mind."

She nodded, her expression calm and collected. "Doesn't matter. I'll find them because there's no way I'll let them get away with this. No one takes aim at one of mine. By the time I get through with them, they'll wish they turned the gun on themselves. As for you, I want you under lockdown. Go home, Luc, and stay there. I need you safe. Until I finish processing the scene, I have to know you're safe."

That was more like Caitlin. Taking control, certain that she could save the world. If she had to lock Lucas in his bedroom so that she knew where he was, she would do it.

But Lucas would never let her.

His lips thinning in frustration, he shook his head. "No."

"I am the sheriff, and if I tell you that you're going under lockdown, *Doctor*, you will damn well listen to me."

If she thought he would let her win just because she brought their titles into it, she was wrong.

"I have work I have to do. You can't stop me."

"I can," she retorted. "I'll do a lot worse before I let some lowlife take another shot at you."

So that's what this was about. He thought she understood. Obviously, he was wrong. "Caitlin. *Cait*," he said, softening his voice in a bid to get her attention. Wild-eyed and fuming, her hand straying to the gun at her side, Caitlin looked ready to run headfirst into a firefight. "I don't think you understand. They weren't shooting at *me*."

That got through to her. She moved back as if he'd shoved her away from him. In her world, Lucas was the only one who mattered. It wouldn't have occurred to her that he hadn't been the intended victim. He was *everything.*

But if the bullet wasn't supposed to hit him, then that meant—

Her composure cracked. "You weren't alone." She blinked. "That Sullivan woman was with you."

For one second, he thought about lying. Caity already had it out for the poor widow. He didn't want to give her any more ammunition. Then he remembered how quickly word spread that he'd taken Tessa for brunch. Just because he hadn't seen anyone around his office when he got shot, it didn't mean there weren't any witnesses. Someone was bound to have seen them together. It would get back to Caitlin and she would wonder if there was more to his being shot than it seemed. With his luck, Caitlin would concoct some convoluted idea that Tessa was the one who pulled the trigger.

No, it was better to tell the truth. Especially since, by Tessa's own admission, she'd seen the sheriff as she walked up to his office. Caitlin knew she was there. And now she would know that she stayed a few minutes longer.

"Yes, she was still there," he admitted.

"Okay. That's it. I want her out. Gone. Today."

That was the last thing he expected her to say. As sheriff, Caitlin was fanatically devoted to keeping the peace in Hamlet. Even though Jack Sullivan was an outsider, his murder cast a dark shadow over their tightknit community. If Caitlin set loose her only lead, she was basically admitting that she was giving up on finding Sullivan's killer.

"But your case," he argued. "Don't you need her to figure out who killed Jack Sullivan?"

"Right now, I don't care. And what if I can't? He was an outsider, he probably deserved it. Right, Luc?"

His whole expression went flat. Caitlin was throwing his own words back at him on purpose. Standing over Mack Turner's mangled remains more than a year ago, he'd said the same exact thing to the sheriff. For what he tried to do to Maria, he deserved far worse than to accidentally run his car off the road and into the gulley. Lucas didn't regret the man's death, and Caitlin repeating his callous words didn't make him change his mind.

"It's not the same and you know it."

"Why?" she demanded. "Because Turner slipped into Maria's room and she didn't want it? Then, yeah, it's not the same because Sullivan's wife is practically begging for it. From you, from Mase, it don't matter who. She doesn't plan to be without a husband for long."

Lucas fought the urge to lash out at her. "This again? It was an office visit, med pick-up—"

"And the coffeehouse visit was just brunch, right? Come off it. She's no good for you, Luc. Me? I would wait for you forever and you know it. That girl doesn't know the meaning of loyal."

Caitlin was wrong. Dead wrong. Since he couldn't explain his absolute certainty, he clamped his mouth shut. Probably a good thing, too, or he would feel pressed to point out that he neither asked her to nor wanted her to wait for him. Divorce was final, he got that. He was beginning to think she never would.

But it wasn't about that. It wasn't about them. So instead of antagonizing Caitlin, he tried to calm her by reaching out to place a reassuring hand on her shoulder. Lucas stretched too far, though, and a shock of pain shot up his arm. Cursing under his breath, he tried to hide his grimace and failed.

Caitlin caught the flash of pain. Knowing he was hurting hit her like a suckerpunch to the gut. She immediately stopped fighting him.

"Okay, I'm sorry. That's not important right now. Finding the bastard who did this is. I don't care if he was aiming for that outsider. He hit *you*, Luc, and I promise you this: he'll pay."

Before he got the chance to reply, Caitlin snatched her communicator off her belt. She turned one knob decisively, changed to another channel, and gripped the receiver button so tightly, her fingers turned white from pressure. Her radio sent out a call, and they waited to see if her buzz would be answered.

Crackle. "Hart speaking."

"Ricky, this is Sheriff De Angelis. You know how you're always telling me that you're willing to lend a hand if I ever need you?"

A pause, followed by a very gruff, yet very hesitant, "Yeah. I remember."

"Great. From this moment on, consider yourself deputized."

RICK HART WAS EX-MILITARY. EVERYONE IN HAMLET knew that. Just like they knew he was born there, left, and came back a different man. He settled not too far from the eastern edge of the gulley. He lived in the small house by himself, spending his days working at the barbershop. His nights? Those he spent down at Thirsty's where he tried to forget the nine years he'd been gone.

A big man, pushing six and a half feet with a bulky frame that was still more muscle than solid fat, he wasn't the type of guy you wanted to run into in the dark. But when it came to having a practiced eye scanning a crime scene involving a gun, there was no one better in Hamlet. He definitely knew his way around a weapon.

Rick was crouching down, staring in the bushes that lined the front of Lucas's office building when they drove up the street, Caitlin's cruiser in the lead.

When it became clear that he had every intention of following her back to the scene, she offered him a lift, not even a little surprised when he climbed back into his Mustang and revved the engine. Lucas always accused her of being the stubborn one in their marriage. Caitlin long ago decided that was only because he was too pigheaded to see just how stubborn *he* was.

Because he had told her that he'd been standing in his driveway when he got shot, Caitlin kept it clear. She parked on the side of the road, Lucas coasting up right behind her. Grabbing her hat and her notepad, she clambered out of her cruiser and just observed the scene.

Before they left her house, she made Lucas give her a rapid-fire interview. Putting her own emotions aside, she seamlessly slipped right into the role of Hamlet's sheriff. Once she thought she had enough information, she drove over to Lucas's office to see if Rick had made any headway in the investigation. It wasn't worth it to fight Lucas over his following her so she barely tried. As long as he understood that she was in charge, and he was the victim, they would get along fine.

On her initial sweep, Caitlin saw the divot in the brick facade where the first shot hit. Her stomach clenched. What if the shooter's aim was better? Would she be standing over his dead body now?

Ducking her head, staring blindly at the notepad she clutched in trembling hands, she tried to conceal that panic that overwhelmed her.

It was one thing when it was an outsider. Turner. Sullivan. She could keep a cool, level head when dealing with their deaths. But to imagine Luc—*her* Luc... she gulped and forced herself to push it to the side. He came to her for help and, goddammit, she was going to do her job if it killed her.

Rick rose to his considerable height when he realized he had company. He lumbered over to Caitlin, towering over her petite form as he moved closer to her.

Very close, Lucas noticed. The newly-made deputy bent down, murmuring something under his breath. Whatever it was, Rick had meant it only for Caitlin's ears. She brushed his concerns back with a flippant wave of her hand.

"Yes, I know he's here. I let him come with me," she said. "Lucas was the one they shot at. I thought he might have a better idea where the shots were fired from, or what they hit."

With a small nod, Rick greeted Lucas with a curt, "Doc."

"Hart. How's the search going? Did you find anything?"

Caitlin's eyes flashed angrily as she bobbed her head up from her notepad, glaring at him. He was well aware that she absolutely hated it when he tried to butt in on any of her investigations; it didn't matter that he was actually *involved* in this one. She pointed at him, then flung her arm out wide. He got the drift and, his hands held up in front of him in a silent apology, backed off.

"I'll just watch. That better, Cait?"

As if he hadn't said anything, Caitlin flipped her notebook shut and tilted her head back so that she was looking up at Rick. "Tell me you found something."

"Yeah. I was gonna buzz you, tell you not to waste time making the trip. Then I figured you might want to check out the scene yourself. I'm still looking for the slug in the bushes, but I got something alright." Reaching into his back pocket, he pulled out a sandwich bag with two spent shell casings. "I saw the chip on the brick and realized that the shot had to come from this direction. Since the doctor would've seen anyone shooting at him, it made sense to me that the shooter was in the trees. It didn't take much searching to find these."

Caitlin took the bag from Rick, holding it up so that she got a better look at its contents. She recognized the casings at once. Hoping she was wrong—*praying* she was wrong—she glanced up at Rick again, this time in confirmation.

He nodded. "Definitely a .40 caliber. You're gonna want to send it out for ballistics to be sure, but I don't think I'm wrong. Best guess, eyeballing it, is that it's a Glock 22."

Her hand went right to her holster.

A Glock 22. Her preferred carry, and the same model worn by everyone in the sheriff's department. She closed her eyes and huffed.

Fan-fucking-tastic.

20

At half past two the next afternoon, the intercom chimed.

Tessa was sitting in the armchair in her rented room, absently flipping through the pages of a magazine three months old. As soon as she heard the soft tinkling sound, she closed the magazine and rested it on top of the chair's arm. She'd been waiting for this call.

Truth be told, she expected it to come last night. As soon as Lucas dropped her off, making her promise that she wouldn't tell Maria about the shooting because he knew it would only upset his sister, she thought someone from the sheriff's department would want to talk to her.

She knew the doctor was only protecting her by leaving her locked in the bed and breakfast, but she already had a good idea how Sheriff De Angelis saw her. It would be a damn miracle if the red-haired she-demon didn't immediately book Tess for attempted murder of her beloved ex-husband.

Tess was well aware she was being bitter. A threatening note one night, being shot at another, all on top of the sudden shock of losing her husband so violently... Tess decided she was owed a little bitterness. If she wasn't the temptress trying to seduce the local men, then she was a black widow who was leaving bodies in her wake. Whatever happened to the kindhearted former kindergarten teacher just trying to have a little love in her life?

The intercom chimed again. It sounded more impatient this time.

With a huff, Tess pulled herself out of the armchair and shuffled over to the bed. Her slippers were crusted with dirt, leaving a trail of flakes of dried mud behind her. Maria offered to wash her slippers after her sprint through the trees. Tess told her no. She needed the visual reminder that, no matter what she thought, she wasn't really safe here.

She engaged the intercom button. "Yes?"

"Tess, sweetie, I hate to bother you, but Sly is at the door. He's in uniform so it's gotta be police business. He says to make sure you're decent because he's here to pick you up." Maria's confusion became even more obvious as she blurted out, "Were you expecting him?"

"Not him, no," she admitted, plucking at the belt poking through the nearest loop on her cozy robe. "I actually thought she might send Deputy Walsh over."

"She? Caity? Oh, no." Maria's trill of a laugh seemed even higher through the tinny speaker of the intercom. "She wouldn't do that. She's convinced you have poor Mase wrapped around your finger. No wonder she sent Sly. Mase would just coddle you, and we both know Caity wouldn't like that. Not after the way he hid the story of the note you got from her."

As if she wasn't feeling bad enough that Deputy Collins was here to take her to see the sheriff. The last thing she wanted was a reminder that Mason seemed convinced that there was something between them—and that Sheriff De Angelis was all too aware of that fact.

"Hey, um, I was kinda hoping they'd forgotten about me. I'm still wearing my pajamas and a robe. Do you think you could tell Deputy Collins that I'll be right out as soon as I get changed?"

"Of course. No worries, sweetie." Her chuckle turned husky. "I'll keep the deputy company until you're ready."

After thanking Maria, she stripped off her robe and tossed it on her rumpled bed. As she pulled on the dresser drawers, looking for something clean to change into, she thought about how Maria's whole mood changed when Tess told her she wasn't exactly *expecting* Deputy Collins.

Maria sure sounded happy to spend some time with the tall, dark, and handsome deputy, she realized.

For the first time since Lucas got grazed by that bullet, Tess grinned. And maybe she took a little bit longer than necessary to get dressed.

HAVING EXPERIENCED THE SHERIFF'S INTERVIEWING style, Tess thought she knew what to expect this time around. Like Sunday, the deputy brought her into the only room with a closed door. She assumed it was an office of some sort for the sheriff, since both times she was told to sit in the plastic chair opposite of a solid oak desk. Sheriff De Angelis sat on the other side, an open notepad in front of her.

Deputy Collins offered her a glass of water, waited for her to refuse, then left the two women alone. At a nod from the sheriff, Collins closed the door behind him.

De Angelis picked up her pen, poised it against the blank sheet of paper and, with a no-nonsense tone, said, "Starting from when you left Ophelia, tell me what happened yesterday afternoon."

Tess did. Going into detail, she explained how Maria needed to take a trip out of Hamlet and, because she didn't want to stay in the bed and breakfast by herself after her fright from the night before, she asked Maria to show her where Dr. De Angelis's office was.

Since she couldn't admit that she just wanted to see the doctor—especially not to his very jealous ex-wife—she made it seem like she was only interested in getting another dose of sleeping pills. Fully aware that the sheriff now thought of her as a pill-popper, she quickly continued. Better a lush and a drug addict than the outsider with her eye on the sheriff's former husband.

Sheriff De Angelis didn't interrupt once. Tilting her notepad toward her so that Tess couldn't see what she was writing, she jotted down whatever interested her. At one point she made a notation, underlined and then circled it. Twice. Tess wished she could remember what it was she had said but she was already three thoughts ahead.

She gamely finished. "—as soon as we got him bandaged up, the doctor drove us back to the B&B. I tried to get him to let me drive—"

The sheriff snorted.

"—yeah, I tried, but now I know that no one is allowed to drive his car except him. Anyway, after he dropped me off, he said he was going to see the sheriff... see you... and tell you all about the freak shooting. At least, I have to believe it was some kind of accident. He didn't say it or anything, but I got the feeling that

Dr. De Angelis thought they were shooting at me. I mean, that's impossible. Why would anyone shoot at me?"

Sheriff De Angelis set her pen aside. Then, opening her desk drawer, she slipped her notepad inside before pulling out a manila folder. She tossed it on her desk where it landed with a soft *thump*.

"I'm not so sure they did."

Tess blinked. "I'm sorry?"

"You just told me how, when I met you outside of the doc's office, you were in the woods. Looking for a stray cat, right?"

"Yes. I thought I heard meowing so I went to check it out. I told you that yesterday, too. And then you told me that Hamlet doesn't have strays."

"We don't, Mrs. Sullivan. And that makes me wonder what you really were doing in the woods." The sheriff paused, either for effect or because she thought Tess might actually answer her. Her lips pressed tight together, Tess didn't say a word. "We found shells a few feet into the trees, not too far from where I saw you. So I'm going to ask again, in case you want to change your mind. What were you doing in the woods?"

Her answer was slow, deliberate. "I heard a cat."

"Maybe you did. But I think it's more likely you were in there checking out the sightlines, maybe loading a gun—or helping someone else do it."

It took Tess a second to understand what De

Angelis was actually saying to her. She couldn't believe it. The sheriff was actually accusing her of somehow orchestrating the shooting with… with some accomplice in the woods. That was absolutely crazy.

"Why would I do that?" she demanded. "Why would I want Lucas to get shot?"

De Angelis frowned at Tess's slip. Lucas. She called him *Lucas*. "I don't know. Why did you strangle your husband?"

"I didn't!"

"Maybe *you* didn't. But, let me tell you, I'm one step closer to finding out who did. Dollars to donuts, same man took a shot at our doc. And I think you know who it was." The sheriff tapped her nail on the top of the manila folder. She was a biter, Tess noticed, the nail chewed down to the quick. *Thud. Thud. Thud.* "Who do you know around here?"

She didn't like the direction Sheriff De Angelis's questions were veering off into. "I don't know what you mean."

"Big city girl, bet you never figured that the sticks has some fine detectives of its own. I don't like to leave Hamlet, Mrs. Sullivan. Doesn't mean that I don't. In fact, I have friends high up in the county. Look what they got for me."

De Angelis opened the file on her desk. Inside was a stack of paper close to a half inch thick. A row of numbers ran down the page. There were about four lines highlighted.

She slammed her palm flat on the top of the paper, covering the numbers. "These are your phone records."

Deep inside her coat pockets, Tess clenched her hands into fists. She kept her expression neutral. "You can't do that."

"Can. Did."

The sheriff offered her a meaningless grin. At least, she bared her teeth. Tess decided it counted. De Angelis looked like she was suddenly enjoying herself.

That made one of them.

"Warrant I got let me go back a year," De Angelis said. "And you know what I noticed?"

"I'm sure you're going to tell me."

"You either loved your husband a great deal, or you were very lonely." Lifting her hand, she pointed down the row of numbers, skipping over the ones in yellow. "Same two numbers over and over. One was Jack Sullivan's cellphone, the other his work number. That's it. Until a couple of weeks ago."

Thud. Thud. De Angelis tapped on the first highlighted number. She rattled it off.

"That's a local number," she said. "No trace on it that I can find, so it must be a burner. In fact, I bet it is. And you know what else? Every Monday, like clockwork, there's a new number to replace the last one.

Same area code, though. So one more time, Mrs. Sullivan: who do you know here?"

Sheriff De Angelis kept repeating herself, just like she did during the other interview. As if she could badger a confession out of Tess. But Tess was prepared this time around.

She fought to relax, reminding herself that she didn't do anything wrong. And she wasn't about to let De Angelis bully her into admitting anything that might get her in trouble. With a shrug, she said, "Nobody. Our car got a flat. It was pure chance we ended up in Hamlet."

The sheriff obviously didn't buy it. "Who are you talking to?" *Thud. Thud. Thud.* "Whose number is this?"

"I don't know. I mean, sometimes my phone gets weird numbers calling it. I don't know who they are. I might answer them. That's all. Look, you said it yourself. All the other numbers are the same. Jack's cell, his work phone. I really don't know anyone else. He wouldn't let me."

De Angelis ran her finger across a different number. She had drawn a large star next to it. "This conversation is from two weeks ago. It lasted more than thirty-four minutes. Who did you talk to?"

Tess thought about it. "Okay. I think I remember that. It was a telemarketer trying to sell me insurance or something. I don't know. Jack worked long hours. I get lonely sometimes. And, yeah, it might be pathetic, it might be sad, but sometimes I pretend to buy into their speeches just to have someone to talk to."

"Except, as I said, I already ran these numbers. Not one is registered to any business, insurance or otherwise."

"I don't know why!" The denial burst out of Tess. Yanking her hands out of her pockets, she gripped the edge of the sheriff's desk. She didn't want De Angelis to see that she was shaking. "All I wanted to do was have a second honeymoon with my husband. Now he's dead... and everyone thinks I'm responsible."

She couldn't take it anymore. Burying her face in her trembling hands, Tess started to weep.

A SOFT RAP AT HER DOOR. READY TO SNARL THAT SHE was busy, Caitlin tore her pointed gaze away from the crying woman in time to see that Wilhelmina had already entered the small office. Her hand was still folded loosely in a fist. Willie must have knocked on the inside of the door—and, most likely, overheard everything that had just passed between her and the Sullivan woman.

One look at the disapproval on her deputy's face confirmed it. Willie shook her head slowly, pursing her bright red lips as she folded her hands in front of her ample waist.

Caitlin gentled her voice. It wouldn't fool the older woman, no. She could at least try not to come off like she was attacking the outsider now that she knew her deputy was watching. "Yes?"

"Report just came in, Sheriff. Ricky's prelim was right on the money."

So the bullet was a .40 caliber, shot through the barrel of a Glock 22. The Glock was standard issue for most law enforcement officers in their state, including the four members of her department. Of course. Because why would anything about this case be easy?

"You sure, Wil?"

"Got the report right here if you want to read it, boss."

Caitlin let out a rough exhale, causing loose strands of her red hair to flutter around a face pinched with annoyance. "Yeah," she said after a second, before pushing away from her desk. "I do."

As she rose from her seat, Sullivan's soft cries seemed to echo in the close quarters. The sound was like nails scraping down a chalkboard for Caitlin. Looking past her, she caught Wilhelmina's eye, nodded at Sullivan's bowed head, and pleaded silently with her.

Willie rolled her heavily made-up eyes, a theatrical gesture that was all the more impressive since she didn't smudge either her eyeshadow or mascara behind her glasses. Caitlin jerked her head at the weeper, throwing in a pout for good measure. Willie sighed, then nodded.

"Mrs. Sullivan, that's it for today's interview," Caitlin said, raising her voice so that she could drown out the weeping. As far as she was concerned, the sooner she didn't have to listen to the incessant crying, the better. "You can go—just don't go far. There's a good chance we'll have to revisit this matter again and soon. So long as you stay on at Maria's place, I'll know how to get in touch with you. If you need anything before you leave the station house, make sure to ask Willie. That'll be all for now."

Then, before she felt compelled to offer the outsider a tissue, she quickly made her escape.

SHAKING HER HEAD AT HOW QUICKLY THE SHERIFF RAN out of the room, Wilhelmina approached Tess. Her knees creaked as she bent low enough to place her hand on the younger woman's shoulder. "You feeling okay, sugar?"

Her whole body tensed and tightened under the soft touch. Tess sniffled, wiping her tears away with the back of her hand before she rubbed underneath her nose. Weak and shaky from her latest crying jag—plus the revelation that she was as much a suspect as ever in the sheriff's eyes—made the deputy's soft question almost laughable.

Did she feel okay? Not even a little.

She was sitting in a police station, once again weighed down with the belief that she was responsible for a crime she couldn't have possibly committed on her own. Where would she have gotten a gun from? And why would she want to shoot Lucas? It nearly broke her all over again to know he'd been hit. And how was she supposed to have conjured up some accomplice when she'd never even been to Hamlet before?

Things stopped being *okay* the second the tire went flat. That was her fault, too. She knew deep down that, regardless of her relief and her freedom, she would never stop blaming herself for causing that.

Brushing her hair out of her face, Tess let out a soft, shaky breath. It didn't matter if she felt okay. She had to let everyone else think that she was.

If she was an outsider, these people were simply strangers. Enough of them had seen her fall to pieces these last few days, and now she had to go and start crying in front of the sheriff.

She nodded, her throat raw. "I'm just ducky."

Wilhelmina gave her a quick squeeze. "C'mon, sug. No reason for you to keep hanging around here. Let's get you back to Ophelia."

The groan was already slipping out before she had the chance to swallow it. How was she supposed to go back? Deputy Collins had picked her up and driven her over to the station house at Sheriff De Angelis's request. It wasn't like she could use someone's radio and ask him to drive her back. If he wasn't on patrol, he was off duty, and nowhere in his job title did it say chauffeur.

Besides, she was sick and tired of having to rely on someone else for a ride. She hadn't had a sip to drink since that night at Thirsty's, nor did she have any desire to return to the bar. There was no good reason why she couldn't drive.

Last night, before she took one of the pills that knocked her out, Tess thought about the strange situation with her missing car. No matter who she tried to ask, no one knew anything about it—or, in the case of Mason, he constantly blew right past it, as if he didn't *want* to answer. She was beginning to suspect that they were purposely keeping her car from her because she was a flight risk.

It wasn't right, though. And it wasn't fair. She didn't think that they should be able to keep her car impounded without at least telling her *why*.

It struck her then that she'd never tried to ask Willie. Though she was as much a deputy as Mason and Collins, she told Tess in conversation that she was the one responsible for most of the paperwork. If anyone knew what happened to Tess's car, it would have to be her.

Trotting along after the older woman like a puppy, she said softly, "Um, Wilhelmina—"

"Just Willie, sugar. I know that name of mine is a mouthful, so just Willie is fine."

"Willie," Tess conceded. Wilhelmina might have told her the same thing right after she found Jack and Mason shepherded her back to the station house. It was another fuzzy memory lost to the haze. "It's something I've been meaning to ask. You wouldn't happen to know what happened to my car, would you?"

"Car?" Pencil-thin eyebrows winged up over the wide swath of blue eyeshadow. "What do you mean?"

"My car. Well, my... my husband's, I guess. We drove into Hamlet in it. I could drive myself back to Ophelia if someone would tell me where to find it."

Either she was an amazing actress or Willie really didn't know the answer to her question. She shook her head, her glasses slipping down her nose. "I don't have half a clue, sugar, sorry. Mason said he was gonna take care of it himself but, shoot, I've got no idea what that boy did with your vehicle." Her hand slid to her belt, long red fingernails tapping the plastic side of her radio. "You want me to give him a buzz? I can find out for you."

Tess could still see the fury in his gaze, hear the

demand in his voice. She quickly shook her head. "No. No, that's okay. He might be busy."

And if she didn't bother him, he might forget all about his plans to come see her tonight.

Willie studied her. Tess couldn't help but quail under the weight of her curious stare. What was she thinking? Did she hear something in Tess's quick refusal? Or did she know exactly why Tess was so hesitant to ask anything of the other deputy?

She didn't know. She couldn't ask. But when Willie gave her upper arm another reassuring squeeze, she let out the breath she didn't even know she was holding.

"Let me get my purse."

"Your purse?"

"It's got my keys. You heard the sheriff, she said for you to ask me if you need anything. Well, you need a ride. I'll take you back myself."

Tess blinked in surprise. "I— you don't have to do that."

"Hamlet is small, sugar, but it's still a hike out to Maria's fancy little place. Plus the temperature's dropping. We might be in for another wicked storm like the other night. You don't want to be caught out in that."

No, she thought, remembering what happened the last time it rained. She did not.

21

Tess continued to hope that Mason wouldn't show. Fingers crossed, toes crossed, the whole deal. Her dreaded meeting with Sheriff De Angelis left her drained, both emotionally and physically. Her eyes ached. Her whole body was tense. All she wanted to do was take some of the doctor's sleeping pills and knock out for another week.

Maybe, by then, all of this would finally be over.

Yeah, right. She highly doubted that. It wouldn't be over until she managed to escape Hamlet. And everything that she knew about Mason—which, admittedly, wasn't much—told her that he would be there at seven o'clock on the dot. So it would be a miracle if she at least managed to escape the earnest deputy.

Nibbling on her bottom lip, she prayed. Now, Tess didn't quite wish a police emergency on anyone. Didn't mean that she would turn her nose up at a fender bender or a quick smash and grab. A bar fight at Thirsty's, even. Just something small and harmless to put Deputy Walsh back on patrol.

The evening sped by. At six o'clock, she gave up hope. Mason would be there within the hour and, as much as she wanted to pull her blanket up over her head and hide, she decided she might as well get this over with.

Because this trip was designed to be a second honeymoon for her and Jack, Tess had conveniently packed a few outfits that could be used for a date night. After she showered and dried her hair, she searched through the remaining clothes in her dresser drawer.

It wasn't easy.

Anything fancy made it seem like she was trying too hard, or that she was reading as much into this meal as Mason apparently was. She didn't want to give him the wrong impression. In the end, she put on a pair of jeans, an off-the-shoulder top and heels. Casual but not sloppy. It would have to do.

She made sure to tell Maria at breakfast that morning that she would be missing dinner, both because she wasn't sure she'd make it back by the nine o'clock curfew and because she felt bad about leaving the other woman alone again. She'd come to look forward to the hour or so they spent eating and simply talking in the serenity of Ophelia's kitchen.

And because Maria automatically assumed she was seeing her brother, Tess had felt compelled to admit the truth about agreeing to go out with Mason. Maria didn't say anything. She didn't have to. The look she gave Tess was enough.

Tess didn't blame her. After the way Mason treated her yesterday, spending time alone with him was the last thing she wanted to do. She just couldn't see any way out of it.

At ten to seven, she decided that if she continued to pace the length of the Lavender Room, there was a good chance she'd jump out of the window again. Shaking off her anxiousness, she opened the door and peeked down the hall, glancing toward Maria's room.

The door was closed. Either Maria had gone out for the evening herself or she didn't want to be disturbed.

Lucky.

So that she didn't have to worry about Mason bothering Maria when he rang the doorbell, Tess decided to wait for him in the foyer. She thought about bringing her purse, decided against it, then grabbed her coat and another outdated magazine to peruse while she waited.

It wasn't long. The clock had just finished chiming the hour when the chirpy doorbell echoed through the room.

Seven o'clock on the nose. She called it.

With a nervous sigh, Tess set her magazine down on the couch, smoothed an imaginary wrinkle from her blouse, then shimmied on her coat. Though it was the last thing she wanted to do, she got up and answered the door.

She had to admit, Mason Walsh sure cleaned up well. He had such an appealing boy next door sort of thing going on. He didn't bother with a jacket, instead wearing a soft caramel-colored sweater over a cream button-down shirt and a pair of pressed khakis. In the evening breeze, she caught a hint of his aftershave. Dark and spicy, she had to admit she liked it.

"You look nice," she told him honestly.

"And you look beautiful."

Tess caught the way his eyes looked her up and down, obviously pleased with what he was seeing. Remembering yesterday, she immediately went on her guard. Mason might be pleased with her now—how long would that last? She was poised, ready for another of his mood swings.

He gestured for her to step out onto the porch. But, before he could help her down the steps, Mason steered her toward the picturesque swing that took up one side of Ophelia's porch.

"Sit with me?" he asked.

As if she could say no.

It swayed a little as she climbed up on the wooden seat. Mason waited until she was situated before he sat beside her. He closed the gap between them so neatly, she didn't think she could slip a sheet of paper between their thighs.

"So," he began, one heel of his boot against the porch as he rocked them softly, "Willie told me that you were down at the station today. I wanted to take a second and talk to you about that."

It seemed as if the ever faithful Hamlet gossip mill had kept him up to date on her trip downtown to be interrogated again. Like she needed the reminder.

"It was just some more questions. I'm used to it by now."

He waved her obvious brush-off away with his hand. "Not that. She told me that there was something you were going to ask me but you didn't want her to buzz me in case I was busy. Before we went out, I wanted to remind you that there's nothing you can do that would bother me. If there's anything you need, I want you to feel like you can always come to me."

"I need that sheriff to stop treating me like a criminal."

It popped out before she even realized she was going to say it. And there was no way she could take it back.

Mason pressed his heel down, stopping the swing in its motion. He stood up, framing her body as he rested one arm along the side closest to him. "Don't let my boss upset you. This is new for all of us. We're trying our best."

She stayed seated. The rocking of the swing after Mason got up was strangely calming. Tess folded her hands in her lap, staring at her nails. "I know, and I appreciate how hard you're all working on my husband's case. But she's still convinced I had something to do with Jack's death. Nothing I can do to make her see reason. I've given up on trying."

She pointedly didn't mention how Sheriff De Angelis was also convinced she had a hand in Lucas getting shot. Tess wasn't completely naive. If Mason knew about the gunshots being fired outside of the doctor's office, she was sure she would've heard from him far before tonight. The sheriff must have kept the investigation into the shooting from her deputy. She could only assume why.

Something told her that turnabout was fair play. Mason kept the night with the note a secret. Now it was the sheriff's turn.

Tess didn't say a word about it at all.

Mason's voice was a rumble deep in his chest. "That's impossible!" He sounded angry on her behalf.

Oh, yeah. That would be *exactly* why.

Still, she huffed. "It's nice that someone believes me."

"I've always believed you."

"You'd have to. You're the one who stuck me in the holding cell. You know I was there."

"No, it's not just that. I *trust* you, Tess. And, okay, I know we just met and, yes, the circumstances are less than ideal, but I want you to trust me, too."

There was something in his earnestness that caught her attention. She'd been picking at her thumbnail, unwilling to look him in the eye in case she saw something there that she couldn't reciprocate. But she heard it instead. And, as much as she wanted to pretend this wasn't happening, it was.

Her stomach sank. Glancing up, there was no hiding the utter adoration splayed across his face as he focused on her.

Why, she wondered. What the hell had she done to make this man think so highly of her and want her so badly when they were strangers a week ago? And what the hell could she do to *stop* it?

She gentled her tone. "Mason, you're very sweet, but—"

But? He didn't want to hear anything that came after a *but*.

Before she could finish her thought, Mason reached down and placed his hands on her cheeks. The move surprised her into silence. Tilting her head back as he leaned over her, Mason pressed his lips to hers. Tess gasped and he took the opportunity to slip his tongue inside her mouth, kissing her with all the passion he felt since they first met but had kept trapped inside for fear of scaring her off too soon.

She didn't struggle. If she had, he would've immediately backed off. But neither did she kiss him back. He nipped at her bottom lip, desperately trying to get her to respond. After a moment that seemed like forever, he felt the hesitance of her response. She was nowhere near as enthusiastic as he was. Mason didn't care. Tess was melting into his caress at last.

He'd won. The deputy, not the meddling doctor. After fighting it these last few days, she was finally admitting that she felt the same pull toward him that he'd recognized that first night in Thirsty's.

Kismet. Fate. She was meant to find her way to Hamlet, this outsider with the golden eyes and a lonely heart. Sullivan hadn't deserved her and now that he was gone, Mason wasn't going to let this chance slip away from him. Tess was his.

At least, that's what he thought. When Tess wiggled up against the back of the porch swing, he followed her until he was kneeling beside her again. Mason wanted to hold onto her forever, until he could be sure he had her heart and everything that went with it, but he knew that wasn't possible. Not yet. Didn't stop him from trying, though. Only when he felt her palms push frantically against his chest did he finally let her go.

Her pale cheeks turned crimson, burning up with color. Scrambling out of the porch swing, she moved until she was a few feet away from him. "I shouldn't have—"

"Yes," he said. His voice husky, his gaze narrowed on her shiny, plump lips. He did that to her. He'd give everything he had to do it again. "You don't have to fight it, Tess. Your husband's gone now. I'm here for you. You can give in."

She ran her pointer finger along the edge of her bottom lip. "It's not that easy."

It could be, Mason thought.

"You don't believe me. I know it's crazy when we only just met, but I've always thought I would know when I found the one I wanted to be with."

"You can't mean—"

"It's you. I know it is. Don't you feel it too?"

Tess couldn't answer him. Regardless of what she did or did not feel, everything was happening too fast. A week ago, she was getting ready to go on a second honeymoon with her husband. Mason was right about one thing. Jack was gone. But Tess wasn't looking for a replacement. She was just looking for a way to get back to her normal life.

"You want me to prove myself," he announced after a moment's silence.

"What? Mason, no."

He continued as if she hadn't said a word. "I can do that. I'll show you that I mean what I say. You think the sheriff is going to pin your husband's murder on you?"

"She's just doing her job," Tess said. She grabbed his sleeve, trying to force him into listening to her. "I'm being oversensitive. Come on. Forget it. Let's go get dinner."

"You won't enjoy yourself. You're such a good girl—Sheriff's got no reason to think you could be behind any of this. I've told her a hundred times this last week. She's as stubborn as an ass. I'll have to try again."

Tess gave another fruitless tug. "You don't have to do that, Mason."

His touch was careful, like she was made from spun glass. He definitely hadn't forgotten yesterday's angry grab.

Slowly, easy, he loosened her fingers from the holes she was worrying into the sleeve of his sweater. "I do. This is something I can do for you. Let me take care of it, Tess. As God as my witness, I'll do whatever I have to do to make her see the truth. And maybe then you'll see *me*."

"Stay," she begged. "I don't want anything to happ—"

"It won't. Trust me. The sheriff will listen. I'll take care of everything. When I'm done, I'll come back for you."

She stood there, stunned, as he ducked his head, managing to steal her lips one more time before he pulled her to his chest and embraced her tightly. It only lasted the length of a heartbeat and then he let her go. She caught the lines bracketing his mouth, determination etched in every furrow, as his eyes bored down on her, like he was memorizing every single freckle and beauty mark she had.

And then he was gone.

TESS CHASED AFTER HIS CRUISER. SHE DIDN'T KNOW why. It was a gut reaction. Something told her it was a really bad idea to let Mason confront his boss after she accidentally riled him up.

But Mason, it seemed, had a lead foot. He was already turning the corner by the time she reached the first street lamp, hobbled by her heels. She grabbed the lamp post, hunched over as she struggled to catch her breath. No way she was going to stop him if he was in his cruiser and she only had her feet.

God damn it, why didn't she have her car back yet?

It would be pointless to keep running after him. She kicked off her heels, stopping only to swoop them up again before racing back to Ophelia. Her head thudding in time to the thumps of her bare feet against the porch steps, she tore into the foyer and ran right to her room.

Her purse was tucked neatly on the desk in the corner. Grabbing it, she dumped it on the bed, pawing through it until she found her phone. A second later, she threw it back on the bed.

The screen was black. Her cell was dead. Not that it mattered. She'd forgotten that there wasn't any service, or even a phone number that she could call. It had been another instinctual reaction to go right for her phone, but it was worthless in Hamlet. She needed one of those radios—

Maria had a radio.

She didn't bother with the intercom. Pausing only to jam her tender feet into her slippers, Tess hurried down the hall that led to her hostess's room. It didn't matter if Maria was home. After watching her habits these last few days, Tess knew that Maria usually left her radio in her bedroom.

She could use it. She *would* use it.

Maria's door was still closed. She remembered herself, then remembered the story of Mack Turner and his attack on Maria in time to keep from barging into the room. Panting slightly, still out of breath, she pounded the flats of her hands against the wood.

"Maria?" The words came out strangled, her voice strained. She swallowed roughly and tried again. *Bam! Bam! Bam!* "Maria? Please, are you here?"

No answer.

She tried the handle anyway. It didn't turn at all.

Locked.

What was she going to do now?

"Tess? Why are you trying to break into my room?"

Maria!

Tess whirled on her. Wide-eyed and flushed, she blurted out, "You have to help me! Please, I need to use your radio!"

Maria hurried forward. She recognized the panic in the other woman's voice, the fright that kept her pupils wide, her eyes staring. She'd felt like that herself not too long ago.

Something was wrong.

Though her first instinct was to grab her bat, Maria forced herself to put her hands on her knees and bend enough that she was eye to eye with Tess. "Shh, sweetie, I'm here now. I'll help."

"It's Mason. He—" Tess stumbled over her words, trying to spit it out. "It's the sheriff... he went to go talk to her."

Maria straightened, bemused. That's what had Tess so worked up? "Caity's his boss. I'm sure it'll be fine. He reports to her all the time."

Tess shook her head. "Not like this. You didn't—okay. *Okay*. This is what happened—"

In between shallow breaths, Tess struggled to explain how Mason came to take her out only to lose it when she told him how Sheriff De Angelis refused to treat her as a victim instead of the villain.

And then, that last look he shot her... the determination, the drive. He got it in his head that he would be her white knight, riding in to save the day. She could live with that, she could deal, except she couldn't deny the desperation in his kiss.

That's what scared her. Because Mason *was* suddenly desperate. And Tess knew better than most that desperation and impulsiveness could be a very dangerous combination.

"He kissed me," she bit out. A lick of color crept into Tess's pale cheeks. "I didn't ask him to. I didn't want him to. But he did and then he left and I'm so very scared because he was talking crazy, Maria. I don't know what he's going to do."

She just knew it wouldn't be good.

Tess didn't say that last part out loud. From the furrow in Maria's brow to the way she released Tess to stroke the silver chain at her throat, she knew she didn't have to.

Maria finally understood.

She nodded. "Mase is going to see Caity? Let's give her fair warning, yes?"

Or maybe she *didn't* understand.

Tess threw her hand behind her, slapping the closed bedroom door. "I'm trying to!"

"He isn't acting like himself," Maria confirmed. Now her pale blue eyes had gone dark with sudden worry. Yes. She did get it. "If he says the wrong thing to Caity, she might fire him. It would kill Mase to lose his job, and Cait, too, if she had to let one of her guys go. No, no, no."

"The radio— that's why I need your radio."

"*Dammi un secundo*. Wait here."

Instead of entering her room, Maria spun around, her long dark hair a curtain that whipped behind her as she ran down the hall. Tess began to nibble on her thumbnail, realized what she was doing and let her hand fall to her side.

One second turned into a minute, then two before Maria came jogging back. She carried her communicator in her right hand.

"I had it with me in the kitchen when I was prepping dinner earlier," she explained. "I already buzzed the station. Sly told me that the sheriff went home. So I tried Caity, but no answer. Come on. I'll take you there. If he goes to the station first, we might be able to beat him to her place. And we can always try buzzing her again in the car."

Tess just managed to snap her seatbelt closed before Maria sped off in her coupe. The roads were empty and Maria drove even more recklessly than her brother. Tess was beginning to think her overwhelming anxiety had rubbed off on Maria until both of them were racing against Mason's cruiser.

Maria wanted to make sure her old friend kept his job. Tess... she wanted to make sure that no one else got hurt because of her.

No sign of Mason as they drove. Normally, the intense speed would've caused Tess's heart to lodge in her throat. Since she was too busy trying to page Sheriff De Angelis over and over again, she barely noticed how fast Maria was going.

The buzzes went unanswered. That only made the feeling that something bad was going to happen even worse. Tess caught herself gnawing nervously on her thumbnail again and let it go.

Just how far *was* the sheriff's house from Ophelia?

She had to trust that Maria knew where she was going. Hamlet was small, and in the handful of days she'd been stuck there, she'd only seen a fraction of what it had to offer. When they pulled up in front of a quaint pale blue house on the corner, she didn't recognize it. She turned in her seat, gripping the seatbelt strap.

There. A police cruiser. Yes!

Maria leaned on her horn, one continuous squeal, as she skid to a fast stop along the curb, leaving burning rubber in her wake. Only one cruiser was parked there. She came within an inch of the bumper, killing the engine before they both climbed out of the coupe. Tess tossed Maria's radio onto the passenger seat, slamming the door behind her as she stepped onto the grass.

"Is this her house?" she asked.

"Yes. And that's her cruiser," Maria said, pointing at the other car. "No sign of Mason, though."

A sigh of relief. The tight knot in her stomach relaxed the tiniest fraction. It felt good to be wrong. "Maybe he didn't come here after all. Maybe I—"

"What the hell is going on?"

Tess gulped. The sheriff sounded pissed. Now that she saw for herself that Mason hadn't come to confront De Angelis, she wanted to get the hell out of there.

She grabbed Maria's sleeve, tugged it once. "Okay, she's fine, still no Mason, and I definitely overreacted. Can we go now?"

"Shh. It'll be fine. Let me talk to Cait."

Moving in front of Tess as if blocking her, Maria turned toward the open door. Caitlin De Angelis stood there, a scowl crossing her pointed face, her red hair dark with damp as it hung in heavy clumps down her back, barely brushed. A towel was in her hand. She'd changed into a pair of jeans and a flowy yellow blouse that made her seem even smaller somehow.

"Maria, was that you honking the horn? What gives?"

She didn't even wait for an answer. Raising her towel up to her head, she wrapped the wet strands of hair, vigorously rubbing at it in an attempt to dry it.

"Jesus, can't a girl take a shower in peace? My radio has been buzzing nonstop these last ten minutes. I finally answer one of the calls, and it's Sly telling me that you're worried about Mase of all people. And now you're killing me with the horn. What the hell?"

"Sly, he's right, Caity," Maria told her. Whether on purpose or not, she shielded Tess's smaller frame as she drew all of Caitlin's annoyance her way. "Something set Mase off, now there's a good chance he's coming to confront you. We don't want that to happen. No. He's a good deputy, and a good man. We all know he'll regret it if he loses his cool. We wanted to stop him before he did."

"We?" Caitlin finished with her towel, tossing it onto the porch chair before she stormed down the couple of steps that led to the walkway. "I don't get it, why would my deputy want to— *oh*."

Her thin lips pulled into a sneer. She'd finally noticed Tess tucked behind Lucas's sister.

"You."

If looks could kill, Tess would be joining Jack.

The sheriff wrinkled her nose, disgust plain on her face. "I should've known. You've been nothing but trouble since you appeared in my town and now you've got the nerve to drag me into it? At my *home*?"

"Cait, that's not fair."

Ignoring Maria, De Angelis stopped in the middle of her sidewalk. As if she couldn't be bothered going any closer to the other two women. She perched her hands on her narrow hips, her stare boring holes right through Tess.

"Look, I don't know what kind of spell you've cast on my guys, but you can just stop it right now."

"Caitlin!"

"Luc, Mase, they're all better off without you."

Unwilling to let Maria defend her, Tess found her voice. "It's not me. I didn't—"

"I warned you not to come between Mason and Hamlet. What were you thinking?"

Her cheeks were on fire. To think she'd come all this way to stop something bad from happening, only to be scolded like a naughty child. Ducking around Maria, Tess stood up, facing off against the belligerent sheriff.

"I was thinking that I didn't want to come between *any*one. Forget it. I don't know why I even tried." Her fists tight, she glanced over her shoulder, past Maria, looking for an answer that she'd never find. Biting down on her bottom lip, she turned back to Caitlin. Tess flexed her fingers, exhaled softly. "I'm sorry for trying to... hell, I don't know. Whatever. I'll just go."

"Tess," Maria called softly behind her, "don't do that. You came here for a reason. You don't deserve to be attacked. Maybe if you explain... go on, sweetie. Tell Caity what happened with you and Mase."

"What did you do to my deputy now?" De Angelis demanded.

That was the problem, wasn't it? What *did* she do?

Tess hesitated. "I just—"

The piercing shot rang out into the gloom of dusk. Unlike the day before, it was only the one time.

Once was enough.

Maria screamed.

Tess, flashing back to the doctor's office, curled in on herself and dropped to the curb.

The sheriff, standing alone on the walkway, glaring daggers at her opponent instead of being aware of her surroundings, was an easy target. Depending on where the gunman was hiding, it was nearly impossible to miss her.

And he didn't.

She opened her mouth again, the softest gasp escaping from her as the force of the bullet slammed her two steps back. Her eyes widened in surprise. Red blossomed on the sunny yellow of her blouse. An instant later, she crumpled to the grass in front of her home.

Maria was still screaming.

The constant high-pitched shriek was background noise to Tessa as her training kicked in. Just like when Lucas had been shot, she tamped down her fear and sprang into action. Scrabbling in the grass, she stayed low to the ground in case gunfire rang out again. When she reached the sheriff, she dropped down and grabbed for her limp wrist, desperately searching for a pulse.

It was pointless.

Sheriff De Angelis was dead.

22

Over the next few days, Lucas called in as many favors as he could. Most he didn't have to. Outrage and grief poured in as news of Caitlin's death spread throughout Hamlet and the neighboring counties. Bonnie's inn was full of outsiders who came to offer help in finding her murderer. When the Hamlet Inn had no vacancies, one or two were invited to stay at Ophelia, including Detective David Rodriguez.

Despite two witnesses on scene, there were no leads. Led by Rodriguez, crime scene investigation teams from the next town over worked around the clock, looking for clues, finding evidence, and questioning nearly every single one of Hamlet's residents.

Because of her position as head of law enforcement, the outsiders took over point on the investigation. No one seemed to argue. They were too busy mourning.

As her former husband, Lucas was one of the first questioned. He tried not to be too insulted. It was rough, especially when he flashed back to that morning in Jack Sullivan's hotel room and Caitlin's insistence that the spouse was usually guilty. Only the fact that this would get the investigators one step closer to discovering who killed his ex-wife kept him cordial during the tedious process.

When they finally let him go, they gave him one nugget of good faith information to tide him over. The ME who was taking care of Caitlin had recovered the bullet. God willing, they'd figure out what gun fired it.

Lucas didn't mind that someone else was doing his job. In fact, that was one of the favors he called in personally. When it came to Caitlin, he wouldn't work on her. He *couldn't*. Not when only a week ago he joked with her about seeing her on his slab. As Hamlet's only acting medical examiner, he was no stranger to dead bodies. But this wasn't just a DB, a gunshot victim. This was his ex-wife.

Someone else *had* to do it.

Luckily, over the course of his career, Lucas had made many contacts and bonds with plenty of others in the same field. Within hours of Caitlin's murder, he had countless offers from those willing to come into town and take over his duties so that, for once, he didn't have to be the only doc. He could grieve.

Not that he spent much time doing that. Keeping busy was a perfect balm to obsessing over this newest and most awful tragedy.

When he wasn't making arrangements with her deputies, Lucas spent most of his time at Ophelia. He tended to his sister, who was traumatized after watching Caitlin die, and he talked with Tessa Sullivan. The poor woman eyed the world warily now, as if she suspected anyone and everyone of being behind these terrible deeds.

As much as it went against everything he believed in as a doctor, Lucas overmedicated them both. Tessa still couldn't sleep without a little extra help. The anxiety that plagued Maria after her attack came back with a vengeance. He raided his limited pharmacy, trying to keep the women calm.

The anti-anxiety meds left Maria drained and more than a little dull, and she spent most of the time sleeping in a vain attempt to cope.

Tess fought sleep until he threatened to shove a sleeping pill down her throat. The first night, she took it. The second, he really thought she'd make him follow through with his threat before she finally gave in.

Lucas couldn't remember the last time he got more

than a few hours down. It didn't matter. He could sleep when he was dead.

He made the mistake of saying that to his sister the morning after Caitlin's murder when Maria pointed out his five o'clock shadow and the circles under his eyes. She burst into tears. He immediately borrowed one of her rooms, showering and shaving so that he looked human.

After that, he put her back on her medicine, keeping her mildly sedated as he pushed on. So many things to do, so little time. The busier he was, the easier it was to simply forget that someone killed Caitlin. It wasn't callous or cold but, rather, just his own coping mechanism. If he stopped to think about what happened, he'd crash. He didn't have time for that sort of luxury. Not now.

Tessa was the only one in Hamlet who understood how he felt. When Maria locked herself in her room, she sat with him in the kitchen, keeping him company. The homey room they returned to Thursday night after he'd been forced to pronounce his ex dead on the scene became the center of their unspoken vigil. Neither could say what it was they were exactly waiting for.

Then, on Saturday afternoon, Maria's radio buzzed. And it seemed as if they'd been waiting for something just like that.

LUCAS STIFFENED AT THE UNEXPECTED SOUND. HE recognized it immediately. It was the emergency signal, the one reserved for the sheriff's department, and it was playing on his sister's radio.

Maria was sitting on the same side of the table as Tessa. Her long dark hair was mussed from the nap she took earlier that morning. Blue eyes were glassy and unfocused as she absently nibbled on the cheese sandwich Lucas slapped together for her. She'd taken to carrying her radio with her. It was propped up next to her plate while she struggled to eat something. When the radio started its chirp, she set the sandwich back down.

No one reached for the communicator. It continued to sound, the frequency growing higher in pitch. Tessa shook her head back and forth. Maria blinked before nudging the radio with her forefinger, moving it away from her. She scooted it in front of Lucas.

He sighed. Picking the damn thing up, he pressed the answer button. "Yes?"

Crackle. "Who is this?"

"Lucas De Angelis speaking."

"Doctor. It's Deputy Collins down at the station. I was hoping you were still with your sister. I thought you'd both like to know." He paused. In a curiously emotionless voice, he continued, "There's been an arrest."

Lucas nearly dropped Maria's radio.

It had been less than forty-eight hours since Caitlin was slain. Her wake was scheduled to be held all day Monday, her burial the morning after that. He expected the investigation to drag out until the collective anger at her murder faded into a sad acceptance that she was gone. Since learning of her death, he prayed for the best and prepared for the worst. After his own questioning, he hadn't had much hope that they could find the culprit without a little help.

Could it be that they had? And so soon?

Maria clasped her hands in front of her in a silent prayer. Tessa, strung as tight as piano wire, seemed to vibrate in place as she silently implored Collins to spill.

His hand shook so bad that his finger slipped off of the receiver button. "Collins? You there, Deputy?"

Static filled the room, then the morose voice of the stunned deputy.

"It was supposed to be routine. They asked us all for our weapons to make sure that none of them matched the bullet that shot the sheriff. But one of 'em did so Detective Rodriguez just came and took him."

Lucas jammed the receiver button, he slammed his thumb into it so fast. When the static died, as if he lost the connection with Collins, he smacked the back of the radio with the flat of his palm. "Who? He took *who*?"

And then the deputy said the words that shocked the room:

"Mason, doc. That outsider detective just charged Mase with murder."

To the surprise of everyone in Hamlet, the charges ended up being two counts of homicide against Mason Walsh.

It was the ballistics tests that did him in. Whether he was cocky or just plain stupid, he used his own gun to kill Caitlin De Angelis. His prints were all over the barrel and the trigger. The bullets fired in testing were an exact match to the slug Lucas's ME friend pulled out of her chest.

Talk about a smoking gun. Thinking he'd never be caught, Mason actually handed over the gun that fired the fatal shot. And then he had the nerve to be shocked when they matched it.

The investigators were thorough. Once they identified Mason's gun as the murder weapon, they had their warrants in less than half an hour. While he was locked up in the county jail, loudly proclaiming his innocence, a team of devoted detectives tore through Mason's home.

By the time they were done, they hit the jackpot. Tucked in a storage bin, hidden in the back of his garage, one of the detectives found a carefully coiled length of rope and a pair of gardening gloves.

Detective Rodriguez brought it to the lab himself. And when the verdict came back that the same type of rope had strangled Jack Sullivan at the Hamlet Inn, Mason earned his second count of murder.

Tess could have let it go. When it was just Caitlin, she almost managed to convince herself that she had nothing to do with it. She'd only known the man for a handful of days. No matter how angry he'd been when he'd run off the night Caitlin was shot, was it really her fault?

And then came the announcement that Rodriguez's team found the rope and the repercussions from that discovery had Tess absolutely and utterly convinced that she was to blame for everything that happened.

After talking Maria into skipping her morning dose of medicine, Tess got her to drive her to the county courthouse about forty minutes outside of Hamlet. The small village wasn't prepared to play host to a double murderer. When Rodriguez came to take Mason away, Deputy Collins accepted that it was a conflict of interest for any Hamlet law enforcement official to have a part in the capture and arrest. He was one of them. It was easier that way.

Since she didn't know how to get there—and she'd just about given up wondering what happened to her car—Tessa asked Maria if she would go with her to see Mason. She first thought about asking Lucas, only to chicken out at the last minute.

In fact, she made Maria promise that she wouldn't even tell her brother that they made this trip. Caitlin's wake was still scheduled to be held the next day. He had a thousand things he had to do. She couldn't expect him to hold her hand. Besides, this was something she had to do on her own.

Though she offered to go in with her, Maria's relief was obvious when Tess refused.

"Thanks for bringing me," she said, climbing out of the car. "Once they let me in to see him, I won't be long."

Maria swept her hair behind her, concern pulling her forehead into light lines. "You sure, sweetie? You don't have to do this."

"Yes. I do. Detective Rodriguez says they're moving him again. This might be my only chance to talk to him before... well, I don't know what's going to happen. But I'm leaving soon, Maria. Before I go back home, I have to see him. I have to know."

Maria's eyebrows rose so high, they disappeared

beneath the fringe of her bangs. "You're going? Already?"

Tess didn't have the heart to tell the other woman that it hadn't been her idea to come to Hamlet at all. But Maria De Angelis had been nothing but kind to her so, with a small quirk of her lips, she nodded. "I have to. It's time. As soon as they let me, I want to go home."

Maria leaned over, laying her slender hand on Tess's arm. "I'll be right out here if you need me. You don't have to face him alone."

"I know. And I appreciate it, but that's something I have to do, too."

Taking care not to slam the door behind her, Tess took a deep breath and started for the building. She expected the paperwork, the metal detector, the curious looks and wasn't let down.

Fifteen agonizing minutes later, some faceless deputy gestured for her to follow him into the cells. She almost turned tail and ran. Digging deep, she ignored her impulse to flee and stepped lightly behind the bulky deputy. He led her down corridor after corridor without a word until he pointed at the third cell in.

Tessa swallowed her gasp.

Mason.

She always heard jail was hell. Here was proof.

The fallen deputy was pacing back and forth, his

shoulders hunched and his hands curled into fists at his side. He looked like a caged animal. Her impression only grew stronger when he froze, his head lifting as if he caught a scent. A heartbeat later, his whole body tensed, then he turned. His big, brown eyes were wild and just a little crazy as he zeroed in on her.

Launching his body at the cell door, he wrapped his hands around the bars. Mason mashed his forehead up against the grate.

"Tess, you came!"

The orange jumpsuit they put him in made his tan complexion look faded and wan. The circles underneath his bloodshot eyes were so dark, they were nearly black. He looked like he hadn't had a wink of sleep since his arrest.

Taking care not to get too close to him, Tess edged closer to the cell. She stopped with more than a foot separating them. "Why did you do it?"

Her whisper seemed to hit him with as much force as a sucker punch to the gut. Mason recoiled, folding over as he shoved away from the cell bars an instant before staggering back. Shock made his features go slack, replaced by utter despair only seconds later.

"You believe them." His tone was empty. "You think I could have done any of this."

She wouldn't let his wounded expression sway her from what she came here to do. "Deputy Walsh, I—"

"Mason. Tess, I'm still Mason. Don't do this," he

begged. "Please."

It really was like that first night all over again. He'd insisted she call him by his name rather than his title even after he brought her down to the station. This time, though, she didn't indulge him.

This time she wasn't the one behind bars.

"Deputy Walsh," she repeated. She wouldn't make this personal. She couldn't let herself. "What else am I supposed to do?"

He raised his voice. "Believe me instead! You've gotta know that I didn't do this. I would never hurt Caitlin!"

"You handed that gun over yourself, you told them it was yours. The bullets matched." Tess paused, taking a second to compose herself. It didn't work. When she spoke again, her voice wavered. "The rope matched, too."

"It's imposs—"

"You strangled my husband."

"Tess, I never—"

"They found the rope. Detective Rodriguez showed me the photo. Did you know that I remember every single detail about what he looked like dead? It was burned into my mind so bad, I've been branded with the memory. I'll never forget. You could show me a hundred different ropes and I would know it again if I saw it." Her chin wobbled. "You had that rope in your garage, Deputy."

"It wasn't mine. I don't know how—"

She never rose her voice. "You gave them your gun. You had to know they would figure it out. Did you want to get caught? Tell me. What reason did you have to hurt them?"

"I didn't! You have to believe me!" In desperation, he yanked the bars again, rattling them. "I'm innocent!"

Spit flew from his mouth. Despite the distance she imposed, the spit hit her dead in the face. Tess took a hurried step away from him. Wiping her cheek, her nose, she shook her head, wrung her hands. And she wondered, if it were possible, would she take back any of her actions that led them to this point? What would she change?

Since she knew the answer to that question, Tess glanced up. She met his gaze straight.

"You have no idea how much I wish that was true, but it can't be. I'm sorry, Mason." The name slipped out. His eyes lit up. She took another step away from him. "So, so sorry. But not as sorry as you're going to be."

With those parting words, she nodded at the deputy waiting to escort her back through the jailhouse.

Mason shouting her name was the last thing she heard before the first corridor separated them.

23

Caitlin De Angelis's wake was held on Monday. She was buried on Tuesday. By Wednesday, Tess was ready to grab her luggage and walk out of Hamlet if she had to.

She was willing to climb the mountain, leap over the gulch, hitchhike as far as she could go, buy a new damn car with Jack's life insurance. Anything.

As if answering her prayers, the intercom rang early that afternoon.

"Yes?"

A rush of static, then Maria's apologetic voice. "Tess, sweetie?" Her voice sounded as throaty as normal, yet tinged with sleep. She must have just woken up. "Someone's here to see you. They're waiting at the front door for you. Do you want me to send him to your room?"

She had no clue who it could be. Lucas wouldn't wait on the porch. Mason—her stomach twisted in guilt. It couldn't be him. She hardly met anyone else in Hamlet, secluded as she had been since the night Jack died.

Maria had been shooing nosy neighbors away for days, using the time to process and grieve and, well, sleep the tragedy away. Whether she meant to or not, she kept them all away from the outsider who brought death into their small community. There was no way she would let someone in to see Tess without vouching for them first.

Caitlin's murder hit her hard. Though her brother divorced Caitlin years ago, Maria still thought of the sheriff as her sister-in-law. Seeing her get killed had broken something in the upbeat, positive woman. Even worse, knowing that her childhood friend was responsible for pulling the trigger. Tess didn't blame her for coping this way. Some people drowned their sorrows in hot showers. Others slept the pain away.

Curiosity got the better of her. That, and boredom. The Lavender Room might be beautiful, but it seemed more like the holding cell in the sheriff's station as another day passed.

Tess nearly tripped over her half-packed duffel in her haste to dash over to the intercom. "That would be great. If you don't mind, let them in."

She couldn't deny the butterflies in her belly as she

waited for the inevitable knock. Except for infrequent meals and whenever Lucas stopped by, she stayed locked inside. With Mason behind bars, she knew the threat was gone. That didn't make it any easier.

Maria no doubt understood. Why else would she suggest sending an unknown man down to the Lavender Room?

The knock, when it came, was assertive and brisk. *Bang. Bang.* Tess took a deep, calming breath and, with a hint of a smile, opened the door.

Sylvester Collins was standing on the other side. He had his hat in his hand, his closely shaved head gleaming like a billiard ball. Standing straight and tall, his copper-colored eyes bright and alert, she could almost ignore the tired frown lines bracketing his severe mouth or the bags under his eyes so deep, she could use them to pack the rest of her clothes.

She felt another twinge of sympathy. Just like Mason, Collins didn't look like he had slept at all since the sheriff was killed.

"Mrs. Sullivan. A moment of your time?"

"Deputy Collins." She was surprised to see him standing there and didn't even try to hide it. "It's so nice to see you again."

"Afternoon, ma'am." He jerked his chin at the pile of clothing on the bed, at the open duffel. "I heard you were looking to leave. Seems that's the case."

Tess couldn't imagine where in the world he could

have heard that. The only person she had told was Maria and that was only because she thought it fair to settle up with her when she finally checked out of Ophelia. She supposed Maria told him.

It didn't matter. The speed with which any news traveled the cobbled roads of Hamlet no longer surprised her.

She nodded. "Yes. I was wondering if I could go. With everything that happened, I didn't know who to ask."

Collins blinked. "I guess that would be me. It's just me and Willie left now, with Rick Hart helping out here and there. We'll have to get a new sheriff eventually but..."

"I'm so sorry." More than she could ever say.

"Can't be helped, but thank you kindly. You've had your share of loss, too. These have been some dark days here. I don't blame you for wanting to go. The sooner, the better, I'd wager. That would be best for all of us."

She didn't think he meant to do it on purpose. That didn't stop Tess from feeling like she was crumbling under the weight of the mountain of guilt on her shoulders. Her bottom lip trembled. "I just want to go home."

"That's why I've come. You're free to go whenever you wish it. In fact, I wanted to let you know that your car is waiting for you down at the station. Seems

Mason arranged for the tire to be fixed before... well, you know." Collins pressed his hat to his chest. His features softened as he looked down on her. "I feel like I should apologize."

A lump formed in Tess's throat. "You don't have to do that—"

"Please," Collins said, holding out his free hand. "Hear me out. You came here for help and one of our own stole so much from you. That's not who we are. That's not what Hamlet is."

She gulped. With a shaky smile, she said, "Hamlet helps?"

"We will continue our best to do so. In your husband's memory. In Caity's." He took his hat, put it back on his head. Reaching into his pocket, Collins pulled out a very familiar set of keys. He handed them to her. "You go on, get home safe. The car's ready to go whenever you are. Don't worry about Mason. He'll pay for what he did."

She took the keys from him, cradling them to her chest. "I appreciate you telling me that, Deputy. Thank you."

"You're a good lady. For an outsider."

She was touched. The fact that his blunt words affected her that way told Tess one very important fact: it was time to get the hell out of Hamlet.

THERE WAS ONE PERSON SHE WANTED TO SEE BEFORE SHE left.

Before Deputy Collins called in with the report that Mason was arrested, they spent those two tension-filled days together in Ophelia. Maria slept most of the time which left Tess and Lucas alone together a lot. And while he never once came out and said that he thought she was to blame for Caitlin's death, she wasn't stupid. He had to be thinking it.

Since Maria was still awake following Collins's visit, Tess asked her hostess if she would mind taking her to the station house so that she could pick up her car. She then tried to broach the topic of paying for the room she rented in Ophelia during the ride.

Maria wasn't having any of it. With red-rimmed eyes that still seemed to glitter with unshed tears, she gave her one glorious glare that killed the conversation before Tess could even tactfully ask how much she owed.

As Maria helped her unload her luggage from the trunk of her coupe into Tess's car, Tess impulsively reached out and gave the other woman a hug. Maria towered over her by more than a head, swooping down to return the squeeze.

"I know you have to go," Maria said, her voice throatier than usual, "and I know that Hamlet is my home, not yours. Still, I'm sad to see you go, Tess. Everything aside, you were a perfect guest, *mia amica.*

Ophelia thanks you. She'll stay open now, for anyone who needs a good bed and a better breakfast." Pulling back, she took Tessa's hand in hers. "Local or outsider, it's all the same to me."

Tess swallowed roughly, trying to get past the lump in her throat. "I'm glad I got to know you, Maria. And I will be sending you a check for payment. I'm told mail really works here, if it just takes a little bit longer. I'll give it a shot."

Maria shook her head grandly, her long dark hair swaying with the motion. "When it does arrive, I'll burn it. I'll take no money from a friend."

"I left you my e-mail address. I hope you'll use it."

"We'll talk." A husky chuckle. "I'm sure you'll be glad not to have to use our radios anymore."

A small smile tugged on her lips. "Between you and me, I'd sell my firstborn for cell service. The second I leave Hamlet, I'm looking for a charger. Maybe one day you guys will finally get a reliable tower."

"Perhaps." Maria reached over Tess's head, made sure the smaller woman was safe, then closed the trunk. "All set, sweetie. *Buon viaggio*." She tapped Tess on the cheek. "And when you say goodbye to my brother, let him down gently. He's a good man, just one that's meant to stay in Hamlet."

Tess knew that very well. She also didn't even bother denying that she was going to stop and see Lucas on her way out of town. "I will," she promised.

It might have been her imagination, but she could've sworn the car smelled like Jack. Someone with much longer legs than hers had driven the car last and it took her a minute to move her seat and reset her driving mirrors. The entire time, she felt like Jack should be in the car beside her.

Once she strapped herself in and fastened her seatbelt, Tess rolled down the windows. The chill didn't bother her. She had to air out the car.

As soon as she was home, she would sell the damn thing. There were just too many bad memories attached to it.

For now, though, she needed it. With a final wave to Maria, she backed out of her spot, almost ecstatic that she was leaving the dreaded station house in her rearview mirror. She never wanted to see that place again.

Not even the small pang of guilt she felt at not saying goodbye to Willie was enough to compel her to set foot inside. Just like the way Jack's presence was still in the car, Caitlin De Angelis would be haunting the sheriff's station.

She couldn't do it. No.

Instead, Tess strained to remember the path to Lucas's office. She was willing to bet that she would find him there. She had to. With him spending all of his spare time at Ophelia, there was no reason for her to discover where his home was. But she knew he was a workaholic—he had to be at his office.

The candy apple red Mustang in the driveway was a pretty big clue that she was right.

Tess parked behind his car. She left her purse on the floor of the passenger seat, making sure to grab her car keys before she climbed out. There was no way she was letting those babies out of her sight any time soon.

Her eyes flickered to the chipped brick on the front of the building. Six days ago she'd been walking down this same driveway, visiting the doctor in his office for the first time. It was amazing how drastically everything could change in less than a week. The sheriff was still alive then. Lucas hadn't been shot yet, either.

No one had ever been charged for that crime. Mason adamantly denied shooting at Lucas and Tess. Of course, he also tried to convince her that he had nothing to do with Jack and Caitlin's murder so there was that.

Tess strode forward. She thought about knocking, then decided against it. With a deep breath, she let herself in.

He wasn't in the waiting room—she didn't expect him to be—and after looking for him for a few minutes, she found Lucas in his lab. He was sitting at a low table, bent over a microscope, staring intently at something on a slide. If he heard the echo of her heeled shoes against the tile, he didn't act like it. His attention stayed on his work.

Tess tried not to let his lack of reaction sting. She cleared her throat. "I hope you don't mind that I let myself in."

"I thought you'd be by sooner." Lucas kept his eye pressed against the microscope. His voice was curiously empty as he added, "The funeral services were yesterday."

"I know."

Tess had almost gone. Just because she signed off on having Jack's remains cremated immediately, it didn't mean that Caitlin wasn't going to have a funeral befitting of her status in Hamlet. According to Maria, the whole town had shown up to pay their respects to the fallen sheriff. It wouldn't have been out of place for Tess to go, if only because she was tied to Caitlin through the tragic circumstances of her death.

Which, in the end, was the precise reason why she stayed away. No matter which way she looked at it, she was the reason why Caitlin De Angelis was in a casket.

"You didn't show," he pointed out needlessly.

"It didn't seem right."

"But you took the time to visit Walsh." He lifted his head up from the microscope, pushing it away. The chair swiveled so that he was facing her. "Maria buzzed me when you came back that night. Why didn't you tell me you were going?"

Looking back, she should have. She knew it. Lucas was just as involved in this whole mess as she was. When his first instinct had been to go after Mason Walsh, she was the one who convinced him that it wasn't worth it. When Detective Rodriguez returned to Hamlet with the news that the deputy was responsible for both deaths, she had honestly thought it was over. Case closed.

But the more she thought about it, the more determined she was to face him herself. So she didn't invite Lucas, and it never occurred to her that Maria would go running to her brother the same way she told Deputy Collins that Tess wanted to go home. Even though she should have. Maria was sweet, but she could always be counted on to pass along anything she was told.

Hmm. Maybe she wouldn't send that check after all.

His eyes were a blast of arctic chill, his beautiful face set in unforgiving lines. She'd obviously upset Lucas by not telling him about Mason. But for all the apologies she'd been handing out, this was one she wasn't going to give.

"I couldn't leave without seeing him one more time. You didn't have to be there."

He didn't say anything. He didn't have to. She could tell from the clenching of his hands and his cold gaze that he wasn't only upset. He was absolutely furious.

"I should've been."

"Doctor—"

"Is that all I am to you? The doctor?"

She blinked. "You want to do this? Now?"

"No. No, you're right." Lucas sighed, rubbing his forehead. "I was out of line. Forgive me, Tessa. I'm sure you didn't come all the way here for me to snap at you over Walsh. I don't like that you went without me, but I get it. You had to have your peace."

Tess didn't think she would ever really have peace. It had seemed like such a good idea to go see the deputy. If she was being honest, though, it only made her feel worse. It was one of the reasons she wanted out of Hamlet so bad. Besides the whispers, the prejudiced eyes, and constant stares that made her feel like the only motive behind the double murder, she couldn't stand that she had some part to play in putting Mason Walsh in jail.

"I did," she told him, without mentioning that she hadn't found it. "It was the only chance I had. I— I'm leaving, Lucas. I'm going home."

"When?"

"Maria helped me pack up my car already. Deputy Collins told me I could pick it up from the sheriff's station and go." Her laugh was hollow as she remembered how quick he was to basically kick her out after Caitlin's funeral. She didn't blame him, but still. "I think the rest of Hamlet wants me out of here more than I want to go. I'm happy to oblige."

Lucas ticked his jaw. "Not all of Hamlet. I'd like it if you stayed."

It felt nice to hear him say that. She knew his goodbye would be the hardest of all, and she remembered Maria's request that she let Lucas down gently. At the time, she thought it was ridiculous—Lucas De Angelis was the type of man who never let anyone see what affected him. But she thought she knew him as well as he seemed to know her by now. He would appreciate her blunt honesty.

"I know. But I can't. I'm sorry, Lucas. I'm driving home tonight."

"Do you— would you ever come back?" he asked.

Tessa's smile was sad yet firm. "I think we both know that I was never made for Hamlet."

Lucas thought about what she said. He couldn't argue with her, so he didn't. Instead, he said, "Do you ever think things happen for a reason?"

"Like fate?"

"If you like."

"No." She shook her head. "I think things happen because they do. One person gets an idea in their head, and they act on it. Did Jack have to be strangled? Maybe. Did Caitlin have to be shot? I don't know. But someone made the decision and it happened and, well, I can't take it back. All I can do is get past it. If there was one thing I learned in the last two weeks, it's that life is for the living. Maybe, one day, I'll be able to do just that."

For the first time since she walked into his office, Lucas seemed at ease. "Good answer, Tessa. And I have only one thing to say to that." He blinked slowly, his thick lashes shuttering the icy depths of his gaze before he locked eyes with her one last time. His lips quirked. "Until we meet again."

"That's so much nicer than goodbye," Tessa told him.

And nicer still because she knew he meant it.

24

Six weeks later

Lucas had just ended another radio conversation with the new sheriff of Hamlet when he heard the irritating chime of the front doorbell ring out in his office. Slapping his communicator down on his desk, he bit out a curse.

Jesus Christ. He'd kill for five minutes peace.

Not that he blamed the other man for finding excuses to buzz. Like his predecessor before him, Collins clearly wanted to have a good working relationship with the town doctor. Lucas just wished Collins' deep voice didn't rub him the wrong way, like the grate of sandpaper against his nerves.

It always had, ever since the first time they met, when the newly hired deputy came to Maria's rescue the night Turner attacked her. Sure, he'd be forever grateful that Collins had been there for his sister when she needed someone. Didn't mean he had to like the guy.

Even if he should—and, albeit grudgingly, *did*—show respect to the new sheriff of Hamlet. At least he tried.

The emergency election had been unanimous; Sylvester Collins was sworn in two weeks after they buried Caity. Lucas had to admit the retired Marine was a good man, one who actually seemed to believe in the drivel Maria painted every year on the Hamlet sign. Plus Collins was good to Maria. He'd answer the sheriff's buzzes for that reason alone.

Rubbing his temples, he debated if he should do the same for his door.

His head felt heavy on his neck. Dropping his hands to his side, he rolled his head back and forth, trying to relieve some of the pressure.

It wasn't getting any better.

He was tired. So fucking tired.

Time dragged. The calendar said only a month and a half passed since Caitlin's murder and Walsh's arrest. It lied. Lucas barely remembered what life was like before a pair of outsiders found their way to Hamlet, leaving nothing but a maelstrom of loss and confusion in their wake.

As if he couldn't stop himself—or didn't want to—

his mind lingered for a heartbeat on Tessa Sullivan before he angrily shoved it away. Then, raising his fingers to his forehead, he exhaled a rough breath as he brushed the strands of his hair, ensuring it was perfectly in place.

There were patients to be seen, and he'd put off re-opening his practice long enough.

With the exception of stitching up a gash in Liam Johnson's forehead last Sunday, Lucas had managed to avoid most of Hamlet. His neighbors were allowing him to grieve and he found himself taking full advantage of that.

It was one of the reasons why he tended to spend most of his time in his office instead of at his house. Too many people thought it would be just fine and dandy to check up on Lucas when he was at home. They were way more hesitant to crowd Doctor De Angelis. And the mountainside of town was quiet and content, the perfect setting for his unsettled mood.

But the bell had rung, once again cutting into his imposed solitude. If someone was at his door, it might just be an emergency. He had to check. The doc had responsibilities that his—

Lucas paused. His stomach wavered, his hands folded into fists. Six weeks and he couldn't keep pretending he didn't know what had him so fouled up. He never thought he'd miss her so much but hell if this wasn't loneliness—

Flexing his fists again, he forced himself to push past that, too. He had goddamn responsibilities that this loneliness wouldn't stop him from seeing to.

With a quick massage to his tightened neck muscles, Lucas fought to erase the scowl that etched its way on his face. Leaving his office, he couldn't stop his thoughts from returning to Tessa once more.

To Tessa and the flippant advice he had given her right when she was trying to process the shock of her husband's murder. He told her that it had to be worse before it didn't hurt so bad; only with pain could she finally heal. Wasn't that the truth?

The bell didn't ring out a second time. No surprise then, when he opened the door, that nobody was standing out on the porch.

But someone had been by, he saw. Because, placed neatly on the ledge outside the nearest window, was a manila envelope addressed to Dr. L. De Angelis.

They didn't have a real post office in Hamlet—just Phil Granger who accepted all the mail from the next town over and spent his afternoons driving around Hamlet in his repurposed golf cart, delivering letters and packages to the townspeople.

For most of the townspeople, he would've held onto the mail until it could be delivered in person. But Lucas was the very busy, very respected town doctor. Even before the events of the last few weeks, no one in Hamlet bothered him if they didn't have a very good reason to. So that meant ringing the doorbell and dropping the manila envelope off on the ledge in case he didn't get an answer.

With a jolt, Lucas recognized the return address. He blinked, narrowing his gaze at the type as if that would explain why this envelope was waiting for him.

It was sent from the outside lab he partnered with whenever he wanted a second opinion on his findings, or when he needed more advanced equipment than what he had at hand in his office in Hamlet. The lab did good work, even if they were usually too bogged down for a quick turnaround, and they insisted on mailing out a hard copy of their findings so that they couldn't be tampered with.

Only... what findings did they have for him? He couldn't remember having contracted them any time recently.

It hit him a second later: *Sullivan's samples.*

He'd forgotten all about taking samples from Jack Sullivan and sending them out. It was routine, something he did whenever he was acting as the medical examiner. It was so incredibly obvious how the outsider died—ligature strangulation performed by an unknown assailant—that Lucas never really thought about it again once Sullivan was gone from his morgue.

Then Rodriguez arrested Walsh for the crime and Lucas accepted that his part was over. It was now up to the lawyers and the judges and the shrinks to figure out why the hell the deputy did what he did.

They already knew how. Rodriguez and his team carted off the rope and the guns before they took Walsh down. The samples wouldn't change anything. He should just file them away, wash his hands clean of the whole thing. The case was over. The outsider detective solved it.

Slapping the manila envelope against his palm, Lucas lasted about three seconds before he shook his head and reached for the metal clasp on the back. He slid the thin stack of papers out of the envelope, quickly shuffling through them as everything the lab found in the samples reaffirmed his initial findings.

Until one word jumped out at him. Lucas blinked. His fingers crumpled the edge of the report. He scanned it again, just to make sure it said what he thought it did.

It did. And he still couldn't believe it.

Fucking hell.

Knock, knock.

Tess was scrolling through her phone, an absent gesture because she was far too restless to do anything else. The soft rapping at her front door stole her attention away from another series of addictive cat memes that barely even merited a second glance, let alone a giggle.

She couldn't remember the last time she laughed. Back in Hamlet, she decided. That small town took so much away from her, kept so much from her. Her laughter too, it seemed.

Knock, knock.

Her grip tightened on the edge of her phone. Her heart sped up, though she willed it calm. By now, she should've been used to random visitors. Ever since she arrived back home and started to make the arrangements to live in a world without her husband—letting those who knew him learn what happened to him—she'd had more than enough people come by.

And to think, when they first drove into Hamlet, she actually thought no one would miss them if they were gone. It was a big world out there. Just not big enough.

Tap, tap, tap, tap, tap.

Nibbling on her bottom lip, she hesitated. Someone wanted her to open up pretty badly. They weren't going away. Even if she thought she should pretend she wasn't home, her car was parked in front of the apartment. All it would take was a nosy neighbor to point it out. And since her visitor was still knocking, eventually someone would poke their head out into the hall.

Might as well see who was out there.

The well-wishers and guests coming to offer her condolences had trickled away after her second week back. And though she had enough casseroles in her freezer to last her a year, she prayed that it was a salesperson or something like that lurking on her doorstep. Jesus, if one more person told her that they were sorry for her loss, she was going to lose it.

In another life, Tess would've tossed her phone to the couch, then peeked through the peephole to see who was out there. That was the old Tess. The new Tess, the one who fled from Hamlet with the ghost of her husband as her passenger… she didn't like the idea of being without the safety net of her phone for any longer than she had to.

Without loosening her grip, she slowly approached the door. She stood on her tiptoes, the angle of the peephole distorting the features of the dark-haired man on the other side.

Tess recognized him anyway. There was no way she could ever mistake those icy blue eyes.

The door was locked. The deadbolt she had installed the night she returned home was tricky and it took her a second to remember how to undo it. She knew how easy it was for someone to get in to do harm. She refused to make it even easier for anyone to get close enough to hurt her again.

He was still standing there when she finally managed to get the door open. His hair parted precisely, that sly dimple that appeared in his right cheek as he offered her a friendly smile that didn't quite meet those guarded, icy cold eyes.

Her heart thumped wildly.

"Doctor De Angelis. What are you doing here?"

Lucas was dressed in civilian clothes. Freshly pressed khaki slacks and a blue button-down shirt without a single wrinkle in it despite the fact that Tess's home was at least a seven-hour drive from Hamlet—five, she considered, if he sped like a demon in that Mustang of his.

If she didn't know he was a doctor, she never would've been able to tell. He was too pretty. A model, maybe. An actor. She'd had that same thought the first time she ever saw him. He had had the face of a movie star, the hands of a healer, and a determination that forever unnerved her.

Standing outside of her apartment, Lucas deliberately adopted a pose to put her at ease. One hand in the front pocket of his pants, the other relaxed at his side as he idly twirled the ring of his car keys around his index finger.

She remembered him telling her once how his patients complained about his bedside manner. Tess called bullshit. Lucas was a pro at projecting a carefree air. And he could read body language like no one she'd ever known.

Too late, she realized she was gnawing anxiously

on her thumbnail. She stopped, dropping her hand to her side. The barely-there quirk of his eyebrow told her she'd been caught.

Damn doctor was like a mind reader. She should've known she'd never fool him. She never had before.

He smiled. "It was a long drive, Mrs. Sullivan. Maybe you should invite me inside."

As if she had a choice. "Of course. Come on in."

The apartment was in a state of disarray. He could almost forgive her for not inviting him in right away. Half-filled moving boxes were scattered around the living room. Haphazard stacks of sloppily taped boxes filled the corner by the brown leather couch. The matching recliner was buried under an avalanche of clothes.

On second look, he noticed that most of the walls were bare. They hadn't always been. He could see countless nails still studded in the walls, the only sign that photos and frames had once hung there.

Either she was trying to remove any reminders of the life she had shared with Jack Sullivan or she was in the middle of getting the hell out of the apartment. After a second, Lucas decided it was probably both.

"Almost done packing?" he asked.

She didn't answer. Instead, she nodded at the couch. "Please, take a seat. Can I get you anything to drink? Water? I might still have a beer or two in the fridge."

"Thank you, but no."

Shrugging, Tess disappeared into the kitchen. She returned with a bottle of water. As Lucas relaxed into the couch, his arms spread across the back, his leg folded so that his ankle rested on top of his knee, she drank him in with her eyes before guzzling half of her water. Suddenly, her mouth was so dry. The plastic crinkled as she took deep pulls.

"Why don't you come join me?" Lucas patted the empty seat next to him.

She recapped her half-empty water bottle and tossed it on top of the massive laundry pile. As tempting as his offer was, she knew better. She could sense the tension in the air. Something big was about to happen.

Keeping her tone light—and staying right where she was—Tess said, "Sorry about the mess. I wasn't expecting company."

"Somehow I doubt that very much." His pleasantness sent chills coursing down her spine. "You had to know that this was coming."

"I... I don't know what you mean."

"Before you left, you said something that stuck with me. Do you remember?" When she shook her head, he told her, "You asked me if I really wanted to do this now. I didn't ask you what you meant by that because I knew. And, trust me, I'm more than ready.

"Hamlet is a very small community," he continued

as she stayed silent. "We weren't prepared for what followed you into town. A man dies anywhere else, there's an entire police force to look into the crime." Lucas ticked them off on his fingers. "Cops, CSI's, lab techs, DA's." He let out a soft snort. "An ME who isn't making it up as he goes along. But not in Hamlet. Caitlin didn't trust outsiders. Most of us don't, but she took her paranoia to a whole other level. We had the five of us." He raised his hand again, folding his fingers down as he named them. "Me. Caity. Wilhelmina. Sylvester. Walsh. We had to figure it out all on our own. Well, *most* of it."

Tess was following along. "The phone records," she guessed. "She couldn't get those on her own."

"Right. But the thing is, the sheriff wasn't the only one who sent out to the outside for help." He let his words hang there for a beat. "Your husband's toxicology reports came in this morning. It was routine for me, sending out samples to the lab after I performed his autopsy. I knew how he died. I just wanted to make sure that everything backed up my initial report." A quirk of his lips, a meaningless smile that didn't quite meet the ice in his gaze. "Imagine my surprise when something came back flagged."

"Oh."

"Tox reports indicate that he ingested a liberal amount of Nembutal. Are you familiar with it?"

Her legs folded beneath her and she dropped

down on the edge of the recliner. The water bottle slipped from her hand. The peak of the clothes mountain tumbled onto the carpet.

"It's a sedative," Lucas told her, as if she didn't already know. "A very strong one, too. Mixed with the alcohol in his stomach, he had enough in his system to knock him out cold for hours.

"Seeing that he took it the night he died, I have to ask myself why he would do such a thing." Lucas's shrug was casual. Easy. "And I don't think he did. I mean, he could've administered it to himself, yes, but it doesn't make sense to me. So next question. Who was close enough to Sullivan to give it to him? No sign of a fight, so he took it willingly. Who would he trust enough that he would accept a drugged drink without thinking twice?"

Tess slumped forward. A pair of panties fluttered to join the pile of spilled clothes on the floor.

She closed her eyes. "Me. It was me."

"I know," he agreed, so readily that her eyelids fluttered open again. "And I've driven all this way for one last question. Why, Tessa? Why drug him?"

Tess's bottom lip trembled. Her eyes turned glossy with the sheen of sudden tears. Dashing them away with a shaky hand, she looking imploringly over at the doctor.

"It's all my fault, Luc," she admitted. "I know I was supposed to stick to the plan and that was it, but I had to. When you did it, when you... I didn't want Jack to feel any pain. You've gotta understand. It was one last thing I could do for him."

That's exactly what he thought. In the hours it took to drive to Tessa, he already worked it all out. She'd never once shied away from what he told her she had to do. After reading the tox report, he kicked himself for not thinking she would do something like this.

It always bothered him that Sullivan hadn't struggled at all, not even as he tightened the rope. Sedatives crossed his mind when he first began the autopsy; he hadn't used them, so he didn't look for them. It never occurred to him that Tessa, with her conscience and the feelings she once held for the man, might have strayed from the plan.

When the results came in and he realized she'd disobeyed him, he hopped right in his car. It might have been hypocritical, but Lucas threw the rest of the plan out of the window. He'd been thinking rationally, clinically, when he first decided that they had to wait at least three months before they could chance seeing each other again. Tessa would move from her apartment and he would leave Hamlet behind and they could just start over together.

And then the report came in. One detail, one small thing had the power of ruining everything he worked so hard for. Her soft heart could've cost them both. He had to see her because this was one discussion they couldn't have on a disposable phone or in coded e-mail messages. Lucas had to assure himself that Tessa was still as devoted to him as he was her.

Of course, when his own impulsive need to see her, touch her, talk to her again led him to pack up his car and leave Hamlet in his rearview, he forgot one major thing. That, no matter what, she held his heart in her dainty, little hands. Seeing her beautiful eyes fill with tears made him ache.

"Come here, Tessa." He opened his arms for her. She pushed off of the recliner, shuffling uncertainly toward the safety of his embrace.

Lucas reached out and grabbed her hand, pulling her onto his lap. As she laid her head against his chest, his fingers ghosted over the tousled waves of her hair. He cocooned her in his arms. He was always amazed at how perfect they fit together. As if they were made for each other.

Tess glanced up at him. His gaze grew so heated as their eyes locked, she felt like she was melting. In moments like these, when he looked at her like that, Tess wondered how she could ever compare this man to ice.

"I missed you," she admitted. Knowing he was hers at last, waiting for him for these last six weeks, it had been torture. She didn't know how she was going to make it another six weeks. So what if he came all this way to scold her? She didn't care. Not when she could hold him.

"I love you," he told her.

And definitely not when he said that. In a matter-of-fact tone because his love for her was something that just was, so simply stated because it was as part of him as his being a doctor. Forget about melting. Tess *burned* for Lucas De Angelis.

She snuggled into his embrace. For the first time since they set their plan into motion, she felt like she could breathe again.

25

When they started their steamy, passionate affair more than a year ago, Tess never anticipated what it would become. Lucas admitted that he'd hoped for it since the moment they first met, though he forced himself to wait until Tess came to him on her own. And when she finally gave in and did? What started out as a spark of attraction, blossomed into a firestorm of epic proportions that eventually burned everyone in its path.

It began innocently enough; at least, for Tess, it did. Six years ago, when she was a fresh-faced undergrad student still taking nursing courses, Lucas visited her college campus as a guest lecturer.

Though he was the only doctor in Hamlet, he was extremely intelligent, highly educated, and had a desire to get out of there as often as he could. He wouldn't leave his sister on her own for long, and Caitlin refused to let him out of her sight for more than a few days at a time, but he used his profession as an excuse to momentarily escape either by taking classes, attending seminars, or giving lectures.

It was during one of those lectures that a young woman caught his attention. Tessa Ryan. From the moment he first laid eyes on her, sitting in the front row as she took notes with a purple pen, Lucas knew she was meant to be his. His one and only. He always understood that his marriage to Caitlin was nothing more than a front; already crumbling, it wouldn't outlast his initial, all-consuming attraction to a light-haired, golden-eyed co-ed.

At first, it *was* innocent, mostly because Tessa was too good, too kind, too naive to understand exactly what Lucas wanted from her. They exchanged emails from time to time, with Lucas acting as her mentor. Even after she switched her major from nursing to education, they continued to communicate because the bond they developed was already too strong to break.

It wasn't long before they fell in love. Though neither one acknowledged it out loud for years—Tess because she clung to her loyalty to Jack, Lucas because he didn't want to push her away—the affection was undeniably there. As constant as the sun, and nearly as blinding.

They couldn't acknowledge it, or even hope of acting on it. Lucas was still married to Caitlin. Tess was in a committed relationship with Jack Sullivan, a relationship that Lucas was intensely jealous of as it grew more and more serious while he languished in a loveless marriage he couldn't quite escape from.

Since she never thought she could have a real future with a married man, when Jack proposed, Tess accepted.

Of course, Lucas immediately tried to convince her to change her mind. Though he'd offered it in passing before, he was dead serious when he said he'd finally divorce Caitlin if only Tess gave up Jack. Tess refused. Lucas had his life. She had hers. He was established in Hamlet and wouldn't leave—as quick as he was to toss his wife to the side, he wouldn't budge on that point. Tessa wanted to finish school. She didn't want to go to Hamlet.

Not yet, anyway.

As much as she cared for Jack, the passion she shared with Lucas wouldn't die. She forced herself to ignore it, going so far as to stall her engagement to Jack for as long as possible until she simply ran out of excuses.

Three years after he proposed, Tess married Jack in a simple courthouse wedding. That day, she promised that she would give her new husband everything she had. He wasn't the one who gave her butterflies in her stomach, but he loved her and did his best to do right by her.

It was enough. It had to be.

She emailed Lucas the morning after her wedding and told him it was over. He showed up two days after she returned from her honeymoon, cornering her in the parking lot at the school where she worked before basically begging her to leave her new husband. Caught up in a jealous rage, he forgot that their fling was supposed to be both carefree and secret.

Alarmed by the depths of his reaction, she refused. It didn't matter that his inevitable divorce to Caitlin was final and had been for years. She owed too much to Jack. She wouldn't leave him.

Lucas went back to Hamlet alone, already plotting how to change that. And while Tessa managed to avoid contacting him for nearly three weeks after her wedding, she eventually rekindled their long distance romance. She wanted to stay away and she tried to—but Lucas was all too willing to wait. A patient hunter, he let Tessa come back to him, knowing that once she did, he'd never let her go.

And he didn't. Emails and stolen phone calls became weekend-long trysts when Jack was away on business and Caitlin thought Lucas was out of town for his work. All the while, he kept lying in wait. His problem? He considered another man's wife to be his. The solution was incredibly clear to him from the start.

Get rid of the other man.

Already hatching his plan, Lucas waited. No one—not Tessa, not his ex, not his sister—could tell the depths of his plotting. After Mack Turner, this one would be a cinch. Methodical and precise, he approached it as he would any other operation. The goal? Separating Tessa from Jack Sullivan. Simple surgery.

The doctor was more than capable of it.

Tessa, meanwhile, struggled in her marriage. Six months later, miserable and growing to despise Jack more and more for the sole crime that he wasn't Lucas, she admitted to her husband that maybe they weren't cut out for this marriage thing. He had to be thinking the same thing. She knew she was making his life miserable, but he adamantly told her no. Jack wouldn't let her give up. There would be no divorce. She was in it for life, he reminded her.

Or just his, Lucas pointed out.

It was surprisingly easy to convince Tessa of his plan. Two months of dropping hints, sneaking phone calls, sending untraceable emails and he had her wavering. After another couple of weeks, she agreed that she didn't see any other way out.

Lucas had always known he was twisted, that a part of him just wasn't right. Everything was either black or white—he never saw shades of grey. He didn't want to die alone, so he married Caitlin. Didn't matter that he didn't love her, or that he knew she was utterly devoted to him in a way he couldn't reciprocate. He wanted a partner. He got one.

And when he found himself haunted and obsessed by a striking student in one of his lectures, he knew he would do anything to possess her.

It utterly amazed him that, in the end, his fragile beauty proved she would be willing to do the same for him.

So they planned Tessa's second honeymoon knowing that a third would follow closely on its heels. Everything, from the nail in her husband's tire to weaken it to the requested stay in a private room, plus the award-worthy performance she put on for Mason Walsh the night Sullivan died, was plotted to the last detail. Odds were good that one of the deputies would throw her in the holding cells if she was caught driving intoxicated. Everyone in Hamlet knew about the drunk tank—but an outsider wasn't supposed to. When Walsh locked her up, he was doing exactly what he was supposed to without knowing it.

It was Tessa who went off script.

Lucas hadn't expected her to insist on calling the Hamlet Inn. Luckily for them, he was able to do some acting of his own as he convinced both Caro and Walsh that he was Jack Sullivan. Though it caught him off guard at the time, he admitted to Tessa later that it had been a stroke of genius. It solidified her alibi, making it airtight since it was "proof" that she had left Jack alive in the hotel room.

He even went so far as to purposely pick the anniversary of his divorce to Caitlin to put his plan into motion because she would be distracted and off her game. The more he pushed, the more he flaunted a "budding" relationship with Tessa, the quicker he thought she'd give up and shunt Sullivan's case off to the side. It almost worked, too, and when it didn't, Lucas didn't hesitate to go to Plan B.

Really, he thought, Caitlin had no one to blame for her death but herself.

All in all, it was the perfect plot. The only evidence remaining that tied Tessa to any of this was the report he received with Sullivan's tox results. And since he destroyed that, burning the letter and its envelope in a rest stop bathroom two hours away from Hamlet, there wasn't even that.

Leaning down, nuzzling his cheek against the silky soft strands of her hair, Lucas told her how he got rid of the one thing that might make someone look closer at the crime. Without a doctor to question the results, the tox report would be buried under hundreds of others like it.

No longer frustrated and annoyed, he took great pleasure in assuring his accomplice that they were home free at last. Breathing her in, snuggling her close, he was at peace for the first time in years. At that moment, everything he planned, everything he pulled off, it was all worth it.

"So that's it then. We did it." She sounded amazed.

"Mm-hmm."

Tessa held onto him for a few seconds more before she abruptly pulled away. He let out a throaty growl at the loss of her warmth pressed up against him. Now that she was in his arms where she belonged, he hated the idea of letting her go. It was even worse when she was distancing herself from him.

Then she went on and said, "Luc, there's time now. We've got to talk."

His stomach tightened. Nothing good ever followed *we've got to talk*. He ran his hands down her shoulder, trying to maneuver her back against his body. "No."

"I'm serious."

"You talk. I'll keep myself occupied."

She slapped his wandering hand as it made a bid to slip underneath her shirt. "Lucas!"

"Okay. Fine. I'll behave." And, to prove it, he wrapped his hands around her waist, moving her so that she was pressed against his middle again. When she relaxed into his hold and sighed as if there wasn't anywhere she'd rather be, Lucas felt magnanimous. Even though he was pretty sure he knew what was coming next, he said, "You want to talk? Let's talk. What's on your mind?"

Tessa didn't disappoint him. "I feel bad," she confessed.

"It's okay. I'd be worried if you didn't." Unlike him, Tessa was still young and naive enough to experience things like guilt. He loved that about her, her inability to accept that sometimes the ends justify the means. To Lucas, the fact that she would abandon her conscience and beliefs to follow him blindly into hell only reinforced how much she loved him in return. He would never disregard her feelings. They were too precious to destroy. "I know we promised each other that we wouldn't. Guess it was easier said than done."

"Yeah."

"But you know we had no choice."

"I know. I *know*." She fisted his shirt in her hands. "It's just—"

Lucas scowled. "Walsh."

The damn deputy had been a thorn in his side ever since he took it upon himself to first comfort Tessa needlessly, then actually fall in love with her. He couldn't blame Walsh for that, not when he knew how easy it was himself, but everything that came after... Walsh had to pay for it.

Lucas had made sure of it himself. And it burned him that Tessa still carried so much guilt when it came to Walsh.

"I know I shouldn't feel bad about him when he did his best to come between us—even though he never knew there *was* an us—but I can't help it. He was harmless. He wasn't standing in our way, not really. You know I would never have let him. He just wanted to help."

Harmless. That wasn't the word he would use to describe Mason Walsh. Conniving. Manipulative. A predator. Attracted by her vulnerability, he saw Tessa as a beautiful woman, a weak one, and he pounced. He wasn't trying to help her—he was trying to help himself *to* her.

It amazed him that Tessa couldn't see that, though it probably shouldn't. She'd always been too innocent when it came to what the men in her life really wanted from her.

Including him.

All he wanted was her. Every last thing she had to offer, Lucas wanted it all. Furious and jealous of the attention Walsh lavished on his Tessa, he wanted to scrap the plan, start over, and make it so that there were three victims by the time they were done. It made it even worse when Tessa fought to spare him. Only her adamant promise that he meant nothing at all to her allowed Lucas to use Walsh as a fall guy instead of adding another body to his count.

He understood exactly what she meant when she said she felt bad. That Mason Walsh was in jail weighed on Tessa's conscience. That he was still breathing weighed on Lucas.

Taking one of her tense hands, he rubbed his thumb over the top until she relaxed her fist, pressing her palm against his chest. She moved her head forward. Taking the hint, Lucas tucked her underneath his chin. Tessa leaned into him.

He rubbed her back, giving comfort and stealing it with the same caress.

"You knew there would be casualties if we wanted our happy ending. We agreed it was worth it. You gave up Sullivan. I gave up Caitlin—"

She couldn't swallow her snort. He felt the rush of air at the base of his throat. "What a loss."

It was a good thing Tessa had her face hidden. He didn't want her to see the amused expression that danced across his. She would accuse him of not taking her seriously. While the opposite was true, he couldn't help himself. That petty slap at his dead ex-wife made him grin. It meant that Tessa wasn't completely wallowing in her guilt. Besides, he couldn't say he blamed her for that, either.

Lucas met Jack Sullivan face to face for the first and last time when he strangled the man—and, thanks to Tessa, Sullivan was sedated. Caitlin was an ever present threat to Tessa the first six days she spent in Hamlet. The sheriff was nothing but a hassle. It was a relief to finally kill her.

Giving up Caitlin wasn't so much a sacrifice as a necessity. Lucas was well aware he couldn't have both women in his life. He made his choice, just like Tessa made hers.

"Are you sorry?" she asked him.

"For what? Killing your husband? Or framing the deputy?"

She didn't flinch. She knew he was just being honest; he wasn't trying to upset her or belittle her feelings. Tessa knew him better than anyone ever had, though Maria used to.

Until Turner, at least.

His sister always suspected he had something to do with Mack Turner's unfortunate accident but, too afraid what it would mean if he had, she started to drift away, using his overprotective behavior as a fence between them. Tessa... she accepted the dark parts of him. Accepted them and loved him anyway.

"For Caitlin," she said simply.

He knew what she meant. Caitlin wasn't always supposed to die. The longer Tessa stayed in Hamlet, the more it became clear to Lucas that she would have to go. Plan A was to off Jack. Plan B always involved Caitlin. Once he had a scapegoat in one of her deputies, his mind was made up.

Fueled by her obsession with Lucas and her jealousy of Tessa, she wouldn't stop until she proved Tessa was involved. She was that dogged, and too much of a liability to be left alive.

"Sullivan wouldn't let you go so we had to make

him. My marriage to Caitlin was over years ago but she still had her hooks in me. If I left her alive, I couldn't be here right now. We wouldn't be free."

She was quiet as she digested his answer. "Sacrifices, Luc. Jack's mine. Caitlin is yours. I guess I'm responsible for Mason. But what about Maria?"

A pang at the mention of his sister, one he managed not to let her see. He wouldn't give Tessa even the smallest reason to doubt him. "What about her?"

"Are you really going to give her up, too? For me?"

He thought, by now, that Tessa understood that there wasn't a single thing in this world he wouldn't be willing to give up for her. Maria would be the toughest, and even that was easier to do than spend another night without Tessa.

"I'll miss Maria, but she doesn't need me. Not like you do. She has Ophelia back, as safe as I could possibly make it, and I know she still sleeps with that bat by her bedside. Besides, Sly'll be looking out for her. She'll be fine."

That was the last thing Tess expected to hear. "Sly? Deputy Collins?" When he nodded, she shook her head in surprise. "Wow. I mean... there was that one time I thought maybe, but— but I didn't *know*."

"Nobody does. They've hidden it very well. But I'm a big brother and, no matter what Caity used to say, a pretty good detective. I figured it out ages ago. I'm glad." Reaching out, he caressed her cheek, letting his hand trail down the slender line of her throat. "I want her to have something even a little as special as what we have, *mia cuore*."

Italian. Unlike Maria, who let the language slip regularly, she only ever heard him speak it when he tenderly called her *mia cuore*. My heart. The same thing he pledged to her from the start, when she was a silly little girl who wanted something she couldn't have.

Except now she had it.

To his surprise, her bottom lip started to quiver again. A second later, she pushed against his arm. "Let me up."

"Tessa—"

"Please, Luc. I want to stand."

Because he would give her the world if she asked it of him, he dropped his arms down so that she was free. Tessa climbed out of his lap and moved out of the living room.

He hated having even that much distance between them.

It struck him that, with Jack and Caitlin dead and gone, he didn't have to stay away from her anymore. Pushing up off of the couch, he shadowed her. She went into the kitchen, bracing her hands against the sink. Folding his bigger body around hers, Lucas rested his chin on her shoulder, breathing in her sweet cinnamon scent.

This delicious morsel was all his. The realization staggered him. Tessa belonged to him now. It made everything he had done worth it.

If only she was as happy about that as he was. She had to be. He would make sure of it.

Lucas loved her too much to accept anything less.

"Tessa. What's wrong? What else has you tied in knots?" She shivered as his murmured words tickled her neck. Chills ran up and down her spine, goose-bumps popping up all over her exposed skin. "Tell me. I'll make it all better. You know I will."

He was so distracting. Part of her wanted to just give in, let Lucas take over as he had been doing all along. She couldn't. This was too important. Tess had to be sure.

"I just... I can't stop thinking about it. I know why we did it. I don't see what we could've done differently and maybe that makes us monsters, but I don't care—"

"You're no monster, *mia cuore*. You want to blame someone, blame me. It was my idea."

"And I was with you all the way, Luc. I still am. I love you. I don't regret a damn thing that happened but... Jesus Christ, what if they believe him? We both gave up so much to have a chance at this, at *us*. I want it to be worth it, but someone might figure it all out. He can't give any details, right? Someone might wonder if he's really as innocent as he claims."

Because, of course, Mason Walsh *was* innocent. And while there were only three people in the whole world who knew for a fact that he was innocent of the murders, what if someone else figured it out? What if he could convince someone?

Lucas thought her worries were charming. Ridiculous yet cute at the same time. When he went along with her idea to frame Walsh rather than give him an "accident" like Turner, he did everything he had to to ensure that no one would ever think that the deputy was anything except what Lucas wanted them to believe.

From the moment the Sullivans arrived in Hamlet, he'd been one step ahead of everyone. It really was the perfect crime. No one would ever guess that the respected doctor had anything to do with the murders. And while they might always suspect the outsider, he'd been careful to shield Tessa. This was all for her, after all. He couldn't stop Caitlin from interrogating his sweet Tessa. He'd never allow anyone else the chance.

Everything he'd done, he'd done for her. For *them*.

Every little detail and interaction was thought up in advance, planned perfectly and executed flawlessly. Tessa's airtight alibi. Acting like they never met before, even going so far as to play out their "first" meetings in front of an audience. The threatening note Lucas slipped into her borrowed room without any advance warning so that her reaction would be genuine.

Of course, he remembered with a scowl, he never expected Tessa would run right into Walsh which just goes to show that even the best laid plans could have a kink or two in them.

Like when he got shot. Now *that* was a kink. He'd provided Tessa with the pair of guns he lifted from Caity's place, instructed her on how to rig them to give the impression that she'd been shot at while in the good doctor's company. No one in Hamlet would doubt his word as witness. But their aim was erratic at best and Lucas was lucky he was only grazed.

It worked better than he guessed, though. It was tangible proof that even the sheriff couldn't ignore. The queen of conspiracy theories never once suspected he engineered his own injury. No sane man would ever consider it a plus to be shot.

Then again, he figured he left the last of his sanity far behind the first time a double murder seemed like a viable option for him to get what he wanted.

As for Walsh, being wrongfully imprisoned for crimes he didn't commit was a better fate than what Lucas wanted for him. The foolish deputy could insist he was innocent until he was blue in the face. It wouldn't do him any good. Lucas buried him in so much circumstantial evidence, Walsh would eventually collapse under the weight of it. He wasn't dead, but he would wish he was.

And that was good enough for Lucas. Served him right. Six weeks later and he was still touchy that Walsh dared to kiss his Tessa.

Massaging her shoulders, he dug his fingers in her flesh in an attempt to banish some of the tension that lingered there.

"We have nothing to worry about," he promised. "I made sure of that when I planted some of the rope in his garage."

Lucas was always so amazed by how stupidly trustworthy other people were. No one locked their doors in Hamlet. People like Caitlin and Walsh were just begging to be set up. Was it so terrible that he obliged them?

Nuzzling her neck, he added, "And then I used his gun to kill Caity after you set him up, egging him on that last night."

He pointedly didn't mention Tessa's change of heart that night, or how she tried to stop Lucas from turning on his ex and the deputy. She really had run off to Caitlin's in a panic, towing poor Maria along, only to serve as a witness when Lucas pulled the trigger from a distance.

After that, she realized they had no choice but to continue in the plan to frame Walsh. When the alternative was targeting him next, Tessa let it go. He insisted.

It was *imperative* that she let the past go so that they could start their future.

"No one will look past that. How can they? It's *his* gun. So let Walsh cry that he didn't do it. No one will believe him. We're home free. You said it before. We did it."

She turned into him, wrapping her arms around his waist. Bright eyes, golden eyes stared up at him in utter worship. "You sure, Luc? Really?"

He looped his arms around her, pulling her close until her cheek was pressed to his chest. He gently kissed the top of her hair. "I'm positive," Lucas assured her.

And then he smiled into the loose curls.

"Trust me."

A NOTE FROM JESSICA

I want to thank you for taking the time to read *Don't Trust Me*. Now that you've reached the end, I would be honored if you would leave a review of your honest opinion. Just some small token that might entice other readers to discover the hidden path into Hamlet. Hopefully, you might want to return there some day yourself!

In fact, I've included a sneak peek at the next full-length Hamlet novel—read on to get a glimpse of *I'll Never Stop* today.

xoxo,

Jessica

I'LL NEVER STOP

Tommy Mathers had charm, he had looks, and he had money. He was also intelligent in a way that scared her to her bones. He knew what to say and how to say it, acting remorseful in one moment and demanding in the next.

The first time she tried to break it off, he bought her a diamond necklace and begged her to give him one more try. She fell for it, and found herself locked in the bedroom of his penthouse apartment after she gave in and spent the night.

Tommy was gone—with her tucked safely in his home, he left to take care of business—and he had two goons guarding the door in case she tried to run. Which she absolutely attempted the minute she accepted that, despite his promises, he was never going to change.

It took three days, as well as giving the damn diamond to a housekeeper in exchange for helping her escape, before Grace realized that if she wanted Tommy to leave her alone, she was going to have to make him. Trapping her in his apartment was the last straw. She finally understood that his so-called love was nothing but an unhealthy obsession with her and this crackpot idea that she was destined to marry him.

Taking nothing but a suitcase of clothes—and stopping only long enough to clean out her savings account—Grace took off running. She was sure, once she was out of his reach, Tommy would let her go.

She was wrong.

So wrong.

He'll never stop.

Her shoulders hunched under the weight of her certainty. She moved—*twice*. Tommy always found her, even after she registered for the address confidentiality program. He had Boone disable her old car, slicing three tires and removing the engine so that she couldn't leave town the last time they met. She abandoned it, buying a used car with her dwindling savings, and started parking away from her new place, in case he was watching.

It didn't matter that her new number was unlisted, or that it was blocked from appearing on other statements the rare times she called home. The speed with which Tommy always got it again made her give up on getting it changed. What was the point? He didn't need her mother to pass it along, though Grace was certain she had on more than one occasion. His genius when it came to computers and the way he thought laws only applied to other people meant that he didn't take him much effort to find it on his own.

The only way she could fight back was with the little things. So she deadbolted her apartment, she made sure she lived on the sixth floor, and she always parked in a well-lit area that was far enough from her place that she could only hope he couldn't find her.

Again.

She was forever aware of her surroundings, too. Even as she carried all of her shopping bags at once so that she didn't have to risk a second trip to the car, Grace's eyes were darting around. She'd learned to trust her gut, no matter what. If she felt like she was being watched, it usually meant somebody *was* watching.

It was a Saturday evening, still early enough that the sun was out. The parking lot was more empty than not, a handful of cars scattered around the space. She weaved around them, searching for the sleek, shiny black finish of Tommy's luxury Jaguar. As ostentatious as it was expensive, she'd never seen him drive around in any other car. If he was close by, she would spot him first.

Considering the speed of the car, the head's up

would never be enough of a warning, but she refused to think like that. Her caution and her care had kept her one step ahead of Tommy Mathers for seven months now.

At the last lot, Grace held her breath and turned the corner. She exhaled in relief when no one was waiting for her. Hefting her bags high, she stepped up on the curb and turned toward the front of the apartments.

Strawberry Village was made up of eighteen different apartment buildings. Each structure was eight floors high, with three apartments on each floor. She lived in the last building, on the sixth floor. In order to get inside, a tenant needed a passcode to enter the front door to each individual building, use the same passcode to operate the elevator (or take the stairs), and then use a key to open a specific apartment. That first step was what had her taking the two-room apartment. It would make it that much harder for Tommy to find his way in.

Her nerves were already stretched thin. It had been more than four days since he last messaged her and she was too used to his volatile mood swings to hope that he'd finally given up on her. Usually, when Tommy went silent, it was because he was focused on another one of his plans.

Glancing behind her, assuring herself that he wasn't lurking just out of her sight, Grace fervently wished that, whatever was occupying Tommy, it had nothing to do with her.

"Grace!"

Her head whipped around at the sound of her name. She was already poised to flee and only just stopped herself when she saw one of her neighbors waiting inside the small vestibule that led into their apartment complex. A welcoming smile on her lovely face, Tessa De Angelis held the door open for her.

De Angelis. Grace knew enough Italian to guess that meant "of angels". Even though it was the woman's married name, she thought it suited her. Tessa was petite and kind, with a set of innocent eyes that seemed more golden than hazel. She perpetually wore an inviting smile and always stopped for a chat whenever they met in the hall.

Stumbling under the weight of her groceries, her heart settling back into a normal rhythm after her scare, Grace hurried toward the open door.

Tessa was harmless. She was safe.

She greeted the other woman with a bob of her head. "Tessa, hi. Thanks for holding the door for me. Appreciate it."

"Need some help with your bags?"

Ice skittered down her spine at the deep voice with the clipped tone. Jumpy as ever, it was all she could do not to react.

She didn't see him standing there in the shadows of

the vestibule. Silly. She should've known better by now. Lucas was never too far from his lovely bride.

It was an automatic reaction. Gripping the handles of her grocery bags tightly, she moved them closer in case he tried to take them. Her lips pressed together; she hoped it passed for a grin. "Thank you, Lucas, but I'm fine."

Tessa De Angelis was harmless. She was safe. Lucas... was not.

AVAILABLE NOW

I'LL NEVER STOP

It was supposed to be one date. After connecting on an online dating site, Grace Delaney agreed to go out with Thomas for coffee—and that was the beginning of the end for both of them.

Thomas Mathers is rich, he's smart, he's arrogant, and, after one evening, he's decided that the lovely ballerina is meant to be his. And because he immediately proves how obsessed he is by breaking into her home and leaving threatening gifts, she knows he's not about to take Grace's no for an answer.

No matter where she goes, he finds her. In the seven months since they met, she's been forced to move twice, change her number three times. The cops won't help her. Her friends think she's just being stubborn.

Tommy would be good for her, they say.

Tommy will never let her go.

He stalks her, tracks her using his wits, his goons, and the best technology that money can buy. How can she escape him?

Simple. By hiding out in a small town where there's no phone, no television, and a retired Marine turned sheriff's deputy is willing to do whatever he has to in order to protect the frightened outsider he's quickly falling for.

Welcome back to Hamlet.

I'll Never Stop *is a full-length novel set in Hamlet. Featuring characters from the previous entries in the series, as well as introducing a new heroine to the small town, this novel is set approximately a year after* **Don't Trust Me** *and will bring the reader back to the cozy small town—where everyone knows your name and, even so, no one is safe.*

This book was released on March 8th.
Available today!

AVAILABLE NOW

OPHELIA

In a small village with a population less than two hundred, there was rarely a need for an inn. There was definitely no reason for one of the locals to open a bed and breakfast when outsiders were few and far between. That didn't stop Maria De Angelis. Though she knew she would never manage to escape Hamlet—and she didn't want to—running Ophelia was her dream.

But when did she decide to do it? Why? Where did she get the name for it?

And what really happened with Mack Turner?

Told in snippets, this novella spans eight years, showing the birth of the idea for Ophelia all the way to the day Maria reopens her bed and breakfast and has Tessa Sullivan for a guest.

The reader gets a closer look at the relationship between Lucas and Maria De Angelis, as well as glimpses of some of the Hamlet residents that are featured in ***Don't Trust Me.***

Available now!

STAY IN TOUCH

Interested in updates from me? I'll never spam you, and I'll only send out a newsletter in regards to upcoming releases, subscriber exclusives, promotions, and more:

Sign up for my newsletter here!

By signing up today, you'll receive two free books!

ABOUT THE AUTHOR

Jessica lives in New Jersey with her family, including enough pets to cement her status as the neighborhood's future Cat Lady. She spends her days working in retail, and her nights lost in whatever world the current novel she is working on is set in. After writing for fun for more than a decade, she has finally decided to take some of the stories out of her head and put them out there for others who might also enjoy them! She loves Broadway and the Mets, as well as reading in her free time.

JessicaLynchWrites.com
jessica@jessicalynchwrites.com

ALSO BY JESSICA LYNCH

Welcome to Hamlet

Don't Trust Me

You Were Made For Me*

Ophelia

Let Nothing You Dismay

I'll Never Stop

Wherever You Go

Here Comes the Bride

Gloria

Tesoro

Holly

That Girl Will Never Be Mine

Welcome to Hamlet: I-III**

No Outsiders Allowed: IV-VI**

Mirrorside

Tame the Spark*

Stalk the Moon

Hunt the Stars

The Witch in the Woods

Hide from the Heart

Chase the Beauty

Flee the Sun

The Other Duet**

The Claws Clause

Mates*

Hungry Like a Wolf

Of Mistletoe and Mating

No Way

Season of the Witch

Rogue

Sunglasses at Night

Ghost of Jealousy

Broken Wings

Born to Run

Uptown Girl

Ordinance 7304: I-III**

The Curse of the Othersiders

(Part of the Claws Clause Series)

Ain't No Angel*

True Angel

Night Angel

Lost Angel

Touched by the Fae

Favor*

Asylum

Shadow

Touch

Zella

The Shadow Prophecy**

Imprisoned by the Fae

Tricked*

Trapped

Escaped

Freed

Gifted

The Shadow Realm**

Wanted by the Fae

Glamour Eyes

Glamour Lies

Forged in Twilight

House of Cards

Ace of Spades

Royal Flush

Claws and Fangs

(written under Sarah Spade)

Leave Janelle*

Never His Mate

Always Her Mate

Forever Mates

Hint of Her Blood

* prequel story

** boxed set collection